RAGING BARONS MC

BOOK SIXTEEN — MAV

This book is a work of fiction. Names, characters, and events are the product of the author's imagination or have been used fictitiously. Do not construe them as real. Any resemblance to actual events or persons, living or dead, is purely coincidental.

This book or any portion thereof may not be reproduced or used in any manner whatsoever without the express written permission of the author. You cannot give for free on any kind of internet site.

This book is for readers over the age of 18 years. If bad language, violence, sexual encounters offend you, please do not read.

There may be mention of physical violence, torture, or abuse, but the series is a lighter version of MC. Hence, for example, rape *will never* be described in the series but may be mentioned.

Business Manager: V. Saunders
Editor: R. Tonge
Alpha/Proofreaders: G. Brocklesby & M Vayer
Proofreader Team One: Editing Diva – R. Fong
Proofreaders Team Two: L. Cameron Brashears & A. Haskins
Beta Readers: S. Hazuda, J Spalding
Reader Group: G. Brocklesby
ARC Team/Street Team Manager: E. Holcomb PA
Book Cover: Oasis Book Covers
Photographer: Paul Henry Serres
Model: Sam Z

NOTE

Please note, this author lives in the United Kingdom, and has American Alpha and Beta readers who correct errors, but, as in other countries, it depends on which state you live as to how your slang or terms differ.

Therefore, although some words/terms you may think are incorrect are correct in one or more states.

No AI programme has been used in the writing of this book, the cover images or design.

REGISTERED

TABLE OF CONTENTS

CHAPTER ONE

: MAV :-

I've been standing on door duty at TJs for the last four hours. My patience is about gone with the idiots that keep walking through the door. I know it's a Friday night and people want to let their hair down after a more than likely busy week, but come on people, stop acting like idiots.

A group of women walked past twenty minutes ago, and one tried to touch my junk. I mean, really! What sort of skank does that to the damn bouncer?

Four men pass by me as they walk inside, giving me a nod as they do. I nod in return, as they are regulars here on the weekend. They have never, to my knowledge, caused an issue. They are some of our better customers.

"MAV?"

Turning as I hear my name shouted I give Colton the *look* to stay on the door as I walk over to Allison, one of the bar staff and servers.

"What's up?" I ask as I lean on the bar so I can hear her clearly over the music, talking, and laughter.

Leaning forward towards me, Allison is side-eyeing a guy sitting at the end of the bar. "I'm not sure, Mav, but I think he's just put something in that group of women's drinks. I wasn't sure what I was seeing, but I thought it best to tell you than ignore it."

"Leave it with me, but you see anything you are not sure of come tell one of us."

"I will, Mav." Allison moves along to serve while I stroll over to Colton.

"Got a live one at the end of the bar. Watch the fucker and if he goes to the restroom, we'll follow him in. One of us watch the door, the other have a little talk with him."

Now, Colton is a hothead, losing his temper fast. Both myself and Knuckles have been working on him, teaching him to channel his strength, mentally and physically. It will be interesting to see how he handles this shit.

"I'll follow him in. You watch the door. You had all the fun last time, and the time before that it was Fist, and he wasn't even on door duty," Colton grins, and believe me, his eyes are twinkling at the thought.

Chuckling more to myself than toward Colton as I recall the Fist incident. The guy ended up with a missing tooth and five stitches, but he never said a word of how it happened when the Sheriff asked. Now Forest is Sheriff, he wouldn't even ask, and if he did, he'd shrug and walk away.

Looking around, I wave to Ruger, Sting and Brag, who are here enjoying a beer. Giving me a frown, they all three stroll over to the door where both Colton and I are waiting.

"What's up?" Brag asks.

"Can you man the door while we deal with an issue?" I reply.

Ruger rubs his hands together, grinning like a fool. "What's goin' on? Can we get involved?"

Now I never realized that Ruger was so bloodthirsty, but he's gotten a manic look on his face that is telling me he wants to have a go at whatever is afoot. "Okay, you come with us, Ruger, and you two stay at the door."

Wandering over to the bar, Ruger and Colton on either side of me. We take a stand and Allison hands us a beer. Colton and I won't drink it, but Ruger takes a hearty mouthful, giving himself a frothy mustache in the process.

Looking at Ruger, I flick my eyes to the guy at the end of the bar and watch as Ruger studies him carefully. "Yeah, got it. He is eyeing up some of the women in that group on the left."

"Allison thinks he has spiked their drinks, so keep your eyes open. When he goes to the restroom we follow," I mumble, making sure to keep the volume of our conversation low.

"Oh, yippee, he needs a piss," Colton says, rubbing his hands together and looking like it's Christmas morning.

The three of us turn and watch him walk to the restroom, and we slowly follow behind him. Colton and Ruger push forward, getting in front of me. Why they are panicking, I don't know because I have no intention of getting blood on my hands, today at least.

Smirking to myself when I hear what Ruger says to Colton. "You take a piss on one side, and I'll take a piss on the other. Once there is only us three we show this fucker what happens when you come into our bar, or town trying shit like this."

"Oh, yeah, I'm up for this," Colton replies, and I take a stance at the door of the men's restroom.

Two men come out of the restroom talking to each other, but with shit-eating grins on their faces. They both give me a nod as they pass me, which lets me know they don't have a problem with what is about to go down.

I hear a cry, but ignore it. Turning a few away from the restroom while hearing banging, shouting, and is that crying? Oh dear, seems someone isn't as brave as they thought they were. A tick in my cheek appears and I'm not sure if it's because I'm pissed I'm not in on the action, or that I'm trying hard not to laugh out loud.

It only takes ten minutes before the restroom door opens and Ruger walks out with a beaten-up asshole behind him, who is propped up by Colton. Walking to the front door of the club, people look at us passing and Colton grins, "Too much beer, you know what it's like. Fell over his own feet in the restroom and head-butted the wall." I'm not sure anyone believes him, but they look like they don't give a shit either. Suits me.

I don't bother watching Colton and Ruger getting rid of the asshole as I lean over the bar counter to speak with Allison. "Any sign of the women having issues?"

Allison shakes her head. "Not that I've seen, and I'm keeping my eye on them. Two of the women left five minutes ago, and I heard Sting and Brag talking about getting them an Uber, so they get home safely."

"Okay, that's good. What about those that haven't left yet?"

"Oh, I took them fresh drinks and tipped the other out. If they only drank a sip or two, they should be good. I'll monitor them, Mav." Allison moves down the bar to continue serving, and I saunter back to the door and bouncer duty.

Sting turns as I reach the doorway and gives me a grin, one that looks like he's holding back more than amusement. "What?" I ask him.

"I let Axel know what was going on, and he said to get the prick to the compound. He wants to have a word with him." Sting gives me another grin, but this time I understand it.

Turning, I look at Colton. "You stay here and watch the door. Brag, will you stay with Colton?"

"Yeah, I can do that." Brag leans on the door frame and folds his arms across his chest, creates a frown on his brow, giving his best *don't fuck with me look.*

Shaking my head at him when he winks at Colton right before screaming starts, and we all turn to look at the dance area of the bar. Two women are fighting and I mean really fighting, none of the hair-pulling shit as they are throwing punches.

Ruger has the guy outside, and I know he'll keep ahold of him. "Wings and Chaos are outside, Mav. They'll help Ruger." Colton says as he steps up to my side just as a punch lands square on one of their noses. We hear the crack and the woman scream. She now has blood pouring down her face. "That had to hurt," Colton states dryly.

"Grab one," I say as I lunge for the one nearest to us. Picking her up as she's kicking and screaming, and I throw her over my shoulder. "Shut the fuck up, now!" I snarl, and it had to sound harsh as she shocks me when she shuts up and lays over my shoulder quietly.

The other one that Colton has is hissing, spitting, shouting, and cursing up a storm. All the while, blood is dripping over her lips and off her chin. "You've got a live one," I state blandly.

"I'll give her live one, I'll give her something that will shut her up for good if she doesn't SHUT THE FUCK UP!" which I have to say he shouts the last right in her face.

Chaos and Wings walk over to us as we exit the club. "Take these two and sort it out. I've had enough shit for one night." I snap, nearly throwing the woman off my shoulder and into Wings' arms.

"Oh, hello handsome," the silly bitch purrs at Wings and he gives me a shocked look, but I turn and head back inside. I've had enough bullshit, as I'd just said.

Back at the clubhouse it's the early hours, and I'm sitting in the kitchen with a coffee and a plate with a microwave warmed pot pie. Meat makes sure we always have something we can heat when we come off shift. I have to admit, although he's a crazy fucker at times he's the best damn person we could have in charge of the kitchen.

Placing the plate in the dishwasher, I head to my room, where I'll have a quick shower before getting into bed. I have been neglecting my training lately and need to get myself back into a routine. I'll be having words with Knuckles to give me extra time, and maybe see about taking on a fight to see how much of my skill I may have lost!

The next morning, I don't appear downstairs in the kitchen until everyone has eaten and gone about their day. Meat is preparing the kitchen for lunch, while the Three Stooges are cleaning up the twins, and talking between themselves.

I pour a mug of coffee and take it outside where I sit on the bench Meat has placed under the kitchen window. I know he's placed it here so he can look at his gardening area and see the treehouse.

Speaking of the treehouse, he's done some modifications on it, but nobody knows what he's been doing to it, yet at least. Even Star has been badgering him to reveal what he's done. I have seen a platform on a nearby tree and I'm guessing he's going to be building an annex.

Hearing my name, I turn and see Axel, Drag and Buzz walking out of the kitchen. "What's up, Pres?"

"Since you were the one who got this fucker caught, you should be in on what the fuck is going on." Axel never pauses in his steps, but he has that mean look in his eye so I don't argue with him. I reach into the open window of the kitchen and place my mug on the sill giving Meat a nod of thanks as I do. Last thing I need is him on my arse... oh goddammit, I thought arse!

Stepping into the shed, I put on shoe protectors from the box on the bench, shuck into coveralls and follow Axel into the main room, where the asshole from last night is tied with chains to a chair which is placed over the drain.

He is looking decidedly peaky, I think to myself. All the color has drained from his face with the fear of what we are about to do to him. I take position against one of the walls and fold my arms over my chest, rest my back against the wall, and cross one foot over the other.

Buzz steps toward the asshole, Axel at his side and Drag lets a punch fly, hitting square in his face. But, as the chair is fastened to the ground it doesn't move, but the asshole's face flies back with blood spraying from the broken nose and split lip.

"Nice hit, Drag, very nice," Buzz states with a drawl, nodding his head while smirking.

I watch as Drag and Buzz punch the guy in various places, even taking him from the chair and hanging him from the chains attached to the ceiling. They have a point scoring system going now, and Axel is leaning on the wall beside me, chuckling at the way they are playing with the idiot's emotions.

"You think he's ready to talk yet?" I ask Axel.

"He's been ready from the start, but Drag super-glued his teeth together so he can't say fuck all until they remove his teeth."

I squint, giving the guy a closer look, and that's when I realize why his cries have been so muffled. He can't open his fucking mouth! Nope, I'm not stopping the chuckle that erupts and giving Drag a nod as he looks at me. He smirks before punching the fucker one more time in his kidneys.

"You got any questions before we stop playtime and get serious?" Axel asks, and I shake my head no, because I know they'll get all the information that they can. Any kind of spiking drinks, drugs or anything else will be dragged out of him. "Okay, give Nell a heads-up that she'll have incoming later today, and I have a job for you when I'm done here."

"Okay, I'll be around the clubhouse. I promised to help Meat move the smoker this morning so I'll be easy to find." Giving the asshole a friendly wave while having a sick grin on my face, I leave the room, discard the coverall and shoe covers before whistling as I head toward the clubhouse.

CHAPTER TWO

-:- MAV -:-

Grabbing a bottle of water, I head out to the smoker to help Meat, but take my phone from my jeans back pocket to give a heads-up to Nell as Axel asked of me.

Tapping out a message, as I don't want to get involved with speaking to Nell if I can help it. She's a little nerve-wracking if you ask me. She thinks nothing of feeding those damn gators, and I mean feeding anything at hand.

Mav: Pres is sending you a gift later

It only takes a couple of minutes for Nell to answer, and I knew that would be the case because she has her phone tucked in her bra on vibrate, so she misses nothing incoming.

Nell: Okay, anything specific?

Mav: Not that I know of. Just disposal

Nell: Oh, good. It's been too quiet around here lately, and I've been sending Graham out to scrape up roadkill. He's not been thrilled about it, but I told him it was that or his ass they were going to be eating. He went out with his bucket willingly then.

Mav: I bet he wasn't happy. Wonder what he told people when they saw him doing it?

Nell: Well, he told one guy that he was being environmentally green and he was cleaning up the roads, so no vehicles slipped on the slime from the dead carcasses.

Chuckling to myself because I can visualize Graham making up shit to shock and terrorize people. I can imagine he was giving them gory details while doing it. My mind is showing me Graham standing with a dead animal, pulling out its innards to highlight someone or other.

Mav: Nice. Well, you take care Nell

Nell: Thanks Mav, you too

Tucking my phone back into my jeans pocket, I look at the smoker and see it's spotless. How the hell he gets it clean like that, I've no idea.

"Don't need you now," I hear behind me, and turn to see Meat stepping up with a tray piled with meat, sausages and fish. Thankfully, the fish is on top of a parchment paper layer. I am not a fish fan and sure don't want it next to any meat I'm going to eat. "Stop giving the fish that look. It's going in the small smoker."

What? A small smoker! I didn't know he had two smokers. Now, the shock must show on my face because Meat points to the left where a much smaller smoker is standing at the ready. Giving Meat a huge grin and a thumbs up, I walk away and leave him to it.

Once I'm inside the kitchen, I give Mia a smile as she's cuddling with Summer. The twins are going to be starting kindergarten, and I'm not sure how that's going to go down. They are a pair of hellions and I feel sorry for the teachers. Trouble with the twins is that all the brothers are teaching them shit they are not supposed to know at their age, because let's face it, four-year-olds are not supposed to be able to go down zip wires screaming with laughter.

I think we all knew the twins were going to be trouble when they started saying, 'Unc Me' and started saying 'Dadda' and 'Pris' instead. Mia, of course, gave everyone hell, but it made no difference. At the end of the day, she adores Meat, and he adores her. Even Star has become a bestie, mind you she calls everyone bestie these days.

Before I can pour a coffee, I hear the back door open and Axel storms past telling me to get my arse to church. Now, I smirk to myself because he has no idea he just said arse, but the giggle from Mia lets me know she heard it, too.

Walking into church, I see Axel, of course, in his usual seat along with the officers, but also myself, Knuckles, Beer and Silver. Interesting, I'm thinking.

"Buzz, after church make sure that piece of shit is taken to Nell. She can do what the fuck she likes with him," Axel is more than a little agitated so this has me thinking that punk in the shed is going to cause us trouble.

"Will do, Pres," Buzz replies, and crosses his arms over his chest while leaning back in his seat.

"That fucker is running shit for an asshole named Mark Milanas. They are testing out the date rape drug they have mixed themselves. Now these fuckers are not chemists. They are little pricks that think they can come into our territory and sell shit like that. Date rape women as they take a fancy to them! I'm not having it, you hear me?" Slamming his fist on the table, making me jump, and that takes some doing.

Drag raps his knuckles on the table as he speaks. "I'll put feelers out. Knuckles, you speak to the bouncers at Club Whisky, and Mav, you do the same at TJs, report to Beer and Silver. They are the managers, so they'll tell you what to do if any incident happens. But if you see shit, you stop it and we'll get the fuckers in the shed."

"Good idea. Nell said the gators need food, so she's okay with sending more assholes for disposal," I add to the conversation. "Oh, she's had Graham going out picking up roadkill for them."

I don't get to say more because everyone, even Axel, is laughing or smirking at that. We all know he's as tough as his sister, but he's far more amusing with his antics.

Axel gives his feral smile. "Well, brothers, let's go hunting for some food for the gators. It's been peaceful around here for quite some time, so let's stir up some shit. I'll report to the rest of the brothers on Sunday. Maybe we'll have more information by then?"

BS stands to leave first, but turns to the rest of us as he speaks. "When I came to the club and the town, it was the best place I'd been in a hell of a long time. Kya and I love it here, and we won't allow these fuckers to ruin it. I'll get out and speak to all the staff at our businesses. They know me well now, as I see them at least once a month when I do my rounds. I'll report back on Sunday."

"Mav, before you wander away I want you to go into town and visit Liam at the Coffee House. Organize a morning for the Ol' Ladies and kids. Tell him to close the place and do something nice for them all. The staff can have a morning of mixing with them and it'll do them all good. Especially if we have to think about going into a lockdown situation. Tell him what's going on and to keep his eyes and ears open for any sign of trouble." Axel stands and I give him a head nod as I turn and leave church.

It was supposed to be my day off, but I have a feeling none of us will have that until this shit is put to bed.

"Mav, hang on." Turning as Knuckles speaks to me, I lift an eyebrow at him. "Have you heard about Gaz?"

"Gaz?" I have to think about who he means for a minute. "You mean Gaz, who you last fought in the underground ring?"

"Yeah. I have inside intel that the fuckers are fixing his next fight. They are going to spike his water, and his opponent is going to kill him." Knuckles has a fierce look on his face, so I know he's not messing with me.

"So, we need to step in! Is that what you're saying?"

"We both know Gaz has only been fighting underground because he was paying his sister's medical bills. Did you know she died three weeks ago? Now, of course, they think Gaz doesn't need the purse and will walk away, so they think they need to get rid of him." Knuckles' face is as hard as granite, and I know this has more than pissed him off a little.

"How about we bring this up in church on Sunday, and see how many brothers fancy going to an underground fight? Maybe get myself a fight, make sure my skills are at their best?" The slow smile that appears on my face shows Knuckles I'm up for it, and I'm damn going to make these fuckers pay. Every fighter goes in knowing they could die, but to be outright murdered is not going to happen on my watch.

"Yeah, could be an idea, brother. I'll put feelers out, and maybe have a match myself. Who knows, we may take out their biggest fighters, then what they gonna do? Especially when Forest swoops in and scoops them all up, you know, when he has a tip-off." Knuckles smirks.

Giving him a nod of agreement, I slap his back as I walk away, whistling under my breath, because I was bored as shit this morning. Now it seems we have drama afoot and I can't wait!

Walking into the Coffee House forty-minutes later, I give Liam a nod to follow me and head into the kitchen. I walk through, past the server and into the kitchen area, and through to the stairs which lead to the apartment above.

Liam is right behind me, but remains quiet until we step into the apartment, which is his now that he's managing the place. "What's up, Mav?"

"Pres wants you to organize a morning for the women of the MC, and the kids, of course. You'll need to close the place for a morning. He said to invite the staff to join in, not just be servers. Everyone is ready for a break, some chill-out time, and he thinks this is a nice way for everyone." I'm really not sure what the fuck I'm saying but trying to do my best to make this sound exciting.

"Actually, that will be nice. I have two new servers so I can introduce them to the ladies, and make sure they show the right respect to them, too." Rubbing his hands together as his face shows the thought he's already putting into the idea.

Liam is a skilled manager of this place. He's introduced different lunch specials instead of only serving paninis of every kind imaginable. But he's also brought in more coffee selections and some unusual blends too, which he now grinds and sells in packets for people to use in their coffee machines, percolators or French press. It has increased the sales tremendously.

"Okay, I'll leave it with you, but keep it under wraps. When you have it all organized let me know and I'll get my end together, but make sure I have a few days to do that."

Liam gives me a nod, and I leave him with a blank look on his face as he's deep in thought. I descend the stairs, walk through the kitchen and out the back door before anyone can speak.

Walking around the building I head to my hog, which I'd left out front, and sigh when I see a woman I've hooked up with twice in the past. She was a half decent hook-up, but that's all she was.

"Hi, Mav, you up for another date?"

"Was not a date. I don't do dates. Now, move along. I've things to do."

Another woman walks past the both of us, gives us a disgusted look before opening the Coffee House door and stepping inside. Now, if she'd asked me for a date, I may have considered it!

"Aw, Mav, come on, I'm ready for another session."

"I've told you, Shelly, it's not happening," I snap as I grab my helmet from the seat of my hog.

"It's Sharon," she snaps back.

"Shelly, Susan, Sharon, I don't care. You can move along and be sure I'm not interested." Slamming my helmet on my head, I straddle my hog and fire her up. I don't give the woman another thought as I head back to the clubhouse to have some well-earned lunch. What a day this has been, and it's still early as yet. Maybe I'll make my way over to TJs later, although I'm not working, and see what I can overhear.

CHAPTER THREE

-:- BLAKE-:-

I'm nervous about my interview as I really need this job. Stefan, my late husband, has left me with debts that I've been struggling to pay. He was a good man when I first dated him, and then married him. He worked hard but got into trouble when he started drinking heavily. It was stupid that he got drunk, had a one-nighter with a woman and she got pregnant.

Stefan got Yax pregnant, and his DNA proved that the baby was his. He moved himself into a home with her, spending half his time there, providing his son a roof over his head and food in his mouth.

Me! Well, I was working, paying our bills and keeping my own head above water, but all the time I was getting further into debt because once Stefan ran out of the ability to borrow more money on his own, he started using my name. Sighing because it doesn't matter how many times I think about it, nothing can be changed.

Leaving my last job after the salary was cut drastically, I have scrambled to find more work. I've done all types to earn money, cleaning, cooking, serving, even walking pets. Now I'm hoping that I can get the job at the Coffee House, which is exactly as described, it sells every kind of coffee you can imagine and every panini to go along with it.

Looking in my purse I check I have the loose change, which happens to be all I have left to live on until I get paid from whatever job I can get. My freezer is emptying fairly fast, with me constantly having to eat what I had been able to freeze, even down to leftovers.

Okay, Blake, stop feeling sorry for yourself. Onwards and upwards. This has become my mantra to survive the days and weeks.

Closing the door of my small house I check the time and start walking. It will take me around twenty-five-minutes to walk to the interview. I'm just pleased it is a nice morning.

Reaching the coffee house I quickly walk inside and step up to the counter. It's quiet with it still being early, and the young man behind the counter looks up from where he has been working.

"Good morning. My name is Blake Carroway and I'm here for an interview."

"Oh, come on through Blake. I'm Liam the manager of the place. We can go through to the kitchen and talk about what's needed where it's a little more private."

Liam is young to be a manager, and it has me thinking that maybe he's a good man if he is being trusted to run this place. I follow him through to the kitchen and he points to a table and chairs on one side. I quickly walk over and take a seat, watching while Liam grabs two cups and fills them from a coffee machine in one corner of the kitchen.

"Help yourself to sugar and cream," Liam says as he takes a seat and places the cup in front of me.

"Thank you." I add a spoon of sugar and take a sip, keeping my eyes trained on Liam. I give him a smile as that is a good cup of coffee.

"If you can fill out the application form before we get into anything else, that would be great." Liam hands me a form and a pen, and I quickly fill out my name, address, and the past jobs I've held.

"I see you are a widow. I'm sorry to hear that, Blake," Liam gives me a look full of pity but he doesn't need to.

"Oh, that's okay. I was about to divorce him anyway, if I'm honest. It's a long story and if I get the job, I may tell it to you one day." I give him a smile to show him I'm not mourning my husband to the point he has to walk on tenterhooks around me. The fact is I did love Stefan with all my heart at one time, but it had gradually died with all the heartbreak he caused.

"Your application says you've worked serving previously?"

"Yes, I worked at Sylvia's Diner for three years, but she remarried, sold the business and moved to Connecticut with her new husband. It was a nice diner and the regulars were amazing. I left when the new owner was far too demanding. She wanted more hours from the servers for the same money, and it was beyond reasonable. I left the diner and took the cleaning job I've mentioned." I point to the application form where the job is described.

"Okay, what I'd like to do is employ you on a trial basis. How do you feel about a two-month trial? You come in Monday through to Friday. Eight-thirty until five-thirty, and yeah, I know that's a fairly long day and it's only a half-hour lunch, but the pay is good."

Liam is watching for my reaction, and I'm well aware this is about as good as it will get for me at the moment. "I am more than happy with that arrangement."

"Okay, it's Friday today, so start Monday morning. Be on time, and I'll make sure to be here to introduce you and get you started."

I stand from the table, holding my hand out to shake at the same time I speak with some relief in my voice I'm sure. "Thank you, Liam. I'll not be late, and I'll not let you down."

With a sense of relief and achievement, I steadily start to walk back to my house. Window shopping as I pass, thinking maybe one day I'll be able to do more than just that. Window shopping that is!

Standing on the edge of the sidewalk waiting to cross the road, I hear a woman behind me speaking loudly. "Heather is looking for someone to take on evenings and weekend work. Not sure she'll get it, but the business has a lot of customers, and with taking on some of the elderly in the community who are struggling to keep their homes nice, she wants someone that is happy to work with them during off peak hours."

"Well, the business has been good to the town. Heather doesn't work as many hours now, but her business partner Alf runs the place like a damn drill master. He took on external contracts too. But he told Bren, who works all over the damn place that he needs someone fast."

Overhearing this gossip is giving me an idea how I can earn more, and use that second income to pay off my debts much faster. Turning I smile at the two women, "Excuse me, but I couldn't miss overhearing what you were saying. I'd like to speak to the person who's looking for a worker."

"Oh, that's cool. Contact Alf at Helping Hands Cleaning Service, tell them you spoke to Ellie. I work for them along with my sister Bren. It's a great place to work and you'll not regret it if you want to work in the evenings and weekends."

"Thank you, I'll go along and enquire." I give her a smile and I've seen the business office in the past so I know where it is, but it's going to take me some time to walk to it.

Turning I make my way in the direction of the business, and I have to admit I have a little spring in my step. Maybe things are going to pick up for me now?

Half an hour later my legs are aching but I've reached the business. The door is locked and rubbing my forehead while I sigh, I notice a contact mobile phone number. Taking my phone out of my purse I snap a picture of the card, check the number is clear for me to use, and start the walk home. I'll give the business a call later when I've had something to eat and a drink.

By the time I get home, have a sandwich with the stale bread I have left, and a jar of jelly in the fridge, I sip the last of the iced tea I have before plucking up the courage to make the call.

Waiting for someone to pick up the call, I tap my fingers on the kitchen table, where I'm sitting with a notepad and pen. If I have to take notes I'm ready, I don't want to be caught napping.

"Hello. Helping Hands Cleaning Service, how may I help you?"

"Oh, hello. I am enquiring as to a position with your company that Ellie told me was being offered. A position where I would be required to work evenings and weekends?"

"Yes, we do have a position along those lines. Have you worked with a cleaning company previously?" Now the gentleman sounds interested so maybe they have been struggling to get someone to fill this position.

"I have worked a cleaning job previously. I've also worked in the kitchen of a nursing home, so have experience working with elderly people." I throw that in as I think it may help if the information I've overheard is correct.

The conversation is thrown back and forth, questions and answers asked and given. The man introduced himself as Alf and said he'd be my boss if he gave me a chance with the position. I gave him my name and the fact I was a widow with no commitments as in family.

"Can you come into the office in the morning? Say ten o'clock?"

"I can, yes," I quickly respond.

"Okay, bring any references you have, and we'll see what we can do about you having a trial with the hours given."

"I will bring what I have, and thank you. I'll see you in the morning."

"Ten in the morning then, Blake."

Smiling, I can't help but think things are looking better now than they did this morning. Noticing the mail I'd brought in earlier I pick up the one that looks like it's hand written, and yeah, it's Yax's hand writing. The woman is a menace and is getting worse as time passes. Tearing the letter open, I grind my teeth because she has to be out of her head.

Dear Blake,

As you are Franklin's step-mother you have a duty to supply an income for his well-being. I will be sending you a breakdown of how much per month you will need to give to me.

I'm not going to struggle to bring up your husband's son on my own. You have a legal obligation to provide a home, schooling and everything else he may need.

I will be in touch again soon.

Yax

I'm not sure this woman is sane because there is no way I'll be supplying a dime to her, or for her son's upbringing. I've never met the child even though he is six-years old. Stefan has been dead for four years now, and yet she's only just starting to want money?

It makes no sense, but if I need to I'll sell the house she lives in, which is in my name. When Stefan got the house I didn't know he'd put it in my name, making sure that Yax could never claim it.

I think Stefan had to know what kind of person Yax is, and that she trapped him knowingly. He, however, didn't want to leave his only child without a father, and that's why he spent half his time with Yax and Franklin.

He really loved his son and didn't want to leave him alone with his mother, but he did anyway when he crossed the street without looking and was mowed down by a passing vehicle. He never knew what hit him and I'm thankful for that.

The good thing is when Stefan died and his will reading happened, it was an up-to-date will, and he'd stipulated that everything he owned came to me. He did mention his son, but left him nothing because let's face it, he had nothing worth leaving. Both the house that Yax lives in and mine are in my name, and always have been. In his way, Stefan tried to secure my future, and ensure Yax couldn't touch what I'd worked hard for.

Stefan knew I was talking about getting divorced, and he understood why I needed to step away from him, and the mess he was having to deal with.

We had completed the paperwork, which I still have showing that Stefan relinquished any claim to anything we'd accrued during our marriage. One of the things I'm sad about was the fact we'd agreed not to have children until we were in a position we could afford to get a better home, and future for any children we may have. Yet he gained a son with someone else.

Even to this day I have no idea why Stefan started drinking as heavily as he did. We were both working, saving well, and our future was looking good...until he started hitting the bottle with his friends. Then things just got harder for us, and the tension began.

Stefan didn't give Franklin his last name, he refused to be tied like that for my sake. But I always felt it was unfair for the child, as he'd not know he was loved by his father, and giving him his last name would have been the right thing to do.

Shaking my head to get out of my morbid thoughts, I throw the letter into the basket where I keep anything I think needs to be followed up on. It may come to a point I have to seek out a lawyer's help to stop this madness.

CHAPTER FOUR

Walking into the kitchen I step over to Axel when he gives me the head nod, telling me to get my ass over to him pronto.

"Morning, Prez, Mia."

"Morning, Mav," Mia replies while keeping one eye on the twins, and one on Summer, who she is feeding.

"Need you to take the package over to Nell's with Buzz this morning. No more information came to light, but Target, Buzz and BS are reaching out to our street contacts." Axel places a piece of toast next to Mia's mouth, and she takes a bite while keeping her attention on Summer.

"Okay, I can do that. I'm going over to TJs later to speak to some of the regulars, see if they have noticed anything out of the ordinary."

"You need to speak to Star. She has a huge fan following at TJs. They all think she's Wonder Woman since she roped Meat."

Hearing a grunt, I look behind me and see Meat with a twitch in the corner of his mouth. Obviously he heard, and he either agrees that Star roped him, or he roped her, but we'll never know the truth of it.

Speaking of Star, she walks into the kitchen, sees Meat and heads right for him. We all watch as she jumps into his arms, wrapping herself around him like a monkey before kissing him passionately. He's holding her up with each of his hands under a butt cheek. Lucky fucker, I can't help but think to myself.

"God's sake, Star, it's breakfast time and I've the twins here. Don't you think I have enough shit on my hands with them, without you showing them stuff like that?" Mia is nearly shouting at Star.

I do notice, however, the twins are taking a keen interest in what their Uncle Meat is doing. I'm not sure I want to know when the little fuckers look at each other with the cutest of smirks on their faces.

Turning back to Axel, I hear a loud bang, and twist back around in time to see the twins standing on the table, Carter wrapped around Hunter like a spider monkey and the fuckers are kissing.

"What the fuck!" Axel bellows while jumping to his feet and grabbing Carter while continuing to shout, "Get the fuck off him."

Now, Star giggles, Meat grunts and Mia just continues feeding Summer as though nothing untoward is happening. I'm keeping quiet. I know how easy it is to get dragged into shit like this.

Wings struts into the kitchen and grins like a fool, but decides not to comment when Axel shoots him a nasty look while snarling, "Don't say a fuckin' word!"

Holding his hands up in a surrendering fashion Wings grabs a plate of breakfast and walks over to a table, but what has me fascinated is Hunter, who is still on the table, but he has his hands on his hips, and a scowl on his face. Now… he's looking like a miniature version of Axel, but what has me spluttering with laughter is when he cocks his head to one side and loudly proclaims, "Wha the uck…" before grabbing to try to get a hold of Carter.

I walk out leaving any thought of breakfast behind, because honestly, you don't want to get involved in any of this. I pass Amelia and Sybil giving them a chin lift to at least acknowledge them.

An hour later, I'm in the passenger seat of the club van. Buzz is driving and the asshole in the back is going to be meeting his maker very soon. I'm interested to see if Nell feeds him as live meat or dead. She is ruthless when it comes to her work, and with Graham, Tank, and Richie on side she can make any eventuality happen.

"This is gonna be interesting. Fucker in the back is a two-bit player, but he was stupid enough to get involved, so he has to pay for his part in all of this shit." Buzz turns to look at me, awaiting a response, I'm sure.

"Yeah, I will never understand why a man would want to date rape a woman. If you can't get a woman fair and square, it tells you that you need to take a long hard look at yourself."

Chuckling, Buzz replies, "Well, this fucker won't have time to do that."

Arriving at Nell's, we head to the building where Graham will be waiting. Buzz had informed them we were on our way, so he'll be ready for some fun, I'm sure.

"Let me out of the van and I'll head inside and speak with Nell."

Buzz stops the van and I hop out, jogging to the back of the house and the kitchen. The dogs are barking, letting everyone know someone is here, so I know she'll be waiting for us.

Knocking on the open kitchen door, I step inside and give Nell a smile. She's making some pastries by the look of it, and the kitchen smells divine. We all know, however, not to mess with Nell when she's cooking, baking or scheming in the office.

"Hi, Mav. How are you these days? It's been quite a while since I saw you last."

"I'm good. What about you? Has that Mafia asshole caught you yet?" I always have a joke with Nell about Vincenzo Vitale.

"No, I keep stringing him along, mind you," giggling she looks up at me, and that's when I notice she has a black eye.

"What the fuck happened to you?" I snarl.

"Oscar jumped up and head-butted me in the face. Honestly, he needs to get some finesse. Ajay is far more careful when he's playing with me. The funny thing was when Oscar hit me, I squealed and Ajay jumped forward, grabbed Oscar by the neck and pinned him down. He didn't let him go until Oscar peed himself."

Chuckling as I turn when Richie walks into the kitchen through the back door. "Hi, Mav. You getting the rundown on the black eye? Honestly, Ajay has only just stopped growling at Oscar every time he looks at him."

I take a seat and watch Nell place the last tray of the two trays of pastries into the oven. Richie starts to clean the kitchen down where Nell has been working, and you can see that they are used to doing this together as they flow around each other without getting in each other's way.

Nell wipes her hands, then sits across from me, but before I can update her on what I know about the asshole, Buzz walks into the kitchen, gives a nod to Richie before sitting himself next to me.

"Tank has taken the asshole to the holding cells. You do as you like, when you like. He's a piece of shit that was popping date rape drugs into women's drinks at bars and clubs around the area. We know the one behind it is Mark Milanas..."

Now, before Buzz can say more, Graham walks into the kitchen, "Fuckin' Mark Milanas! Well, well, well, he's filth that needs to be fed to the gators. I'm sure Teeth and Jaws would enjoy a piece of him."

"You know the fucker?" Buzz asks.

"I know who he is, but I don't know him personally. He was sent to prison for a while for assaulting a man while he was protecting his wife. Seems the asshole needs to be a dickless dead man." Graham grins before proceeding, "Oh, wait until I tell Vitale, he's gonna love this."

We all watch Graham disappear out of the kitchen, into the hallway, and presumably the office. Nell sighs and as I turn to look at her, Tank steps into the kitchen sporting one hell of a smile.

"What?" Nell asks as she rubs her temples.

"Nothing much, he tried to break free, so I had to teach him it'd take a better man than him to get away from me." Holding both his fists in the air we can all see the grazes on them, and the blood.

"Graham's gone to contact Vitale. Why? Who knows! You have beaten the crap out of the prisoner, and I've not even seen him yet." Nell stands, and without another word walks out the back door shouting, 'Oscar, Ajay, with me.'

Tank chuckles as he takes a seat at the table. "She's gonna sulk for a while now. I know she wanted to mess with this fucker first, but Graham has been messing with her for a month. He'll be sorry, he never learns. Bringing Vitale out here is going to earn him a big payback from Nell."

"Come on, Mav. We've gotta get back. I've a shit ton of things to get done today." Buzz throws a soft punch at Tank's shoulder as we pass by him, and I give him a chin lift. As for the asshole, I could give a shit what happens to him.

Reaching the van, both of us come to a halt, and I'm sure our mouths have dropped open in shock, because we are watching Nell chase Graham around the yard swinging a golf club. Now it doesn't seem to bother him much because he's cackling like a witch come Halloween.

"Let's not get involved, Buzz," I mumble, and his grunt tells me he's in full agreement.

Later that evening, I'm standing in TJs at the bar watching everyone. I'm looking for anything suspicious is what I'm actually doing. Knuckles saunters over with none other than Gaz. The fighter who has a mark on his back.

"How you doing, Mav?" Gaz asks.

"I'm good. I hear some fucker wants to take you out."

"So, it seems. I've told them I'm not doing any more fights, but they are not taking no for an answer. I'll be leaving town on Friday of next week. Nothing to stay here for now, and with the threats, it's time to move on." Gaz I note is watching everything, and everyone, keeping himself as safe as he can I'm positive.

Colton walks over from where he'd been standing on the door and slaps Gaz on the shoulder. "Hi, how you doing Gaz?"

"Leaving town as soon as I can. My time here is done, but I'm being followed, so can't jump ship as they say without giving myself away." Gaz has a pissed off look on his face, and I can totally understand why.

Knuckles leans on the bar next to me and gives Gaz a questioning look. "Prez asks if you want to stay at the clubhouse until next week, and he'll get you out of town, and the state, if that's what you need."

"Actually, if anyone can sneak me to the airport, I'll get out of here as fast as I can. I have friends in the UK who I'll stay with for now. They are solid, and I can restart my life with them." Gaz stiffens as two men enter the bar. Colton, seeing them, walks over and asks them for ID, giving us a flick of his eyes to get Gaz out of here.

"You take him out the back way, Knuckles. I'll stay here and have Colton's back. Good luck Gaz, get the fuck gone and stay safe." I don't look at either of them as they walk away towards the kitchen. I keep my eyes on the two fuckers that are starting to give Colton a problem.

"I said, no ID and you can't come in. Now, get the fuck out," Colton snarls.

"I would listen to him if I were you. We have been teaching Colton here to not lose his temper so fast and stay calm under all circumstances. But that doesn't include door duty here, or any of the club properties. You know this bar is part of the Raging Barons MC, right?"

"Who gives a shit? You're just little men playing with bikes," one of the assholes states, and I look at Colton, shrug my shoulders and head butt the asshole as hard as I can, breaking his nose in the process.

Colton throws his punch and lands it squarely on the other one's chin, but both myself and Colton turn when we hear, "No, not again, it's my fucking turn."

That's when I step back and allow Fist to step forward and start throwing punches. Since I'm now redundant in this fight, I saunter back to the bar. With my back against the bar, I rest my elbows on it and watch the mayhem that is happening in front of me.

"Oh, that had to hurt," Helen, who usually works in the kitchen, murmurs from behind the bar.

"Yeah, probably did," I add, as I had noticed that Colton had punched the broken nose, which has more blood spraying over anyone in the vicinity.

"Why do these women always have to scream? Can't they just get up and walk away, you know, in an orderly fashion?"

Glancing at Helen who is frowning at the half-clad women who had obviously come tonight to catch themselves a man, and she's right, they are standing screaming like idiots.

"Hi, Mav."

Looking to my right where I heard the greeting, I give a broad smile as Kenzie walks up to me. Now, my cousin is one hell of a woman and I'm more than happy she is with Jig. They are a great couple, and I think they are going to have a huge family from the way they've been talking. The size of the house Jig is having built says they are aiming for more than one or two kids.

"Hi, Kenz. How you doing? You too, Jig," I best not leave him out of my saying hi, or he'll be throwing a tantrum, I'm sure.

"What's going on? Why are these women screaming?"

"Well, Colton and Fist are having a throw-down with those two assholes. They are not going to be much good when this has finished. That one..." as I point to the one Colton has a stranglehold on, "has a broken nose which has been pummeled, so he's gonna need some plastic surgery to fix that. The other one Fist is beating on is that one's friend, and if you look closely, I think Fist just busted his arm."

Kenzie is frowning as she turns to Jig, "Why don't you and Mav stop the fighting or take it outside, and I'll shut up these damn screamers."

Not waiting for our agreement Kenzie rushes over to the table of women and bellows, "SHUT THE HELL UP!" Much to my surprise they actually do shut up, look at Kenz as though she is crazy. When one opens her mouth to scream again, Kenz moves fast and she has her finger nearly poking the woman's eye out. I can't hear what she's saying now, but the woman steps back while all the color drains from her face.

Jig helps drag the two assholes outside and I stay as I am, again looking over my shoulder when Helen speaks. "Boy, there is never a dull moment here."

She could be right, I'm thinking. But I'm not interested in sticking around for more fun. After the two were taken outside it's a bust on finding anyone doing anything untoward tonight. I warn Helen to watch for anything shady, and when she agrees, I give her a nod before giving Kenzie a wave as I leave.

CHAPTER FIVE

: BLAKE :

Today I am going for my interview for the cleaning position. I'm good at cleaning because I've done more than enough of it over the years. I take out the letters, receipts and list of how much I have to finish paying before I'm debt-free. Placing them on the kitchen table, I take a seat and for a few minutes stare at the things in front of me.

Sitting with a glass of water that I've taken from the tap before sitting at the table, I lament that it's not a nice bottle from the fridge. I have no more of my favorite bottled water left, so beggars, as they say, cannot be choosers, and have to be satisfied with what they can get their hands on.

Looking at the three statements for the debts Stefan created in my name, I see one I've nearly paid to completion. Two more payments and that one will be finished. The next one I'm looking at as I scribble figures on a notepad, I estimate if I pay what I'll save on the first one, along with what I pay now, I can have this one paid in full in ten months. The third one will take me probably two years!

If I can get this second job, I will use the entire salary on these debts. It will be such a relief when I am clear of all the mess Stefan left. Four years and I've been living on peanuts while throwing every cent I can to get things paid. I've also the mortgage on the house Yax lives in, and it is coming to the point she either pays me rent on a lease agreement, or she'll have to move out so I can sell it.

I'm happy as I can be that things are all paid in full for this month. My utilities are paid, and I'm thankful that I had taken insurance on both mine and Stefan's lives to cover the mortgage on the house I live in. The only thing that has saved me in a lot of ways, is the fact that I don't have a mortgage on this house anymore.

Noticing the time, I quickly get ready to walk into town for my interview. Ten minutes later, I lock the door and start walking, to only be stopped by one of my elderly neighbors.

"Hi, Blake. How are you?"

"Good morning, Bitty. I'm good, thank you, and yourself?" I ask. Now I like Bitty, but she is friends with a couple of other ladies that I'm going to describe as *bat shit crazy*.

"I'm good. I am thinking of selling my place because I'm hardly here anymore. Oh, what was that awful Yax woman doing hanging around outside your house yesterday?"

That has taken me by surprise, because I didn't know Bitty knew Yax, and I sure didn't know that Yax had been hanging around the house yesterday. "Well, you know the story with her and her son, Franklin. She seems to have it in her head that I am responsible for paying for her son's upkeep."

Bitty laughs before shocking me and spitting on the ground. "That's what I think about that awful woman. You know she has a man living with her in that house you own, don't you?"

"No, I did not, but thank you for telling me. That is very interesting."

"Yeah, well, I'll keep my ears to the ground, and you know I have friends all over town. We watch out for each other, now that we are older. Of course, I have a whole MC at my back."

I giggle at the look on Bitty's face, because anyone would think she was the Queen of England the way she is puffing out her chest, lifting her chin and looking mighty regal.

"I have to run, Bitty. I'm going for an interview."

"Where at?" Bitty asks before I can move away from her.

"The cleaning company, you know, Helping Hands," I reply as I start to walk backwards, hoping she sees I have to get moving.

"You tell them Bitty said that you are under my wing. If Heather is there for your interview, you tell her she'll be eating rocks if she doesn't employ you."

"Oh, okay, will do. Thanks, Bitty." I turn and start to speed walk because I have to make up time, or I'll be late and that would be a terrible impression to give.

A while later I take a seat where indicated, which is in front of a desk where Alf is looking me over. He gives me a warm welcome and the lady who I overheard talking about the job gives me a finger wave as she passes the office I'm sitting in.

"Okay, Blake. First, can I see your references?"

I pass the envelope with all my references inside. I have seven and they are all good ones, showing I am reliable, honest and can work unattended. I am rather proud of my working experience, even though they are lowly in some people's eyes. But to me, it doesn't matter as a job is an honest way of making a living, no matter what that job is.

I wait calmly and quietly as Alf reads each one of the references. He eventually places them back into the envelope and passes them back to me. "I'm impressed with those, Blake. You have continually shown excellent character, and the cleaning, nursing home and serving ones give their personal contact numbers as well as the company's. That, to me, shows how much they valued you as a worker and an individual."

"Thank you."

"No need to thank me Blake, you have obviously earned the praise they are giving you. I'd like you to start on Wednesday if you can. It will give me time to get your clients organized. I will go around with you the first time you meet them, then they won't be frightened to open the door to you.

"The job entails cleaning kitchens, bathrooms, utility rooms, and if needed, anywhere else. The people you are being placed with see no one after they have had their lunchtime meal. We have included hot meals for any of our customers who can't get a hot meal for themselves. I don't give a rat's ass what anyone else wants us to do officially. We included a little on the cost of our service to our commercial clients, which covers the meals. Hence, our elderly customers don't have to pay for a meal each day.

"I need you to check their fridge, freezer, and cabinets. If you think they don't have enough food, offer to shop for them. If you do any shopping, I will give you a bonus at the end of the month to cover your time and effort."

"I can do that, and would do it without you needing to give me a bonus." Alf gives me a considering look, searching for something in my face, I'm sure. I calmly look back at him, showing I have no hidden agenda.

"Let's put you on a three-month trial, and then we can part ways if we feel we are not a good fit. If you are a good fit your salary will increase a little more."

"Okay, that's good. Do you want me to come here and go with you to the customers? Oh, there is one problem, but you may not employ me after I tell you."

Alf leans forward, clasping his hands together on the desktop. "What's that, Blake?"

"I don't have a vehicle. I am okay to walk from one customer to the next, but is it a problem?"

Tapping his fingers on the desk while obviously thinking, we both turn when a lady walks into the office and gives me a bright smile.

"Hi, are you Blake?" she asks.

"I am, yes," I return the smile, trying to maintain a good impression.

"Well, you've got the job. I've been told by Bitty that you are solid, you need the job and that you are her friend. She also told me she'd spit in my food at the clubhouse if I didn't employ you."

I'm so shocked that I'm sitting here with my mouth hung open. Alf looks about as shocked as me, but then both he and this woman throw their heads back, laughing.

"Those three are beyond anyone I've ever known. Honestly, Heather, how the three ended up in that clubhouse I'll never know, but I bet they are trouble at times," Alf chortles.

"I'm not sure I can take the job because I don't have a vehicle at the moment," I quickly let her know that I'm on foot these days, because I don't want them to employ me, and then they are embarrassed to say they can't use my services.

"That's not a problem. Alf, have you placed Blake on a trial basis?"

"I have, Heather. Three months. Blake's references are excellent and I'm sure we won't have any problems."

I realize that Heather is the owner, along with Alf, that I've heard of. I have not heard a single bad word about her, and if I've heard right, she is the woman of Forest, our local Sheriff. I don't think they are married? But then I don't know them so they could be, but either way, it isn't my business.

"We have the Nissan NV200 out back, and nobody has used that in quite a while. It'd be better to be used than left to rot," Heather is looking at Alf with a raised eyebrow.

"Yeah, okay, Blake can use that, and I'll give her the usual contract we put on the vans with the stipulation it's returned, if at the end of the three-month period we part ways." Alf looks at Heather, who nods her head in agreement.

"Okay, I've got to get to the clubhouse this morning, but I'll see you soon, Blake." Heather quickly waves at Alf and disappears. She is a bit of a whirlwind.

An hour later, I'm driving home in the van I've been allocated, and I have the broadest smile on my face that you could imagine. Even my cheeks hurt with it. This, I hope, is going to be a tremendous step up for me and my circumstances. It's going to be tiring working two jobs and from morning to nearly midnight, but I need it and that's all that matters.

Parking the van, I climb out, lock up and turn to walk towards the house when I hear my name called. Turning, I can't hold back the frown that flashes onto my face. Yax! What the hell does she want now?

"What do you want?" I ask, standing with my back to my front door because no way am I going to have her get inside.

"I need you to give me money for Franklin."

"Not happening, Yax. You are already living rent free in a house I own, which I allow out of the goodness of my heart. I'm paying a mortgage on that place, and if you want to continue trying to squeeze money from me, then I'll see a lawyer about you signing a tenancy agreement."

"You can't do that. Franklin is your stepson. You have responsibilities towards him." Yax is getting red in the face, and I can see something behind her eyes that I'm not liking.

I open my mouth to respond when again, Bitty appears from nowhere. Now she said she was going to the clubhouse, so I'm shocked she is still around. But what she says next has my blood starting to boil.

"Oh, hello, Yax. Is Benny still living at your house? I hear he is the real father of your son Franklin, and not Blake's poor, dead husband. Is that why Benny is living at your house with you and his son?"

My head spins toward Yax, and I can see another flash behind her eyes. Oh yes, there is something going on here, and I'm not going to be made a fool of any longer. "How long has this man been living in the house that I own?"

Yax swallows hard, before muttering. "Not long."

"He's been there a year or more, Blake. I have proof because my friend Marjorie lives directly opposite Yax, and she has photographs on her cellphone of that man coming and going. That right Yax, over a year? He's Franklin's dad and you are screwing Blake over for a free roof over your head." Bitty is nearly nose-to-nose with Yax and is so angry each time she speaks, spittle flies hitting Yax in the face, who jerks back trying to not get hit by it.

"I'll be seeking legal advice, Yax, about Franklin's DNA and for you to either sign a lease or get the hell out of my house." I turn and open the door, giving Bitty a smile. "You want a cup of coffee, Bitty?"

"No, I have people to see, but I'll find out more information for you about this bitch, don't you worry," pointing at Yax, who is rushing down the street. "I'll be having my boys look into you and your man, Yax, so I'd start packing, ready to run if I were you."

"Thanks, Bitty," I say, as soon as Yax is far enough away.

"Don't thank me. I'm more than happy to take that bitch down. That poor son of hers is going to have no life at all. He's not your husband's son, Blake. She saw him as an easy one to fool. She bragged about it while out of town at The Nitelife, in Midville, which is only fifty-minutes away. She was overheard by Marjorie's granddaughter Carolyn, and of course she told her Grammie, because Marjorie loves gossip."

"I'm going to have to find out the costs of legally getting a DNA from Franklin, and to have Yax removed from my house. I don't want her living there anymore." I rub my face with the palms of my hands and give Bitty a smile as I thank her again and head inside.

How I'm going to afford this I have no idea, but I'll have to look at how much I can save in various places, like utilities. I'm pleased that the van for work is not my responsibility regarding gas. I have an allowance and I'll walk everywhere, apart from my cleaning duties. That way I cannot get into any kind of trouble because I have it.

CHAPTER SIX

It's Saturday morning and I need to get my butt in gear, as I promised Jig I'd help him and Kenzie place furniture in their house. The house is damn awesome, but it needs a lot of furniture. I don't care about that, it's the amount of lifting I'm going to be doing to help move all that furniture as it's delivered that's worrying me.

Walking into the kitchen, I grab a bowl of oatmeal, toast, and a mug of coffee. Taking a seat near Knuckles and Jo, who are eating quietly, I turn my head as Mia gives an announcement.

"I just want you all to know that the twins are enrolled for kindergarten, and will start next week." Mia is beaming, and we all know she's proud of the twins, even though they are hellions now. Before anyone can give congratulations, the twins walk into the kitchen with Amelia behind them. They are both holding a teddy bear, which isn't at all odd, until they lean them against the wall and start to dry hump them.

Mia squeals, stamps her foot and scans the room, coming to a stop when she looks at Knuckles and Jo. Jo has her head down, trying to look like she's seen nothing, and it has nothing to do with her at all. Knuckles, however, is grinning at the twins' antics, and to everyone's amazement he throws his head back, laughing.

Mia isn't taking this well. She picks up the apple she'd placed next to her plate and throws it at Knuckles, missing him and hitting me on the shoulder. I jump to my feet, hold my hands in a surrendering fashion, and damn, I see Mia picking up anything from the table she can and throwing it. Thankfully, missing me this time.

Jo jumps up from the table and runs out of the back door, leaving Knuckles to his fate. But to be fair, he isn't worried at all. However, when Axel walks into the kitchen and sees Mia upset, Knuckles scurries out the back door after Jo.

I'm not hanging around here. I grab my dishes, take them to the drainer and leave them, quickly making my way out of the kitchen and over to Jig's place. It's got to be safer moving furniture than staying in this kitchen.

As I walk over to Jig's house I can't hold back the chuckle as I remember the twins humping the teddy bears. I can just imagine the fuckers are going to be competing when they get older. I'm not sure how Mia is going to survive the twins, but I hope Summer is a sweetie that doesn't become a rootin' tootin' gun-toting redneck.

"Hi, Mav." I look over to the new house and see Kenzie standing out front waving with the biggest smile on her face. BigDog of course, is next to her, watching for anything he may have to protect his momma from.

"Morning, Kenz." I give her a hug and mess up the top of her head, which I know irritates the hell out of her. "I advise you to stay out of the clubhouse for now. I'm sure Mia is on the warpath, and keep clear of Knuckles and Jo too..."

"Oh, Jo and Knuckles are here." Kenzie points over her shoulder towards the front door, and I sigh, knowing if they are caught here, Jig and Kenzie will get roped into the mess.

"What's wrong?" Kenzie asks, and I whisper in her ear what happened in the kitchen. Looking up at me, I see the grin start to form before a full-on laugh bursts out of her. "Oh, my, I would have paid to see that. Poor Mia, she is going to have her hands full with those two, I'm sure."

"I don't think she is going to... I think she already has." I can't hold the smirk that forms until I hear grumbling and heavy footsteps behind me. Turning, my eyes widen when Mia is stomping over to us with a fucking cleaver in her hand.

"Come on, Mia, let me make you a chamomile tea." Kenzie throws her arm around Mia's shoulders with not a worry about the cleaver, and I stand well away because I don't want my junk cut off, because Knuckles can't keep his in his damn pants.

Jig steps out of the front door and gives a cautious look at Mia and Kenzie, but keeps quiet. I think he's going to survive this, as he gives Mia a smile and steps over to me.

"Don't ask. Let's get this furniture moved." I make my way into the huge cabin, or house, as Kenzie likes to call it, and look to Jig for where we are going to start.

I'm not a bit surprised when Kenzie says she's going to speak to Heather about getting cleaning help. The place is huge, and going to take some looking after.

The morning passes fast, and I have to admit to myself that although I keep myself fit, I'm pleased to be handing over the afternoon help to Garth, who apparently has today away from work, but was overheard saying so and got himself hogtied to helping here.

I like Garth and the more contact I have around him, the more I think we should drag him in as a brother. I may just bring it up in church.

Later, and after lunch of course, I'm riding into town behind BS, who is going to be visiting the club's businesses. We are all hoping to hear anything being whispered about women being drugged, and any suspicious people seen around town. Wings, for some reason, jumped onto his hog and tucked in behind me as we left the compound. He was mumbling about being bored, and Chaos was working too many hours to get into any mischief with him. I roll my eyes because honestly, do they think they are still teenagers!

Pulling into the front of the Bespoke Furniture Shop, BS places his helmet on his seat and turns to speak to us both. "You two wait here. Keep your eyes open. If you see anyone that is friendly to the MC ask them if they've seen anything."

Staying astride my hog, I lay my helmet between my legs on the tank. Turning to look at Wings, who I thought was behind me. Well, his hog is, but Wings is walking down the sidewalk, giving winks and smiles to every woman he passes. Sighing, because I know he's gonna cause trouble.

Nothing unusual going on here. It's damn boring if I'm honest. Folding my arms across my chest, I continue to watch everyone walking down the sidewalk, going into and out of the shops.

"MAV...MAV..." Turning to look behind me when I hear my name shouted, I frown as I watch Wings sprinting up the sidewalk.

"What's up?"

"I found out that two women have left town after they were date raped last month. This, it seems, has been going on for longer than we thought. I'm going to keep digging around as I've made a few contacts since I got here. Well, me and Chaos. We go to a poker evening once a month at old Benny Bradshaw's. Surprising what you find out from the older generation. They are more observant than you can imagine." Wings is snarling and I can understand why because this is showing we were negligent in our observations of the town.

Before I can reply to Wings, BS walks out of the furnishing shop and stands a moment at his hog. "Lucas from the wood supply saw something last week. He called Terry and Jorge to him and followed the guy he had seen peeking into a woman's window. They cornered him and dragged him into the backyard of old man Gonshaw's place and beat the fuck out of him. They've not seen him around since, but they are keeping ears open for anything."

"Fuckin' hell, we've been missing shit going on. We need to get to all our people and find these fuckers, take them down and clean up," I snarl.

BS nods in agreement. "This is the third thing I've heard in two days. We need to discuss this in church tomorrow. Find out what Pres wants us to do."

"I know what I want to do, and that's feed some fucker his own balls!" Wings straddles his hog, fires her up and takes off before I can even place my helmet on my head.

"He's a fuckin' hothead," BS shakes his head, then looks at me. "But you can bet he'll find out faster than anyone else what's going on. He'll speak to the women he's been *friendly* with."

I chuckle, because Wings is known for his following of women. "They all seem to think he's someone that needs to settle down. We all know it's going to take someone like Star to settle Wings down. Can you imagine putting up with his shit on a regular basis?"

BS shakes his head as he smirks. "Oh, it'll be fun when he finds his woman. I can't fuckin' wait."

Back at the clubhouse I'm grabbing a bottle of water from the fridge when I stop to listen to Mia, who is telling the Three Stooges the twins are going to be starting Kindergarten. Now I can't help but inwardly smirk because whoever is going to be looking after those two hooligans is going to have a hard time. If I had to describe them, it would be to say they are from the Little Johnny jokes— Yeah, little Johnny one and two!

Sunday and after watching the women's training session with Chaos, Wings and Meat, I'm surprised to see Graham had joined them. When the fuck did he come here to train with the Ol' Ladies?

Target takes a seat on the bench next to me, and he's watching Winter enjoying herself messing with Kenzie. They seem to have gotten themselves into a friendship, and it's great to see. My cousin deserves happiness, and now her brother and his family are further away she's sunk into the MC family with enthusiasm.

"I'm going to do a second wave over my informants later. If we need to follow through with anything, you gonna be available?" Target asks, and I turn to look at him, with a raised eyebrow that is clearly asking if he has any doubts. "Okay, okay, sorry. I'm going to check every one of them, and it may take me a few days, but I'll find each of them."

Walking into church an hour later, I take my usual seat and relax back, place the ankle of one leg onto the knee of the other and fold my arms across my chest, calmly waiting for Pres to arrive and open the meeting.

Knuckles takes a seat next to me on the left and Colton on the right. I give them both a chin lift but remain in my relaxed position. Colton is buzzing for some reason. You can feel it flowing from him. I give him a fast study but not sure what is going on with him.

"Sit still, Colton." Knuckles gives him a firm look, which he has to do by leaning back and glaring from across my back.

"I'm trying, but you know I don't like waiting." Colton obviously has something going on, but I'm not getting involved unless I have to.

Last scheme he dragged me into, we ended up on compound duty for a month, pulling every weed we could find. Axel thought it highly amusing, as he had us doing it in a costume of a Knave that he rented from Lily's shop.

Pres walks into church with Drag and Buzz behind him. Surprisingly, he also has Graham! Now what the fuck is going on?

Once everyone is settled, the door is closed and Axel picks up the gavel, slamming it down and declaring the meeting open. I'm not sure if we'll be able to keep using this room as church, because we've so many members now that if you don't get a seat early, you are packed standing against the walls.

Axel speaks, and everyone pays close attention, some leaning forward in their seats. Sentry, I notice, is standing next to the door, obviously living up to his name.

"Okay, first, I've looked at all the officers' reports and with nothing particular to give you all, I'd rather we don't waste time on that. Anyone have a problem with that?" Nobody speaks, so Axel continues. "As you can see, we have Graham in attendance, which is not the norm, but he found out a little more from our *friend* we took over to Nell's place. Graham, do you want to fill everyone in?"

"The man was not wanting to give anything extra, but Tank got him talking. It seems this Mark Milanas wants to start himself a trafficking ring. He's eager to get a full take on how well the date rape drug works. Then he can drug and have his men test out the goods before they are sold on," Graham is snarling, and anyone can see he's about ready to burst out of his skin with anger and disgust.

I grit my teeth so hard it is a wonder I don't crack the molars, but I can hear the disgust and pure rage from my brothers. Colton can't seem to sit any longer, and he shoots to his feet. "I want in on torturing these fuckers. I've heard where two live and I'm ready to drag them to Nell's and feed the gators a hearty meal."

Pres shakes his head, looking at Colton. "It's okay, Colton. You'll get to share in the fun. Now, take a seat."

The calm way Pres spoke to Colton has all of us looking at him with more than a little interest. That is not the normal reaction we'd expect from him. However, when you look closely at Axel, the man, and not the Pres, you can see he is past angry and only holding himself together by a thread.

"By next week's church, I want all the information of who is involved, where they are and when would be the best time to strike. I want this motherfucking Mark taken down, and I'll hand him to Jaws myself if necessary." Turning once more Pres looks at Graham. "Anything else?"

"Well, it seems he thinks he is capable of taking down Vitale..." Before Graham can continue, the room is in an uproar, and I mean with laughter. If this idiot wants to push Vitale, I'm more than happy to sit back and watch it happen.

"If you want a piece of Mark, you've got to get to him before Vitale does. He is aware now because Nell contacted him last evening and filled him in. To say he wasn't happy would be an understatement, but he was on top of the world, as somehow, during the conversation, he got Nell to say yes to a date." Graham throws his head back, laughing, "Honest to goodness, Nell's face was like a deer caught in the headlights when Vitale quickly cut the call. She hadn't realized what she had said yes to for a moment, and when she did, she went into cursing mode and stormed outside."

"You want in if we find this fucker?" Pres asks Graham.

"Of course, so do Richie and Tank. Nell is happy to get rid of the evidence. In fact, she mumbled something about cutting off balls to push into a rectum, and a dick to shove down a throat." Graham has a lopsided grin on his face at the memory of the incident.

"Graham, keep us updated and we'll do the same. Buzz and Drag are going to be on top of all the information we get. Come round next week for church and we'll put everything out for how and what we are going to do." Pres shakes hands with Graham, and the latter exits church, closing the door quietly behind him.

"I want everyone to get every single thing you can about this asshole, and every one of his men. I don't care who, or what they are, they are living on borrowed time. Forest, get reports ready to cover our asses, and Chaos do your thing with the ladies to see what they know." Axel gives Wings a dirty look when he complains he has more women to speak to than Chaos, as the ladies love him more. The bickering begins and everyone enjoys the stress relief it's achieving. "Anyone got any other business?" Axel asks while hiding the smirk he is struggling to hold back.

"We need to look at the fight ring again. We've not had anyone at the underground ring lately, but we helped Gaz get away from them. He's now in the UK and won't be coming back. But we need to get into this because I have a feeling this Mark is more than likely trying to recruit men there." Knuckles is waiting for Pres' reaction.

"Who are you thinking of going in as a fighter?" Pres asks.

"I'll do it." Colton shoots to his feet once more, and once more, I drag him back down.

"Hey, I'll do it. I'm older than you, and I used to be more involved with it than you, too." Fist grins, knowing full well he's annoying shit out of Colton.

Wings speaks out, "I'll do it. I can take any of the fuckers down."

"I'll do it, too, and I've been fighting longer than you, Colton," I snap.

"Yeah, me too," Chaos adds.

"Fist, Wings, Mav, and Chaos, you're up. Colton, you pretend to be their manager. Knuckles, you are the support person in any way needed." Pres is not grinning as he has his eyes on Colton.

"Manager, fuck, yeah... You four have to listen to me now," Colton chuckles, claps his hands, then rubs them together as though he's won gold.

"Okay, keep me updated. Fuck off and have a decent day. But by next week I want a full report on everything. This Mark and his band of idiots, and the fighting ring." Pres smacks the gavel down then points at Knuckles, "Me and you need a conversation in my office about teaching my twins shit that is stressing Mia out."

Knuckles and all of us know it's about the incident where the twins were kissing and dry humping. I have to admit I keep having a chuckle each time I think about it.

CHAPTER SEVEN

-:- BLAKE -:-

The comment from Bitty regarding Franklin has me searching through the paperwork I have tucked away safely, with my late husband's birth and death certificates.

Sitting at the kitchen table, I find the DNA paperwork. With my eyes, I scan every word, looking for anything that seems out of place. If this is a forgery, which it has to be, if what Billy said is true, then there has to be a way of finding that out.

As it's Monday morning I have little time as I have to leave for work in a few minutes, so this will be my chore once I get home this evening. Placing the paperwork in the top drawer of the dresser in the hallway, I pick up my jacket and head out of the house.

The walk to work will take me twenty-five minutes, so I don't have time to waste. I'm looking forward to working in this job. It is a nice place and has a great reputation. The boss, Liam, seemed friendly and I think I will get along with him well.

Arriving at work, I walk into the shop and smile at Liam. "Good morning," I quickly say as I reach the end of the counter.

"Morning, Blake. Come on into the kitchen. I have to ask you to work in the kitchen today, as we are going to be busy. Mondays are usually quiet, but a group of ladies have booked three tables. They are elderly and we never rush them as they come in once a month and have their knitting circle meeting here." Liam gives me a pained look, and I can't help the smile that appears at the thought.

"I can look after the kitchen. Washing up and keeping things clean will not be a problem," I try to put Liam at ease, even though he is throwing me in at the deep end.

"This is Marg. She'll be helping in the shop along with myself and Millie," Liam introduces them, and after we've given each other a smile and nod, Marg rushes out of the kitchen and into the shop.

"You can see what needs doing, I'm sure. But if we bring through a canister that needs filling for the paninis make it a priority, you'll find everything you need in the fridge." Liam points to the commercial fridge and I give him a nod of understanding. "If you struggle to find anything, or just struggle, give one of us a shout and we'll come through. Elaine will come in for two hours later this morning to help, and she can give you instruction in here if you need it."

"Okay," is all I manage to say before Liam turns and walks out of the kitchen, leaving me to do whatever is needed.

Taking a deep breath in, I turn a full 360 degrees, checking the counters, cabinets, cutting table, and sinks, then grab an apron folded on a pile at the end of the table, where I'd had the interview last week.

Right...so let's get on and do something, I think to myself before walking over to the sink and running the hot water. I'll wipe all the counters as I clear them, rinse the few dishes and fill the dishwasher...yeah, that's where I'll start!

The morning rushes past. I've filled the dishwasher many times, cleaned counters, and refilled the canisters with the fillings for the panini. I also chopped lettuce, tomatoes, cucumber and anything else you can imagine, along with rushing to the rescue when Liam, or one of the servers, needed something urgently. I even was sent to the storeroom to grab supplies, which was a little spooky as it was a cellar, basically.

Liam gave me a lunch-break along with Elaine and we sat at the table in the corner of the kitchen. I had a breakfast panini and a large mug of Americano. The caffeine hit the spot perfectly, as I had been flagging.

"How are you getting along this morning, Blake?" Elaine asks, shaking me out of my thoughts.

"Good. I think I've kept up with everything?" I question it slightly because I'm not sure I know all I'm supposed to do, but with Liam just dropping me in the kitchen and disappearing, it was a learn on the job type of thing.

"I honestly think you've shown you are more than capable of fitting in here. You were dropped into the kitchen this morning and left to get on with it. But you have kept up with the shop's demand for fillings, clean cutlery, and crockery. When I first came to work here I was followed around for days," Elaine giggles at the memory, "I flooded the kitchen after leaving the tap running in the sink, and of course it then took quite a while to get it mopped and dried thoroughly. You have run the kitchen single-handedly, kept up when we've shouted through, or come to you for something, and not a word of complaint, and not even questions of how to. Amazing, Blake, you've been amazing."

I can't help the smile that crosses my face with the praise she's given. It's been a long time since I've had nice things said to me, or about me. Shaking my head because I do not want to go down the road of having a pity party. It helps no situation, it only makes the depression worse than it would have been.

Liam walks into the kitchen an hour later as I'm filling the washing machine with aprons and tea towels. "No, you don't need to do that, Blake. Throw them all in the large basket in the storeroom and they'll be collected by Heather's company, who now does all the laundry."

"Oh, okay. I didn't realize." He must see the confused look on my face as he steps forward to explain.

"We use the washing machine if we have any major spillage. We get it quickly into the machine with the strong stain removal detergent. It helps stop any stubborn stains from forming."

"Good idea," I smile as I respond, but step toward where my jacket and purse were left when I started my shift.

"Take care and I'll see you tomorrow," Liam smiles as he steps back into the shop, with Elaine following him while giving me a finger wave.

I need to rush home and get something to eat, changed out of these kitchen smelling clothes before taking another look at that DNA paperwork. Something is bugging me, but I can't pinpoint it.

Rushing out of the back door of the Coffee House, I make my way onto the sidewalk and start the walk home. I'm not looking where I'm going as I have my head down and thinking about the day, when I'm barreled into and knocked to the ground.

"Hey, bitch, you need to send me money for Franklin, or something bad's going to happen to you."

Looking up as I climb to my feet with the help of a large hand, I first give Yax a nasty look, and second turn my head to thank whoever has helped me get to my feet.

Now, I'm standing with my mouth hanging open because this man is tall and well built. The first thing I notice is his eyes. They are the darkest brown I've ever seen. He has a neat beard and mustache, that shows he cares for himself. He has one of those earrings where you see a hole right through the earlobe. A tunnel? Gauging? Who knows, but it had to hurt. He has short hair, but how short I'm not sure as he has a baseball cap on and facing the right way around. I want to giggle at that thought, but keep it to myself.

"Are you okay?" The man asks.

"Yes, thank you," I reply as I turn to look at Yax, who is standing in front of me snarling about money.

The man next to her, who is scowling at Yax, snaps. "Shut your mouth. We saw you intentionally push her onto the ground. I don't care who you are, or what you want, but fuck off before I lose my temper."

"Now, BS, is that any way to speak to a woman?"

"She's not a woman who has any right to any respect. Seen too many like her over the years. Never work a day in their life, living off other people's hard work. What respect does that earn someone?"

"How dare you..." Yax I can tell is going to spill her vileness at this man, but she must decide to be quiet as she sees the nasty look on his face. Whirling around she rushes away, and it's nearly jogging, which amuses me as she is wearing what you can only describe as stripper heels!

"Are you sure you are okay?" I'm asked again by the man who helped me stand.

"Yes, thank you again. She's not a nice person, and you more than likely saved me from having a huge drama happen right here on the sidewalk."

"You've skinned your knee by the look of it. Do you live nearby? Oh, my name is Mav, and this is BS."

"Oh, I'm Blake. I'll put a bandage on my knee when I get home. I need to get walking or I'll be later home than I intended." I give them a smile before quickly setting out for home. If it wasn't for that DNA paperwork I need to check out, I'd have a bath and go to bed early. But I need to get clean and eat before I can climb into bed.

By the time I'm home, my legs are screaming from the walk and standing all day. I will need to make sure I get enough rest or my legs are going to suffer. I also need to sort out my knee, which is just a scrape if I'm honest, but it needs cleaning.

An hour later I've had a shower, put on joggers and a tee and am eating the last of the frozen leftovers I've defrosted and heated in the microwave. My eyes are flicking over this DNA and I can't put my finger on it, but something doesn't look right!

Knocking on the door grabs my attention, and not having anyone that would be interested in coming to see me, I'm wary that it's Yax again.

"Blake, open the door. My old ass doesn't want to be standing out here."

Rushing to the door, I open it and nearly get mowed down by Bitty, who dashes past me and takes a seat at the kitchen table. Closing the door, I retake my seat at the table and give Bitty a questioning look.

"Look girlie... You have no one that comes to visit you, apart from bitch features. So, you'll have to put up with me, 'cause I like you and I'm thinking of adopting you." Bitty is giving me a bright smile by the end of her speech, and right before she grabs the DNA from the table. "Oh, I'll take this to Specs. He's my tech man. He can find anything, and if this is dodgy, he'll find out."

I'm not sure what the heck is going on, adoption? Tech man? You know what? I'm too tired to even be bothered. "Do you want a drink, Bitty?" I ask, giving her a weak smile, because if I'm honest I'm too tired for more than that.

We have our drinks, then I wash up and tidy the kitchen as Bitty tells me all about packing up her house, ready to sell it. She's going to move in permanently at the clubhouse as she has her own room, and all the stuff in her house is just that, stuff.

"Tomorrow night I'll bring takeout and we'll eat together, but now I have to get gone. I have people to see and things to do."

Like the whirlwind she is, Bitty has gone before I can say anything at all. Looking at the table, I see she's taken the DNA with her. I have no idea what she has in mind, or what this person called Specs can find, but anything may help me get out of this mess with Yax. The last thing I need is to be landed with having to make payments to her for Franklin. But, if I do then the house will be sold as I can't afford to pay anything more than I am already.

Turning out the lights after checking the door is locked, I wearily make my way upstairs. I double check my alarm is set for work in the morning, and lay my head on the pillow, breathing out slowly as I calm my aching body. Sleep isn't long coming...

CHAPTER EIGHT

-:- MAV -:-

It's halfway through the week already, and we've learned no more about the date rape assholes than we did last week. Walking into BS' office, I lean against the wall, because he's on the phone with someone and it looks serious. I wait quietly, and after giving me a chin lift he continues with the, 'Yeah', 'Okay', 'Where?'.

Folding my arms, I allow my mind to wander while I wait for him to finish his call. I'm wondering who that woman was that I saved from falling a couple of days past. She was a stunner, that's for sure.

"You want to come into town with me, Mav? I've got a man to see about a dog," BS states, giving me a chin lift to follow him out of the office.

Walking behind BS as we head through the common room, I turn to look at Mia, who has called my name. "Mav!"

"Yeah, what's up?" I ask as I pause before walking out the front door.

"Next week the twins start kindergarten, you know, since they had their birthday and are all grown up." Mia has fuckin' tears in her eyes...is she kidding? They are five, not leaving home! Now I may be an underground fighter, bouncer, and prior military, but I'm not brave enough to take Mia on.

"And?" I ask, because I have no idea what she is getting at.

"Well, I'm putting you on duty to travel with me to and from kindergarten with the twins." Mia is looking at me with what can only be described as caution.

"If you need me to be an escort, that is not a problem. Just give me the times and I'll arrange everything around that duty." Now, I can see her take a sigh of relief, and she gives me a tremulous smile. "Why didn't you ask Meat?"

"Well, he's busy with his modifications to the treehouse. He would have done it as he is their godfather, and he spends a lot of time with them. Between you and me, Mav, I think that's why they are such little shits." Mia has a scrunched up nose at the last of her comments, and I know she's trying her best to bring the boys up decent and well-behaved. But, you know, let's be honest, they are living most of the time in a clubhouse. There is not a hope of them being perfect kids, they are always going to be hellions.

"I can do it, Mia. It'll do them good to mix with other kids and get away from the clubhouse."

"COME ON, MAV, WE DON'T HAVE ALL DAY!"

Before walking out the door, I give Mia a kiss on the top of her head and a quick hug. Then scramble fast as I see Axel heading our way.

Later, I'm sitting astride my hog, I watch BS speaking with a young woman. She doesn't look like she lives on the street, too well dressed and clean. The woman is flinging her arms around as she speaks, and I see she has tears in her eyes. Something has gone on with her, but I'm not close enough to overhear their conversation.

I scan the street while BS is busy, and notice a dodgy fucker watching from the corner of a building. I step off my hog, stretch as though I'm pulling my back into line, and before anyone knows what's going to happen I'm off, sprinting towards the fucker who is standing with his mouth gaping open in shock at my sudden move.

Turning, he starts to run, but I'm already in full stride, and I'm damn fit, training every week on multiple days. I can outrun most of the brothers, as I have an easy pumping action with my arms and legs working in harmony.

I'm nearly at him when a van pulls up, and he throws himself into the side door, which is open, and the vehicle shoots away. I jog to a halt, but not before I notice there is no license plate on the van, so no way to find it, or who owns it.

Back at my hog, BS is sitting astride his, waiting. "What was all that about? I was getting ready to follow you."

"Fuckin' hell, BS, I nearly had him. But a van pulled up, and the weasel threw himself into it and they were gone. No plates either."

"Come on, let's get back to the clubhouse 'cause I need to speak with Pres." BS fires up his girl, and I'm only a minute behind him.

Back at the clubhouse, I follow BS into the office and take a stance beside the door. I listen to the conversation between them but keep quiet as I've nothing to add to what is being said.

"Miranda was approached by a sleazy asshole as she came out of the grocery store. He asked her for a date, and she turned him down. He followed her to her car and said next time she was at Club Whisky she'd be calling a different tune."

BS' comment catches my attention because that shows something vile is about to happen. "I'm going to speak to the bar staff, bring Silver up-to-date, and see if we can catch this fucker. If it's the one I chased, then I know what he looks like."

"Who did you chase?" Axel asks, and I fill him in on what occurred while I was waiting for BS to finish speaking to Miranda.

"BS, fill in Silver and Beer. Make sure all bar staff, including servers and kitchen staff, know what the fuck is going on. We need to catch this bastard and bring him down. If he thinks he can come into our businesses and start shit, he's got another think coming, and a deadly one!" Axel snarls, and both myself and BS know that is our president speaking and we best make it happen.

"I'm at Club Whisky tonight on duty, but I'll ask Knuckles to come along. Colton is over at TJs as we are giving him more responsibility, where we are not looking over his shoulder," I chuckle because I know it's hard for Colton not to get into a temper at the least little thing, but he has improved of late.

"Okay, you get Knuckles on board, and I'll speak to Ruger, Sting, and Brag. They've been moaning of late that they are bored," BS grins, then continues, "I'll speak to Graham too, see if he wants in on a little action."

"Good idea, BS. Find out how the date night went for Nell and Vitale while you're at it." Axel laughs, and both BS and I know that Nell is bound to have caused some form of trouble on the date night.

Walking into the kitchen after I have arranged for Knuckles to come with me to Club Whisky in the evening, I overhear Bitty speaking to Mia, along with Amelia and Sybil.

"That bitch is trying to stitch Blake up. I just know it. I've got Specs looking at the DNA report. How much you want to bet it's fake?" Bitty snips.

"I'm not betting because we all know what Yax is like. She's the image of her mother, and she was the most horrible of women. I was pleased when she left town and we all know that was because two wives were after her blood for messing with their husbands," Amelia calmly adds to the conversation as she sips her herb tea.

Mia, I notice, is taking all this in, like a sponge that needs water. "So, you're saying that this Yax person is pretending that the boy is

Blake's husband's child when he isn't? And that he's dead, so she's trying to squeeze the widow for money?"

"Yeah, that's right." Bitty nods and looks at Mia expectantly. I also notice that Sybil and Amelia are looking at Mia in the same way.

"We need to get the girl gang on board with this. It stinks, and we've not had a mission for a while, so let's give Bitty's friend a helping hand." Mia grins, hugs the Stooges, then rushes out of the kitchen.

Bitty holds her hand in the air, and to my shock Amelia and Sybil high-five with her, and walk away grinning as though to say, 'Mission accomplished'.

I'm not getting involved in this shit, but I wonder if it's the same woman who I rescued from the fall? I'm sure she said her name was Blake...

Hearing shouting, I head out the kitchen door and walk towards the treehouse. Now, I don't know if something has annoyed Meat, but he's walking around with a fuckin' G-string on and nothing else. Looking around, I search the area to see if Star is anywhere in sight, but not seeing her, I make my way over to Meat and Star's home.

Knocking on the door, I shout, "Star, you home?"

"Yeah, what's up?" Star asks as she opens the front door.

"What's goin' on with, Meat? He's walking around the treehouse with only a G-string on."

Star rolls her eyes, then storms past me mumbling about treehouses don't have nurseries, and she's not even pregnant, so who needs a nursery, anyway? 'Oh,' I think to myself and decide it's not worth the hassle to get involved, so jog over to the clubhouse and disappear into the kitchen once more.

"What's going on?" Mia asks as she looks up from where she's feeding Summer.

"Meat wants to build a treehouse nursery. Star doesn't want one because she's not even pregnant." I keep walking because I don't want to get involved in Meat's issues, because he could get you hung, drawn and quartered without trying.

Thinking back to when Meat first came to the MC, I can't hold back the smirk. He would walk around that treehouse for hours naked, with a weapon on his shoulder at the ready for whatever may occur. Axel would spend half his time covering Mia's eyes with his hand. It was amusing, as she'd do all she could to get a good look.

Later that evening, Knuckles is standing beside me at the door of Club Whisky. We are looking at everyone, whether man or woman, for any sign of shiftiness. Turning to speak to Knuckles, who is staring at a middle-aged man who is chatting up a young woman.

"See anything?" I ask.

"Nope. I've been watching that asshole, but he's made no attempt to touch her drink, even when she turned to speak to her friends." Knuckles responds.

"Did you speak to Silver?" I ask as I notice Dylon and Sherman on the bar talking quietly to each other.

"BS did earlier, so he knows what's going on. The staff have been informed and will watch closely. Silver is going to ask about more doormen, so we have time out with this going on." Knuckles turns and gives the group of men a look over as they line up to enter the club. Checking pockets and giving them the low-down on anything they see looks suspicious to let us know.

The rest of the evening goes smoothly, and it seems whoever is running this date rape gang may know we are on to them. That's good if they get out of town and stay out. They can move states, but if we find out where they are, we'll quickly inform the nearest MC to them, and what they are doing. I'm positive someone or some MC will catch up with these fuckers, given time.

CHAPTER NINE

Arriving home from my second day working at the Coffee House, I quickly shower and change into joggers and a tee. Bitty is coming tonight with a takeout meal. She didn't say what type of food she's bringing, but I'm not bothered by what it is as I'm hungry, and my fridge and freezer are both empty.

Knocking on the door grabs my attention and I quickly rush to open it, giving Bitty a bright smile as she pushes past with a large crockpot in her hands.

A huge man follows her inside, and he's carrying a box which he places on the kitchen counter before kissing Bitty on the top of her head, giving me a chin lift, and walking out the door, closing it quietly behind him.

"That was Meat, he gave me the food to bring for our takeout. We don't want to be eating that trash we have to pay the earth for. Come on, let's get this crockpot switched on again, and empty the box of goodies Meat gave us." Bitty is like a whirlwind and although I'm trying to help she is grinning as she keeps blocking my hands as they reach to pick something out of the box. Laughing now, she speaks again. "Well, we have some goodies here, and I told Meat I wanted things for your fridge, so we'll put them away first. You stand at the fridge and I'll pass them to you."

Twenty minutes later, and the large box is empty. I'm amazed at how much was packed in that box, and even the way he's wrapped frozen things, so they stayed cold at the bottom, with fridge items on top of them.

I take a seat at the table and look up at Bitty, who is serving us both a bowl of beef stew. There are biscuits to go with the stew and smashed potatoes that have cheese and chives mixed into them. It's delicious looking and I can't wait to try it.

"Now, while we eat, I want to speak to you about a few things. One the DNA thing, another is the fact you need help and a family."

I stop eating to look at Bitty. "What do you mean by help and a family? And has your friend found something with the DNA?" I ask hesitantly, because I'm sure Bitty is more than a little on the crazy side after some of the shenanigans I've seen her getting up to in the neighborhood.

"You are busting your ass, Blake, to pay the debts Stefan left you. You have that house Yax is living in, and girl, get it sold. You don't need to be supplying her with free accommodation any longer. The DNA report is false. Specs dug into it and it's a completely false form. It's a group of people that scam others out of what they have. Whether it be adding a name to someone's will, or taking a name out. Or, in this case, a false DNA report. Fake marriages, deaths, you name it, they do it. Well, they did until Specs had a face-thingy-meeting with some of his tech friends. Now, I'm not going to tell you what they are up to, but know that this shit is not real. Franklin is not Stefan's son. He is the son of the fucker that has moved in with her."

Now my face must show the shock at Bitty saying the F-word and she chuckles at my expression before continuing to speak, "I know, I know, I shouldn't curse, but honestly they are enough to make a saint curse, a nun drop her habit and a gay turn straight."

A giggle bubbles in the back of my throat after hearing Bitty's tirade. It rises slowly until I can no longer hold it back, and a full-on laugh bursts out of my mouth. I laugh so long my eyes are streaming with tears. I notice that Bitty is smirking at me while she continues eating, as though this is a normal conversation for us to be having.

Once I've calmed myself, I give Bitty a watery smile. "You are such a delight, Bitty. I've not laughed like that in a long time."

"You're welcome. My girls will be here in a few minutes, I'm sure. So, let me quickly say the rest. We are going to get Yax and her man out of that house, get it sold so you have the cash from the sale. I want to sit with you and go through all the debts you pay that Stefan created, because Specs can get rid of them. Now, about this adoption...you are too old, of course, for a real adoption, but that doesn't mean I can't claim you as my daughter. From now on, you are officially mine and I don't give a monkey's tittie for anyone else's opinion on the matter."

Again, I'm just lost for words. I'm not sure what to say or do, but the sincerity in her voice is so clear that a tear runs down my cheek, and I cheekily grin, stating, "Mom!"

Jumping to her feet, Bitty rushes around the table and throws her arms around me. "I always wanted a daughter..." said while sniffling back tears.

The front door bursts open and two women storm into the kitchen, banging the door closed behind them. I've seen them with Bitty but I've never spoken to them, but why they have burst into my house, I don't know.

"Why are you crying? Why are you hugging Blake? Why are you called Blake when it's a man's name?"

"Amelia, shut your cake hole," Bitty snaps, and the other woman giggles as she winks at me. But I watch in silence as they both grab a bowl and fill them with stew before sitting at the table.

"Well, you going to answer my questions or what?"

Bitty shakes her head while pointing at the woman, "This is Amelia, and that is Sybil. They are like sisters to me, and part of what the boys at the club call the Three Stooges. I was crying because Blake has agreed to be my daughter and called me Mom for the first time. I don't know about the name Blake either?"

All three are looking at me, and I give a small sigh. "My name is Blakely Carroway. But as you see, everyone calls me Blake, and it's been like that for so long I never say my given name anymore."

"Blakely, that is nice, I like it," the woman named Sybil says, and gives me a wink. Maybe that is what she does, winks at everyone?

"Okay, down to business," Bitty says, and turns to the other two women. "We have to get Yax, her man and the child out of Blake's house. We need to do it so the child isn't homeless, of course. But we need it done and sold so Blake has the cash for her future."

"Where are you working?" Amelia asks taking me by surprise.

"I just started work at the Coffee House, and I'm going to be working for the cleaning company from tomorrow," I reply.

"Heather's company? My dear, you are going to be tired out. Exhaustion is no joke." Sybil looks at Bitty while giving her a look I'm not sure of.

"I need the jobs to get my name cleared of debt. I'm doing okay, and working the two jobs will get me clear sooner, rather than later. I'm looking forward to working with and for the elderly people that Alf has allotted me to."

"What are you going to be doing?" Amelia asks.

"Well, cleaning, shopping if they need anything, and I will make sure they have their meals from Heather as they are doing delivery things now for them." I take my dish to the sink and start running the water because it does take longer than a few minutes for it to get hot.

"Alf runs a good business. I've spoken with Heather about the things he's doing now that they didn't do previously. She is leaving more and more of the business to him. She still cleans at the clubhouse, but to annoy Wings more than anything I think," Sybil grins.

"Who is Wings?" I ask, and I'm thinking there are some weird names being thrown around because wasn't that other man called Meat?

"He's one of the MC brothers. He's one of the enforcers too, a big, strong, man who has every woman's panties melting around their ankles," Amelia states while resting her chin on her hand as she rests her elbow on the table.

Enforcer! Oh, what have I let myself get involved in? Bitty is never going to disappear now that I've called her 'Mom'.

"So, leave it with me and I'll speak to Specs again, and some of the other boys and find out how we are going to evict that piece of shit, Yax," Amelia rubs her hands together, and has a glint in her eye I'm not sure I like the look of.

"When is your day off?" Bitty asks.

"Hm, I work Monday through to Friday at the Coffee House during the day, and I work evenings and weekends at the cleaning job," I respond, and not sure when I have a day off now I think about it.

Bitty picks her phone up from where she'd placed it on the counter earlier, "Sundays, the cleaning company is closed, so you must have Sunday free. I'll check on that. I'm making a note to remind me. You know we can do like Harry Potter and have rememberals on our phones. They let you know appointments, and stuff."

"Do I have one of those on mine?" Sybil asks and pushes her phone over to Bitty.

"I don't know, you need to ask Specs, he will sort it out for you." Bitty pushes the phone back again, and for a minute I'm thinking they are going to start fighting.

A loud banging starts on the front door and before I can get up, Amelia grabs her cane and rushes to the door. Now, I'm thinking why does she need a cane when she can move that fast?

Before I can really consider that thought the door opens and I see Yax with a man standing behind her. "We are here to speak to Blake. She has to start paying for Franklin's upkeep. He is her stepson and she has responsibilities."

I slowly stand and take a step toward the door, but am pushed back when Bitty grabs my arm. She shakes her head to indicate I stay where I am and nods towards Amelia and the door.

Tap...tap...tap...Amelia's cane is tapping, and it's like a drumbeat, it is attention grabbing. But when she speaks, my mouth falls open in shock. "Get your skanky ass gone and take your no-good-asshole man with you. You ever come to Blake's house again and I'll have the MC on your arse, and bury you where no one will ever find your disease-ridden butt."

"Hey, there is no need for that." The man steps forward and before I can get past why Amelia said arse she swings her cane and smacks him upside the head.

The man screams in pain, Yax screams in fright, Sybil steps forward with a can of pepper spray in her hand and Bitty is cheering as though we are at a football stadium.

Tap...tap...tap...Amelia's cane starts beating that tempo once more, and looking at Yax I place my hand over my mouth to hide the smirk that is happening. Yax grabs the man and drags him down the path away from the house. Amelia leans forward pointing her cane at them, "Come back again and there will be more than my cane for you to face..."

I'm not sure what the heck is going on, but I know I'd rather be on the side of these three than against them. I plop into my seat at the table and stare at Amelia, as she calmly takes her seat at the table and asks, "Do we have any dessert?"

CHAPTER TEN

Sitting in the kitchen drinking a coffee and checking in with Chaos, who has an idea for everyone to go on a ride over the weekend. I'm going to get my name down for that because I've been at the club, the bar, or here at the clubhouse for months, and I'm well ready for a break.

Meat hands me a plate with a grilled cheese sitting in the middle. I look up and give him a nod of thanks before grabbing it and taking a huge bite. I don't know what else he puts on top of the cheese, one of his concoctions, but fuck, it's good.

Bitty takes a seat beside me and I give her a side-eye, because I'm not sure what that look is on her face, but it smells of trouble. Before I can speak Mia, Sybil and Amelia take a seat.

"I thought you were all looking after the twins and Summer?" I ask, with more than a little suspicion in my voice.

"Oh, Star has them in the playroom. Now...we have something we want to discuss with you." Mia says quietly and leans forward. But it's the shifty way her eyes are flashing to the door that leads to the common room that I'm worried about.

Leaning back in my chair I fold my arms over my chest and give Mia my squint-eyed look. That tells her clearly I'm onto the fact she's up to no good.

Bitty gives a small giggle before placing her hand over her mouth to contain the glee I can see in her eyes. "What are you lot up to?"

"Well, you know Bitty just got herself a daughter? Doesn't matter, she has, that's all that counts. Well, seems her dead husband got mixed up with another woman, on a one-nighter, but produced a son. Which we know now is all a lie. He isn't her dead husband's son…"

Now, I'm not a dense person as a rule, but I'm not sure I'm following what Mia is saying, and looking at the other three who are nodding in agreement with all Mia is saying I decide to not even ask, and remain quietly listening.

"Anyway, we want this terrible woman out of Blake's house, and in such a way, she can't get into trouble for evicting her, with a child being involved. So, are you up for coming along and finding out what we can? Then we can decide as to how we are going to get Yax and her man gone," Mia leans forward and looks me in the eye. Waiting for my response, I'm sure, and for fuck's sake, she is the President's woman. There is no way I can allow her to go without having her back.

"Okay, I'm in."

Meat grunts where he's working at the island, slicing steaks and placing in marinade. I can see he has a slight upward tip to his lip, which shows he's finding this highly amusing. "What about Meat, he's a good one for recon missions?" Yeah, I'll throw the fucker under the bus.

Meat stops slicing and looks over at me. I give him an innocent look, but he knows as well as I do what I'm up to. Amelia must realize too, and she's totally in on the idea. "Yeah, Meat, you are good at recon. You can come with us, too."

"Go where?"

We all turn and see Star, who is holding Summer over her shoulder and patting her back lightly. But when Summer belches louder than any baby should, followed by a tremendous fart, we all look at Mia, who starts to giggle, "Just like her daddy!"

That is how forty-five minutes later, I'm following Mia out of the compound. Mia is on her trike, and looking damn proud of herself. Meat is driving the SUV with the Three Stooges excitedly sitting inside, and all of us are heading towards the house that Blake owns. I've a feeling this is the Blake that I caught, and the woman who we are going to spy on is the one in the street causing trouble.

As we reach the street, a bike pulls up and I see it's Graham. Now, what the fuck is he doing with a bike? A damn fine Harley he has too. It's an Electra Glide, and in damn good condition.

"Where are you all going?" Graham asks as he takes his helmet off.

Mia grins, "You want in on some trouble, you follow us. No questions asked, no lies told."

Before anyone can say anything at all, Mia is off and we are all right behind her. I look over my shoulder and see Meat is right behind me. The Stooges are grinning like fools in the SUV and must be giving Meat some grief, but he doesn't seem to give a fuck what any of the women do. He's always on their side, whether they are right or wrong. He just loves the women of the club and sees them all as his responsibility.

Pulling up at the side of Mia, she quickly places her helmet on the handlebars and gives me a grin. "Come on, Mav. The others can follow."

I sigh to myself as I follow Mia two streets through the back of gardens and dodging dogs that think we are invading their territory. Mia doesn't give a shit, and I keep looking behind me, but no sign of the others. Mind you, I can't see the Three Stooges climbing fences and shooing dogs out of the way. Graham is another matter. He is climbing fences and catching up to us fast.

"What's going on?" Graham asks as he finally reaches us.

"We are going on recon duty. This bitch is going down, and we are going to get the evidence we need to get her out of this house. Bitty's daughter owns it and we need this woman gone so Blake can sell it and free herself of some debt. Debt that isn't even hers, I might add." Mia is on the ball with this, and knowing how bad she had it with the prison stint and all, she is a tremendous support when she finds any woman having an injustice thrown at her.

"Did you tell Axel where you were going, Mia?" I have this terrible feeling in my gut that she has sneaked off, and that's going to leave all of us in hot water when he finds out.

"No, of course not. You think I'm a fool? He'd have said no, I couldn't come and do recon." Mia snorts as though I'm an idiot for suggesting it, but she continues speaking. "Star is keeping him busy. He'll not notice I've gone missing."

"So, you are dodging Axel to come here and check on what's going on with this woman?" Graham asks.

"Yeah…" Mia replies but stops mid-reply when we see the Three Stooges and Meat stomping up to the door of the house that we are watching and bang on the door.

"Are they not supposed to be doing recon? You know watch, but not be seen?" Graham mumbles.

"Yes," Mia growls, and I look at her because she sounded just like Meat.

"Let's wait here and see what happens. They have Meat with them and he'll not let anything happen. But we are a backup that the people in the house don't know about, so a secret weapon at this point." I had to make it sound good, or Mia would stomp her way over to the fucking house and cause mayhem.

The door opens, and Bitty pushes the man who opened it in the chest as all three of the Stooges rush past him into the house. Meat grabs the fucker by the collar and slams the door closed behind them. I look at Mia, who is frowning and keen to go over to the house, but I speak to Graham to divert Mia's attention. "What happened to Nell's date night?" I innocently ask.

Graham immediately knows what I'm doing as he gives Mia an innocent smile. "Well, they went for a meal, and Vincenzo chose a beautiful Italian restaurant. All dressed up in his black suit, which we all know is the normal attire for him, anyway. But, he brings an enormous bunch of flowers with him, including lilies which Nell is allergic to. So, she gives him a dirty look, takes the flowers and hands them to Tank, telling him to get rid of them before she feeds the idiot to the gators."

Mia giggles and rubs her hands together. "Was Nell okay?"

"Yeah, she stayed back from them, so none of the pollen got on her. But she went for the meal and in the restaurant, a woman at a nearby table kept speaking to Vincenzo. The idiot, instead of ignoring her or telling her to go away, kept responding. Now, you all know Nell, she saw that as disrespectful from the woman and her date.

"Nell excused herself to go to the restroom, and she climbed out the window, sprinted down to the nearest park and found herself a quiet area where she called Richie, Tank and myself to come and fetch her home."

"Oh. My. God. The idiot, what sort of date talks to another woman while you are at the table with your date? What happened?" Mia has forgotten all about the house across from us, as she is now fully focused on the tale Graham is telling.

"Vincenzo must realize after a while that Nell isn't coming back from the restroom, and goes to see where she is. He can't find her, so has his men start the search. They find her before we can get to her, but she's hopping mad. She throws every insult she can at him, and everything at hand, which happens to be rocks and earth. Vitale's men are inching nearer and that's when Nell inches her skirt up and grabs her Glock from the holster she has strapped to her thigh," Graham is grinning as he is telling us the story.

"No...Oh, good for Nell. I need to go visit. I've not been over since I had Summer."

"She'd love that, Mia. She doesn't have enough friends. As you all know, she tends to stay on the property with the three of us, but we are not always great company." Graham leans against the wall of the house we are hiding beside and gives the house across the road a sharp look. "What do you think they are up to? It's boring being on your recon."

"We'll go over in a minute. Just finish your story."

I grin because Mia is not interested in what is happening right now across at the house. She is interested in what happened with Nell and Vitale.

"Oh, she shot one of his men in the shoulder, one in his thigh and pointed the gun at Vitale, snarling that if he takes one step nearer she'd blow his dick off. That he had his one chance and blew it, and why didn't he go back and play with his new piece at the restaurant. She wouldn't let him get a word in, and when we arrived he was about ready to grab her, but she jumped on the back of Richie's bike as he was the nearest to her and we all drove away. She's ignored every contact he has made since then." Graham is grinning so seeing it happen had to be highly amusing.

"I'm going over to see Nell next week while the twins are at kindergarten. I need to hear all the details, and then I'm going to enroll Nell into the girl gang. I don't care she's not an Ol' Lady of the club. She's my friend and she's going to be enrolled."

The door on the house opens and the Three Stooges followed by Meat leave, and they all look smug. I side-eye Mia as I notice she's giving them all a look that says they best have left something for her to deal with. Graham is looking from one to another, and I innocently ask. "How come you've got a hog? And why have the other two got hogs as well?"

Graham smirks, "Well, we have all that property and we were fed up of dragging out the truck all the time, so we got ourselves a bike. We love them, we can check out the property on them easily, and we love riding them. Nell loves them but isn't keen on having one of her own, but I reckon I could persuade her to have a trike like yours, Mia."

"Well, if she is part of the girl gang, then she will need her own bike, or trike, don't matter, she just needs whatever she's happy with. I'll talk to her next week." Mia scoots over the fence, dodging the yapping dog and both myself and Graham clamber after her, but why she couldn't just walk up the sidewalk I don't know!

Back at the clubhouse and in the kitchen once more, I listen to Bitty, who fills Mia, myself and Graham in on what happened at the house. "We pushed our way inside, and oh my, it was disgusting. There was trash everywhere, the kitchen was disgusting, and every room will need to be fumigated in my opinion. Our boy Meat had that asshole pinned to the wall, and made sure he paid full attention. Amelia and Sybil checked every room, and Yax, along with her son Franklin, were not home. We told that piece of shit he had two weeks to find somewhere else to live, taking his woman and kid with him. Also, they best not mess with Blake again because come two weeks the cleaners will be in, and the house up on the market for sale.

"I let him know that the DNA was false, that the debts were paid and him, along with his piece of shit woman, best get out of town. Amelia whacked his shins for him with her cane, and that made him pay attention.

"Now, I have to speak with Specs, who is doing something magical, and then we can tell Heather about this cleanup job. I don't care if they are out of the house because I'm taking my boys if they are not to just throw them out. I have friends who can make sure Franklin is safe and has a place to live with people that actually care."

Mia is grinning so widely her eyes are nearly closed. She's enjoying every minute of this, and I know she's had some of that postparty whatever it is after having Summer, so she deserves a little fun.

"Momma...!" We all turn when we hear one of the twins shouting to Mia, but what we didn't expect was the ribbon in his hair, and the fake tattoos on his arms and chest. He's got shorts on and his sneakers, and that's it...what happened to his other clothes I'm not asking. Ribbons, tattoos, whatever next?

CHAPTER ELEVEN

-:- BLAKE -:-

This has been a busy week now that I'm working at the coffee place. I like it and it's only been my third day. Wednesday has come around fast and I start my cleaning job tonight.

Arriving home from the day job as I think of it, I quickly make a drink and change into an old pair of black pants, and a tee which I won't mind getting cleaning fluids on if I have any accidents.

I've not seen Bitty or the other ladies since we had the kitchen experience, as I like to label it. My mind sees it as some kind of event because I've had nothing like that happen to me previously, and it was fascinating watching the three of them. They are more like sisters than friends, and you can see the love they have for each other, although they pretend they don't.

Alf has been with me for my first three clients this evening, and they were easy, as they are still mobile and doing most of the housekeeping themselves. I cleaned up the kitchen, bathroom, and wet mopped the utility rooms if required, but apart from that it was just nice to speak with them. It's more than obvious they are all lonely.

Now, Ed! What can I say about him that probably hasn't been said before. He's my fourth client, and Alf left me to deal with him alone. Ed's a widower, losing his wife a few years back. He has a walker, but he's not using it at the moment, the dust on the thing tells me that, and the fact he walked toward me in greeting with a huge smile on his face tells me he isn't reliant on it either.

It is now ninety minutes since I started, and Ed has followed me around talking a mile a minute. It's more than obvious to me that the four clients I've been given need someone to do more for them than the half an hour to an hour of cleaning. I'm going to have to think about this.

"Have you finished for the night, Blake? It's getting very late and you should have finished here nearly an hour ago."

Turning, I give Ed a smile. "Hey, you trying to get rid of me? I wanted to make sure you had a clean bed and everything was as it should be. Now I'm putting you a meal in the crockpot. I'll put it in the fridge and in the morning take it out and pop it on the low setting and it'll be cooked for you, giving you a nice hot meal later."

"Oh, that's good of you. I've been eating the meals that Alf told us all about. They are decent, but it's not like home cooking." I close the fridge door. "You know it's nearly ten-thirty and you should be home." Ed gives me a good looking over, and I'm not sure what he's actually looking for, but it must be okay as he gives a satisfied nod to himself. Honestly, these elderly people are strange and I hope it doesn't rub off! I can imagine myself as a Bitty, Sybil or Amelia in my old age, if it does.

"I don't have anyone at home to worry about, so don't you go fretting about that. I have the vehicle that Alf gave me, so I won't be walking the sidewalks either. You don't have to worry Ed, I'll be careful. Now, tomorrow make sure all your laundry is ready for me when I get here and I'll get it in the washing machine. It can be forgotten about until I've done the other chores I want to get done." I grab my purse and van keys and quickly make my way to the front door. "Lock up after me, Ed, and I'll see you tomorrow."

"Okay, girlie, go careful," Ed is a sweetheart, I'm thinking, and I can see him being a friend as well as a client.

At home at last and it's been a long day. I run upstairs, shower, put on my pjs and walk back downstairs into the kitchen and make a cup of rose tea. It's one I have for calming before I head to bed. I find this gives me a better feel than chamomile does, and like the distinct flavor of it too.

Sitting on the bed a while later, I'm writing shopping lists for each of my clients. They all four need something, and I may as well do a shop at the all-night grocery so I can make sure they are all going to be eating as they should. They get a meal each day from Alf's and Heather's company, but they look like a home-cooked meal would cheer them up somewhat. I may do it for them twice a week?

Setting my alarm, I turn out the bedside lamp and lay my head on the pillow. Maybe it is all work, but I at least have people to speak with, and kept busy so I don't have to think about being lonely myself anymore, and that's my last thought as I drift to sleep.

Walking into the day job, I quickly get the kitchen ready for the morning mommas to arrive. I call them that in my mind as they have left their children at school and are now having a coffee, panini and a gossip with other moms.

Liam steps into the kitchen from the shop area. "Morning, Blake. We are not having the normal opening tomorrow. We are having a coffee morning for the ladies of the MC. If you come in at the same time, we are going to close once they leave, so you can have an afternoon free to do as you want, as soon as we have cleared up, that is."

"Oh, okay. I can do some shopping then, instead of..." I stop myself revealing more, because the last thing I want is my boss feeling sorry for me, or letting me go because I'm working another job.

"Instead of?" Liam asks, frowning slightly.

"Nothing, just thinking out loud." I turn my back to him and empty the dishwasher, which I had filled as the last thing before I left yesterday. I'm relieved when Liam walks back into the shop, and I can get fillings ready for the paninis.

The rest of the day and evening pass as expected, and I find the clients I will be seeing are a delight. Now they don't have Alf in their space and watching my work, they are following me and talking. I hear about how many children they have, whether they see them or not. Past marriages, husbands that have left them, or died, family they never see, or hide from, the latter having me smiling broadly at the lengths they will go to, to not see these people.

I have Sundays free and I'm wondering if I can get all four of my clients into my small kitchen! If I can manage it I will invite them, and fetch them to have a meal and the afternoon with me. I wonder if Bitty will let me use one of her chairs because I only have four and I'll need five?

The next morning I'm filling the dishwasher for the second time when the door opens and Bitty walks into the coffee house kitchen. "Come on, Blake, I want to introduce you to all my family, and now yours."

I'm more than a little taken by surprise because there are women everywhere. The shop area is full and each woman apart from the Three Stooges as I've been informed they are called lovingly, are wearing leather vests. It's like walking into a room with cult members that have congregated.

"Come over here, Blake," Bitty grabs my arm and starts introductions, "This is Mia, she is the first lady of the club, she is the presidents ol' lady, and they have the twin boys over there playing, Carter and Hunter, and this beautiful girl, Summer."

I give Mia a smile, and an ever bigger one to the twins, who are, for some reason, stripping off their clothes. Mia scowls and shakes her head. "Honestly, they are worse than Axel. He can strip his clothes off faster than you can fart, but these two are even faster. I'm going to have to speak to Meat about this. Star, you gotta get your man under control. I don't want the boys stripping off and shaking their manhood at every girl that walks past them next week at kindergarten."

Bitty points. "That's Star, and she's married to Meat, who is our chef, gardener and general reliable male. Now, Meat likes to strip off regularly too, and let me tell you he has one…."

"No, Bitty, don't discuss my man's package. First, the boys are here and of course are earwigging, and second it's my package and it's staying mine," Star replies, but we all hear her mumble to herself, *that man can use his package any way he likes as long as it's with me.*

Pointing from one to another, I'm introduced to Kya, Paisley, Gemmy, Jo, Eden, Tilly, Destiny, Carrie, Winter, Kenzie, Raven and of course, Heather, who I've met. I am never going to remember all these women's names! There are also two other children, Harrison, who is Eden's son, and Quinn, who is Tilly's daughter. It has your hormones throbbing as all five of these children are so cute. Even the twins, who are now naked and painting on the wall, much to Liam's displeasure.

One of the twins lets rip a huge fart, and the other twin bends down to look at the first twin's butt. He takes a huge sniff before covering his nose and giving a nasty look at the first twin. First twin shrugs, then farts again before peeling with laughter as he throws himself on his back, but he's holding onto his tiny manhood as he's laughing.

I look at Mia and she's looking from one twin to the next in total shock and disbelief. "Well, he is a bit gassy this morning," Destiny giggles, followed by all the other ladies.

"I'm going to have surgery so I can't have more kids. I can't survive any more twins, and it's a huge risk. How can anyone manage two more like those two? Nope, I'm going to have to see about having something done," Mia is mumbling, more to herself than anyone else.

A male voice speaks out, and it's the first time I notice the man who caught me from falling. He's standing near the door making sure no one enters, I think? "Come on, Mia, Axel will never agree to that. You know he wants six kids."

"SIX! If you or anyone else thinks I'm having six of his kids, you have to be out of your mind. Two is more than enough of the crazy that I'm breeding with Axel. Honestly, could we not have had normal children like everyone else? Oh no, I had to have two boys that are clones of their father, and, and, and....Meat," Mia nearly screeches.

"Don't pick on Meat, the boys have nothing to do with him," Star pipes up, giving Mia a dirty look.

"I didn't say he had, but he's teaching them all that shit. Like bungee jumping from the treehouse, zip lining, and he even has them crawling under cargo netting for god's sake." Mia is gradually standing and coming nose-to-nose with Star.

The man who started all this, well I think he did with his comment, grins, gives me a wink, then wades in to cool the situation. I turn and scoot back into the kitchen where I think it's safer to be at the moment.

What a morning this has turned out to be. The arguing, laughing, and general mayhem happening in the shop area has me hiding in the kitchen, although Bitty keeps trying to get me to go sit with the other ladies. I think Liam knows what I'm doing as he keeps smirking at me. Elaine and Fran are also here helping, and I don't miss them looking at me when I refuse to go back out front. Elaine grins and whispers, 'Chicken' as she walks past, but I can see she's more than a little amused. I let it pass because in her shoes I would probably be laughing too.

I head out to the grocery store once I leave work and pushing the cart around, I pick up everything I'm going to need to make a large pan of stew, that I've every intention of sharing with my clients. I also pick up from my list what I want to get them all. I'm using the last of my money before I get paid, which thankfully is tomorrow. That's the good thing about my starting this week, I don't have to wait a full month to get anything paid into the bank.

I hear what can only be Yax in the next aisle and I spin my cart around and hightail it to the end where I peek around the corner to see Yax, her man and Franklin. Just when I think I'm going to be able to sneak to the cashier and get out of here, I hear my name shouted by, of course, Yax.

"BLAKE!"

I'm not hanging around and letting go of my cart, I turn again to skedaddle and smack into what feels like a wall. I bounce back and windmill my arms to try to stop myself from falling when I'm grabbed by a pair of strong arms and held against the wall. Slowly looking up I inwardly groan when it's the man who saved me from falling last time I was around him.

"BLAKE! You are not running again. We had people come to the house..." Yax must realize I'm not on my own when she suddenly stops speaking, and eyes this man from his feet to his face and back again.

"Lady, I know who you are, and what's going on, and I'm telling you now to fuck off and leave Blake alone. Take your son and your man and get out of town, because give it a few more days and we'll be having another visit to you, and you'll not like the visit." Looking at me, the man winks.

"Blake, we need the house…" Yax again speaks.

"Are you deaf as well as stupid? You've had one visit, you do not want another one. Man, take your bitch and get gone. Leave town because I can promise you will not like it if you stay. You have a kid you need to make sure is good, but this bitch isn't going to help you in any way at all. Get rid of the trash, man, and move on, take your son with you."

"Fuckin' hell," the man curses and grabs Yax by the arm, and drags her along after him. What is sad is watching Franklin with his head down following behind.

"I'm Mav. Not sure if I've told you before, but I know you are Blake. You are Bitty's new daughter, and I'm sure you will be dragged along to the clubhouse soon, where you'll meet everyone."

"Um, I'm not sure about that. I don't have a lot of spare time. But I am thankful that you were here when Yax cornered me again. I keep trying to dodge her, but she seems to be everywhere."

"Bitty has Yax under control, and I'm sure she'll have something else up her sleeve, she'll just pull out like a magician with a rabbit in a hat, to have Yax run out of town. Come Saturday evening, I'll come pick you up, and we'll go to Club Whisky, have a drink and something to eat. See you Saturday, babe."

My mouth must be hanging open at this point. I've never been asked out on a date quite like that before, and not sure I'm going to be going either. Babe? I'm not a babe!

CHAPTER TWELVE

Friday afternoon and I've gotten myself a date with the lovely Blake. I left her with her mouth hanging open in shock, but no way am I stupid enough to leave her swinging in the wind with unattached brothers in the MC.

I have a few things to get done today as I'm working the door at TJs tonight. Colton is along with me, but I want to speak to Garth about helping on door duty. He is bored as shit working at the Swap Shop, and nothing much is happening there apart from women walking in and out exchanging or buying stuff.

I'm going to get him into the club as a brother, given time. He's a great man, and prior military, so an excellent addition to the fold. His wife, Hannah, is a real help at the shop. She works hard although she only works three days a week.

Sentry owns 51% of the shop, and we've left him to his own devices as the club owns 39%, and Paisley as a silent partner 10%. It's worked out well, but I don't think Garth needs to be standing at the door when I can get him working with us on doors at Club Whisky and TJs, which will earn him more cash. I'm going to visit the shop and speak to him as soon as I get the chance. I'll need to clear it with Sentry too or I'll be in trouble for stealing his staff member.

Walking into the playroom, I close the door behind me and give Sybil, Amelia, and Bitty a conspiratorial look. "Okay, tell me all you know about Blake and you don't need to fill me in on the Yax thing because I know she's in a house Blake owns. I just don't know why."

Bitty gives me a firm look before she speaks. "Blake is a widow. Her husband died in a vehicle accident, but he had what he thought was a son with Yax. He hasn't, as the son is not his. I had our boy Specs dig and find out if the DNA report was true or not, and surprise me pink, it was not true. So, we are getting rid of Yax, her man and sadly the boy, Franklin. You know most of this, Mav."

"Yeah, now is Blake seeing anyone? Does she live on her own? Is she naturally accident-prone?"

"Wow…hang fire, Mav," Amelia gives me a questioning look. "Are you after seeing Blake, like you know, romantically? Because if you are, then you need to get permission from Bitty. She is her mother now, after all."

"I don't know about permission, but I'm taking her out on Saturday night to Club Whisky. We are gonna have a meal and I'm going to find out about her. I won't rush her. I need to know if she has anyone sniffing around, and if she has anything that I need to be aware of." I'm doing my best to find out all I can so I don't put my big foot in my mouth at any time.

"Not that I know of, Mav. She is working two jobs. One at the Coffee House, and one for Heather's cleaning company. She's a hard worker, has been paying debts she shouldn't have been, and I'm sure she has been struggling alone." Bitty sniffs as she shows disgust when she states the last part.

"Okay, so nobody I have to persuade to leave her alone then? That's good."

"You treat her right or you'll have all three of us to answer to." Amelia taps her cane on the floor, which I'm sure is to make a point.

"Of course I'll treat her right. Come on, Amelia, since when did I not treat a woman right? Fuck's sake…" I'm not happy at her comment, but realize I'd cursed when I hear, 'Fu's ake.' Goddammit, I forgot the twins were in here.

The door opens and Mia steps inside, gives me a wide smile, which I return as I quickly slide past her and scoot out, making my escape because I know Hunter is going to drop me right in it.

"Momma, uk's ake," I hear as I rush away from the playroom, but I see Axel standing in front of me with his arms folded across his chest. But it's the shit-eating grin on his face that tells me I'm safe from a tongue-lashing about cursing in front of the boys.

"MAV!"

"You best get to your business, Mav, you know, before Mia catches up with you. I think Meat needs a hand with his extension on the treehouse." Axel is loving the fact we are all getting into Mia's bad books of late. I know it's that she leaves him alone when she is cursing us out. Which is rather hypercritical, but I'm not stupid enough to tell her that.

Walking through the kitchen and outside, I make my way over to the treehouse, where Meat is standing on his walkaround in a roman centurion's outfit. But the icing if you like, is Star next to him wearing a cherry red stola over a cream tunic. She has a wig on and jewelry that has her looking damn authentic for the period.

"You need any help today, Meat?" I shout to him, although I can see the trap door is closed, which is him telling everyone he's not available. Looking down at me, he frowns, grabs Star around her waist and pushes her into the treehouse, slamming the door behind him. Effectively telling me to fuck off. I sigh and make my way back to the clubhouse, where I dodge Mia and the Three Stooges in the kitchen.

BS grabs my arm and drags me into his office as I was passing to go to my room. "I need you to come with me to check out an empty shop. The one at the end of the main street. One of my contacts has seen someone going in and out. I've spoken to Wings, Knuckles and Colton. We can sneak over there tonight once it gets dark and take a look. You in or not?"

"I'm in. What about getting Graham in on the action? He's bored as fuck at the moment."

"Get me involved in what? You're right, I'm bored. Nell has everything wrapped up nicely, and apart from working on the property to keep it tidy, we've nothing going on. So, whatever is going on, I'm in," Graham states clearly. Where he appeared from I don't know, but he seems to come around here quite a lot of late.

"What are you doing here again?" BS asks, and we both watch the smirk grow on Graham's face.

"I came to fill Axel in on Nell's date, and the fact Vincenzo is chasing Nell even harder than normal. He's invited her to one of his mafia events, and from what one of his men tells me, if she goes, it's Vincenzo's way of saying she's his woman to his men. I know Nell has no idea at the moment, but I want to be a fly on the wall if she agrees, then finds out this shit."

BS and I look at each other, then at Graham, who can't hold back the laughter and throws his head back, laughing loudly. I don't hold back my smirk because I've got to agree I'd like to be a fly on the wall, too.

Feeling my phone vibrate, I take it out of my back jeans pocket and see it's a message from Chaos.

Chaos: Not going on a ride this weekend. I'm helping Winter set up a new range out back of the property.

Mav: OK. No problem.

Chaos: Another time, Mav. Any news on the fight?

Mav: No, I'll catch up with Colton and let you know.

Chaos: OK.

Putting my phone back in my jeans pocket, I turn to BS and Graham. "I've got to go as I am working out with a couple of the brothers. See you later, Graham." I give them both a chin lift and quickly make my way outside.

I give a hand to Drag and Buzz after leaving BS and Graham, who are working on a new workout routine. Being the one who's taking the hits from these two is never fun, but it teaches me a few tactical moves ready for the fight coming up. If it happens!

These two can fight and they keep each other sharp. I've seen Chaos, Wings and Target working out with them, too. They all are fast and fierce, not giving a quarter to each other.

"You ready for this fight thing if it comes off, Mav?" Buzz asks, and I give him a chin lift as I respond.

"Yeah, we all are ready, and I'll tell you I'm more than happy to not have Colton as a bona fide manager, 'cause shit, he's a mean one." I chuckle as I think of the last session we had where Colton was giving Wings shit about moving faster.

"I wish I'd put my name down now. I could do with a good fight. Nothing much going on around here these days. I'm not complaining about it as such, it's just boring. I've spoken to Reuse about helping at the tattoo shop now and again. I need an outlet because with the club being at peace, I'm bored following Axel around all day. He's in his office a lot of the day, checking on the officers' reports."

Drag surprises me with his comment because I had no idea he went to the tattoo shop. I know he gets along with Reuse and Hashtag well, but not sure about the woman called Siggy as I've not been to the shop since it opened.

"What can you do at the tattoo shop, Drag?" Buzz asks.

"I can stand on the desk, use a broom, whatever is needed. I can watch some of the women coming in and out, too." Now, he has a huge grin on his face saying the last, and I'm sure he's found himself a few women for a one-nighter that way.

Buzz looks at me and I shake my head grinning, but know better than to comment, but I chuckle more to myself than anyone else, as I make my way back to the clubhouse kitchen where I'll grab a bottle of water to take with me to my room. It's time to shower and change after that workout. It doesn't take me long before I'm back downstairs and heading into the kitchen to drop my empty water bottle in the recycle bin that Reuse had positioned in the kitchen.

"Mav, I'm going over to Nell's. Can you come with me? I'm leaving the twins and Summer with Jo and Sybil. I don't want to stay long but I need to get out of here for a while." Mia asks, giving me fluttering eyelashes, which I admit has me chuckling.

"Okay, let me drop this bottle and then I'll get the truck keys. Meet me out front." Turning, I head to PT's office to grab the truck keys.

Once I have the keys, I walk through the kitchen, drop off the bottle and head outside to where Mia is waiting at the truck. Axel is standing with her. Well, he has her pinned to the side of the truck and looks like he's getting rather frisky, much to my amusement and Mia's displeasure.

"Axel, get off. I'm going out for an hour to Nell's. Mav is driving, so I'm not on my own. I'll be safe. Now get off..."

Axel is smirking, knowing full-well that he's annoying Mia on purpose. He has this knack of getting her angry, then whisking her upstairs or to their house on the compound, where he soothes her down again. We all know how that soothing goes, and how Summer came to be.

Once Mia had freed herself from Axel, we quickly make our way to Nell's. All the while, I'm hearing Mia mumble under her breath about Axel being an *arsehole, an idiot, a sex maniac,* and other hot and angry comments.

Deciding to divert Mia's attention, I ask, "Have you heard anything from Shar lately?"

"No. But the last time I was talking to her, she was thinking about traveling. Maybe travel around Europe, visit the UK, and even Australia. She's worked hard, but she's ready to move on. I know she's restless and trying to find where she belongs. She knows she can come to us anytime she wants, but I don't think she will." Mia sounds a little on the sad side, but knowing Shar, she'll bounce wherever she lands,

"I thought she was going to get with Hammer, but it didn't work out. She'll be okay Mia. She's a strong woman and a survivor."

"I know."

I let the subject drop, and arriving at Nell's, I watch Mia become animated as she enters the kitchen, and takes a seat, throwing one question after another at Nell. I sit back and rest my head on the wall, making sure my seat is opposite Mia, so she doesn't feel I'm on guard.

I close myself off to their gossip until I hear Vincenzo's name mentioned, then I have to admit my hearing takes a turn for the better.

"Well, he's a dick, and I know he's a powerful man being fit physically, but it's mentally I'm talking about. He controls all his men without hardly trying. They respect him and what he is doing for them all. You know he's cleaned up and got rid of a lot, and I mean a lot of evil men and a few evil women. My gators never ate so well." Nell places a rack of muffins onto the table that she's obviously made earlier. I don't wait to be asked if I want one. I grab one and take a massive bite.

"Damn good, Nell." I hum as I finish this one and grab another. I close off to the rest of the gossip until Mark Milana's name is mentioned. Then my ears really do prick up.

"I've heard this asshole is selling drugs that are used for date rape, and I've had two or three men here, you know, for interrogation. It seems that this Mark is trying to get into the fight scene, but also wants to get into trafficking. He wants to be a billionaire...yeah, you heard, not a millionaire, but a billionaire...!" Nell sounds exasperated.

"I'll speak to Axel. We can't allow this and if you hear anything let me know, and I'll do the same." Mia is looking like she's found a new hobby, and I'm not sure any of us want her to get too involved with Nell, interrogations or the gators!

I'm going to have to watch Mia, and if I need to, I will inform Pres, and I'm sure Mia isn't going to be happy with me when she finds out I've informed on her. Oh, happy days!

CHAPTER THIRTEEN

It's Friday lunchtime and I'm getting ready to have a break from working. I am enjoying working the day job, the people are nice to work beside and Liam is a good boss. He doesn't ask any of us to do anything that he wouldn't do himself. He often takes out the large trashcans we have in the kitchen, and doesn't complain if he gets covered in anything nasty either.

I pour a tall glass of cold water and take it outside where I sit at the small bench we have behind the shop. Closing my eyes a moment, I count my blessings that I am able to pay all the utilities with no issue. I'm going to sell the house that Yax is living in. There is no point my keeping it as I would never live in it, and I certainly don't want to be a landlady.

Hearing my name, I turn and smile at Bitty, who is bustling over to me from the side of the shop. "Hello, Bitty."

"I'm getting too old to be coming into town all the time. I'm going to introduce you to the people at the clubhouse, then you can come and see me. I've asked the realtor to look at my place and hopefully I can get it up for sale soon. Now, I have the news that Specs has gotten rid of all the debts, so you don't have to pay them anymore, forget them. The only payments you need to make are the mortgage on that house Yax is living in, which we'll get rid of soon, and your own utilities, grocery shopping, etcetera."

"What do you mean he got rid of them? Gone, as paid?" I'm shocked and worried that this may come back and bite me on the ass.

"Specs found all the debts in your late husband's name, and yours, and he had them all gotten rid of. Puff, gone…"

Bitty is grinning at me as though she's a magician that just waved her wand and everything in the world is right. But looking at her, she's nobody's fairy godmother I'm positive on that. I've seen her do too many things to even think she is anything but innocent.

"Puff, gone? I'm not going to get into trouble with the Sheriff, am I?"

Giggling like a teenager, Bitty winks, "Forest is one of us, Blake. He'd never arrest you or we'd make sure he and Heather had more issues than they could cope with. I'd even consider getting Meat, Wings and Chaos onboard."

I've heard the name Meat, and know he's the man that came to my house with the food. But there are so many odd names that I'm not keeping up that well. I'm not going to ask. No Blake, I think to myself, just keep your head down and say nothing. "Am I really free of debt?"

"Yes, you are. Now, you don't have to work two jobs if you don't want to. You can kick one to the curb and have a bit of an easier time," Bitty grins, giving my hand a squeeze where I had it laid on the table.

"I'll keep my jobs as I like them both. I've been meaning to ask if I can use one of your chairs as I'm going to ask my clients to come for a meal one Sunday. I don't have enough chairs as I need five and I only have four."

"Of course you can. In fact, I've been meaning to ask if you want anything from my place before it's sold. My dining table and six chairs are in better condition than yours, and if you want the set, it's yours. Oh, my washing machine is only a year old, if that's better than yours?"

"I would love your dining table and chairs, and the washing machine too if that is really okay? My washer has been leaking for a while and I have to keep mopping the water that comes from under it every time I use it." I blush a little at that admission, but I'm not going to withhold the truth from Bitty. She's being the support I've not had in a long time.

"Okay, well I'll get the boys to come over and sort it out. It will be Sunday afternoon more than likely as they have training, and then they have church on Sundays. We can't rely on that mind you, so don't take it as gospel."

Church? Blimey, I didn't realize they were religious...maybe they are a cult after all!

Once Bitty has gone back to wherever she appeared from, I make my way back inside and finish my shift. Walking home later that day I ponder on how busy the place has been. I never realized how busy a café can be, which is basically what it is, in my opinion anyway. It is staggering to have seen how many people have been in for a drink and panini in just one day. I've washed so many cups, saucers, plates, mugs and trays that it's been like a factory line of dirty dishes.

Eight-thirty and I've gotten Audrey, Pru, who is Prunella, and Robert organized and they have agreed to come for a meal at my home once I have Bitty's dining table at the house. I've left them all with a chicken stir-fry which I threw together from the groceries that I purchased. I have a few groceries for each of them, and they were so grateful that it left me with tears in my eyes.

Knocking on the door I hear Ed shout, 'Come in, Blake'. Entering the house, I walk into the kitchen where Ed is covered in flour and what looks like strawberry jelly.

"What are you doing?"

"I'm baking. Well, I'm trying to bake. I have this recipe that says it's quick and easy, but I'll tell you it's a damn lie. This is harder than mixing cement in the yard." Ed is giving me such an irritated look that I can't hold back the giggle.

"Come on, let's clean you up. Then you can show me the cake you wanted to make."

Spending quite a few minutes, we enjoy talking as we clean the kitchen before making the batter for the cake and getting it into the oven. Ed obviously has enjoyed the experience, even though he kept eating the batter from a spoon as we were pouring it into the cake tin.

"Now, you didn't need the jelly at all, so what had you using it?" I can't hold back asking.

"Well, I just thought it's a cake, so why not throw in some strawberry flavor by using the jelly that has been sitting around not being used since...forever." Ed gives me a shrug of his shoulders, and I don't even try to hide the grin I'm wearing.

Wiping the counters and glancing at Ed I ask, "Not this Sunday coming, but the one after I'm going to make a lunch for all my clients, that of course includes you Ed. Would you like to come to my home, have a home cooked meal and a little company? I'll have a cab collect you all and bring you to my home. That way, you'll not have to worry about anything."

"Girlie, of course, I want to come. Not sure about sitting with all the other old coots, but I can suffer being around them for you."

Ed has a delighted expression on his face, so I know full well that he's only blustering. "Well, that is good, because it would not be the same without you." I grin to myself as I notice Ed puffing his chest out as he takes a seat at his kitchen table.

The rest of the evening I spend with Ed, far longer than I should be here. But he is such good company that I enjoy listening to him talking about his wife who died and their travels. They didn't have children as they wanted to see the world, and they both worked hard so they could have two months of the year traveling.

Ed owned a diner, and his wife worked alongside him. They had a trusted employee who would step up when Ed and his wife traveled.

"Ed, so if you owned a diner, and you did most of the cooking, how come you can't make a cake?" I know I shouldn't have asked, but the question flew out of my mouth before I could stop it.

"Well, I did all the meat, fries, and stuff like that. Sophie did all the green shit and other sides. The desserts we had brought from the bakery each day. So, in fact, we never had to do any baking. Even the bread we used for the burgers was fresh each day from the bakery."

Taking the cake out of the oven, I turn it out onto the wire rack and the smell is divine. Looking at Ed, who is sniffing loudly while his eyes are closed, obviously enjoying the sweet smell too.

"Okay, Ed, while this cools, I'm going upstairs to clean the shower. I didn't have time yesterday, but I want to do it tonight as tomorrow when I come, I want to get your laundry out of the way."

"I'll put the TV on and wait for you to get done. Then we can have a piece of this cake before you go home." Ed bypasses his walker, which is in the kitchen near the door. My eyebrows must raise a little and Ed gives me a wink once he sees what I was looking at, but he makes no comment as he walks into the living room.

For some reason, he reminds me of the Three Stooges. It seems these older people have far more going for them than they like us to know about. But I'm going to be an older person one day, so I'm going to learn all the tricks I can, while I can.

The cake is lovely and I have a second smaller piece while Ed has two enormous pieces. "You know you'll have some for a snack tomorrow if you don't eat anymore."

"Yeah, I'll have it with my morning coffee. Then there will be a piece left that I can have after that horrid meal Alf will send over. It's a peppered steak on Saturdays. It's okay, but it gets boring having the same thing every week," Ed grumbles.

"Do you want me to mention that to Alf or Heather when I see them?" I ask.

"Yeah, why not."

"Okay, then, I'll do that." I grab my jacket, give Ed a smile, and after saying good night, I quickly get to my van and make my way home.

Saturday came around quickly, and knowing all my clients will eat peppered steak today, I didn't worry about making meals for them. I'll make sure all laundry is done and everyone has everything they need for Sunday while I have the day off.

By the time I'm home again, my feet ache and my back feels like it's split in two. I take two pain-killers and drink a bottle of water before heading to the bathroom, and filling the bath with a sprinkle of Neroli and Jasmine bath oil into the water.

Laying in the water, my head back and eyes closed, I sigh contentedly. I allow my mind to wander and think about Bitty and her having the debts removed. It's an immense relief and I'll have money to spare for the first time in years. I have to get Yax removed and sell the house. Then I will truly have a way to save for my future.

My eyes fly open as I remember Mav and the date he said we were having. I don't know if he's coming here, or I'm supposed to meet him at Club Whisky because that's where he said we were going. I jump out of the bath, and grab the towel, wrapping it around me quickly as I empty the bath and make sure everything is tidy. I know I can be a little OCD, but when you've had to look after yourself most of your life, you learn to keep life easy.

After drying myself, I wear clean underwear, find my newest pair of skinny jeans, which are at least a year old, and a fake cashmere top. It's the best I can do until I get new clothes in the future. I throw my hair into a loose bun and think that'll have to do. I hardly wear makeup, just a touch of mascara and lip gloss.

Downstairs, I place a tissue, lip gloss, and a few dollars in my purse. I've enough to get an Uber if needed and even pay for my own part of the meal. I'm always going to be ready to watch my back since Stefan had let me down.

Knocking at the door has me taking a deep breath, letting my nerves flow out of me before opening it and giving Mav a smile. "Hello, I'm ready." I don't pause as I close and lock the door, dropping the house key into my purse.

"You look lovely," Mav quietly states, and grabs my arm as I trip over his foot. Which I have to tell you has a massive biker boot on it. He's wearing black jeans, a button-down shirt and the leather vest which has all the writing on. The cult vest as I think of it.

I climb into the SUV that he guides me to and helps me sit inside before closing the door. After he removes his vest and places it on the back seat, then gets into the vehicle, we quickly make our way to the club, talking quietly as we traveled.

Walking into Club Whisky a while later, I trip over something on the ground and nearly fall onto my hands and knees. Mav grabs me around the waist and rights me once more. I'm not sure why I seem to be so clumsy of late! "You're really trying to fall at my feet, aren't you?" Mav chuckles.

Now, I'm not one to take offense, but I think if someone trips or falls, you don't make fun of it, so I scowl at his response even though I know he's joking. Looking where I'm going I see a lot of men wearing the same vest as Mav is wearing, and without thinking, I mumble, 'It's a cult!'

"What's a cult?" Mav asks, but before I can reply someone steps between us and I scurry to a nearby empty table where I quickly take a seat, and think that solves the tripping incidents for now.

The evening progresses well, and we have what is called a basket meal. Mine is fried chicken, fries and onion rings, and it is great. "I've not had a basket meal before, and I love it."

"They are good, and there is a wide choice now too. We have the best desserts around if you want to try one?" Mav is licking his fingers and I'm fascinated watching how he sucks, then slides his mouth down a finger. I swallow hard because this has my mind wandering to some naughty thoughts, which I'm brought out of when Mav asks, "You okay, Blake?"

Dang, he noticed, and he's amused. The sparkle in his eyes tells me he knew exactly where my thoughts had wandered to. Thankfully, before I can reply, a lady sits at our table and gives Mav and me a huge smile. Then a massive man sits next to her, throwing his arm around her shoulders. He looks me right in the eye and smiles, and that is when my eyes notice the dimples...

"Yeah, she's got the look. The dimples did it, didn't they?" The woman asks me.

"Sorry, that was rude of me, but my eyes just saw the dimple pop on his cheek and it took my attention."

"Happens to everyone, don't worry about it. I'm Jo and we met at the Coffee House when Mia had the coffee morning. That was the morning one of the twins had gas, and I mean he had it bad."

"Oh...I remember the twins and the gas incident." I grin because it still amuses me that the one twin had smelled the butt of the other.

"I wanted to say hello before we head out. Bitty told us all that she claimed you as a daughter," Jo giggles. "You will have to watch those three. They are trouble and can rope you in for any mischief they have planned. I know because they have got me involved plenty of times."

Laughing a little, I reply, "For now, Bitty has not gotten me in any trouble. In fact, she's done the opposite. But I will take what you have said and watch what Bitty is doing."

"Okay, my man, I have a scene to play out," Jo says to her man and gives him such a look that I feel myself blushing. They both jump to their feet and nearly run out of the club, and I'm watching in total amazement, I have to admit.

"Sex. That's what she's talking about. She's an author, writes hot as fuck sexy stories, but she has Knuckles play out all the sex scenes with her, so she has them right. Well, that's her excuse. I think she just wants in his pants," Mav chuckles.

Before I can respond a woman walks up to the table from behind Mav, so honestly he doesn't see her coming. But she throws herself onto his lap, wraps her arms around his neck, and before he or I can say or do anything, she's kissing him.

Now, I'm no idiot and not going to be disrespected, so I'm on my feet before you can say 'Jack shit' and I'm out the door looking around for a cab. I know they hang around waiting to pick up customers, so make my way over to one quickly and jump inside, telling the driver my address.

I know I was rash running like that, but he didn't push the woman off quickly as you would expect when on a date with someone else. It told me he knows her and they have been intimate. No way am I sitting and watching that on a date. He needs to get his act together and his past just where it should be, in the past, before he contacts me again. I need to see and speak to Bitty tomorrow. I'm thinking she'll have some good advice for me on this subject, and I'll be quite happy to go along with what she suggests.

CHAPTER FOURTEEN

-:- MAV -:-

I'm so taken by surprise I don't react quickly enough, and fuck, I'm going to pay for this. I jump to my feet and watch as Sharon falls to the floor squealing 'Ouch', as if I give a shit about her.

"BLAKE!" I shout as I run after her out of the front door of the club, and see her in the back of a cab while it pulls away, leaving me watching my date leave.

Storming back inside, I see my club brothers staring in shock at what they just witnessed. But what has me stopping in my tracks and my mouth hanging open is Raven, who had been having a meal with Grease.

"What the shit do you think you were doing? How dare you assault Mav like that?" Raven is right in Sharon's face, but it's frightening because she is not screaming or shouting. She is deadly quiet. Turning to look at me, Raven surprises me even more, "Mav, I reported this as assault to Forest, and he's sending Ty and Aaron to arrest her. I'm a witness, and so is everyone else."

"No, I didn't assault him. I just kissed him," Sharon whines.

"That's classed as sexual assault." Raven is getting angrier as the minutes tick by, and I look at Grease, who is watching Raven with pride in his eyes...we are all fucked! We watch our women being bold and independent and we glow with pride. What happened to bikers being in charge? I blame Axel for this because it all started to go downhill when Mia came on the scene. Mind you, I'm not brave enough to say that out loud. I want my balls to produce kids one day, and not be sitting in the bottom of Mia's purse.

"Go find Blake and speak to her. Go on, move it, or you'll lose your woman before you even get her. What a first date this turned out to be," Raven snaps, which shakes me out of my stupor, and after giving her a chin lift of thanks, I dash outside and to the SUV.

It doesn't take me long to get to Blake's house and I know she is safely inside as a light is on in the bedroom. I shout her name, but she's not answering, and when I step back and look again at the window, the light has been extinguished. Fuck...fuck...fuck!

Walking into the clubhouse, I head right to the bar and grab a bottle of beer. Taking a seat, I swallow half the bottle in one go. I'm well and truly in trouble now. I know that Billy claimed her as a daughter and she's gonna be hot on my ass, that's for sure. Sighing because I know tomorrow is going to be one hell of a day.

"What's up?" Turning my head, I give Brag a look that has him cringe. "Oh, fuck, what did you do?"

"Actually, I did nothing, and that is the problem," I reply, and not sure how this is going to sound when I explain it. Brag takes a seat next to me at the bar once he's taken a beer for himself.

"What didn't you do?"

"I took out Blake on a date. Our first date too. We had a basket meal, and it was going great when fuckin' Sharon appeared from nowhere, threw herself in my lap, wrapped her arms around me and kissed me."

"Oh, fuck...that's not good." Brag's eyes are round with the shock of the scene I'm painting for him. "What happened?"

"Well, I was so shocked I didn't move for a minute. I didn't fuckin' kiss her back, Brag. But when I jumped up, Blake was gone. She'd run out the front of Club Whisky and bolted in one of the cabs that hang around looking for a fare."

"Oh, that's not good," Brag repeats, and is shaking his head in disbelief. "You know Bitty is going to be after your ass now, don't you? Oh, and Kenzie too, as she and the Stooges have been big friends. I hope she doesn't set BigDog on your ass."

"Goddammit..." I snarl as I rub the back of my neck. I'm in deep shit in more ways than one.

The next morning I'm dodging Bitty, who keeps giving me odd looks. I'm doing my best for it to not be known what happened last night. I need a chance to catch up with Blake. I've arranged with Wings to take my place at training this morning while I go over to see Blake.

"What's going on?" I hear Bitty ask, and fuck me, Raven and Grease have walked into the clubhouse kitchen. Now they don't usually come in the kitchen before training on a Sunday, but of course, today they have. It is, however, the look they are giving me which is alerting Bitty to something amiss.

"Well, Bitty...you see...there was a mishap while I was on my date."

I get no further when Bitty drops the spatula she was using to concentrate on Raven, Grease and myself. Now, Grease is smirking at me, obviously taking great delight in the shitstorm I'm sitting in. "What mishap?" Bitty snaps, placing her hands on her hips.

Amelia, Sybil, and Meat all step over to Bitty and look over her shoulder at all three of us standing here in front of them, but the glare is aimed at, you guessed it, me. Fucking hell!

"Look, it wasn't my fault. Sharon came up to where I was sitting at the table with Blake. She came up behind me, so I didn't even know she was there. She threw herself into my lap, wrapped herself around me, and kissed me. I was so shocked I had a delayed reaction before I stood up and chased Blake, who had left the club and jumped into a cab." I quickly make my case and see Bitty grinding her teeth. I hope they are not false teeth because if she breaks them you can bet she'll blame me, and I'll end up paying for new ones. Damn, where did that thought come from?

"I'm going to speak to Blake and Kenzie. Don't you think you are going to walk away from this free and easy. Your cousin isn't going to be happy about this as she likes Blake from what she's seen of her." Meat smirks from behind Bitty and walks back to the stove, humming under his breath. Fucker, I think to myself, because it's obvious he is taking delight in my predicament.

"Hey, Bitty, come on, it wasn't my fault. Raven had Sharon arrested, and was the witness to what happened." I do my best to smooth over the anger on Bitty's face, and I see it has eased somewhat, especially when she turns to Raven.

"I did. She was arrested for sexual assault, and you can ask Forest when you see him, Bitty. They hauled her ass away, and she was screaming and crying, making a real fuss she was. We watched it all happening and we are waiting to see what is going to happen to her now." Raven is grinning and Grease is chuckling. They are both finding this highly amusing.

"Leave Blake alone for a couple of days, Mav. Let me get the details from Forest and then I'll speak with Blake. If you are innocent, that is." Bitty gives me a raised eyebrow and I hold both hands out in a sign of surrender. I know I stand no chance with her at all. She'll check all the information before she gives me the go-ahead to speak to Blake again. "You just wait until I know all the details."

Giving Bitty a nod, as I know I'm defeated at this point, I walk over to a table and take a seat. Placing my elbows on the table, I stare at my hands while I run through everything that happened. There was no way I could have seen what was about to happen. I was just slow to react. Sharon, what a stalker she has become. I hope Forest can get rid of her. It's about my only hope without doing something radical. But Nell is someone I can speak to if I get to a point of urgency.

Star walks into the kitchen with Carrie and Kya. They take a seat at the table next to mine and I can't help but overhear Star telling the others that Meat is building a nursery onto the treehouse so he can have all his godchildren stay with him. Now, I'm not sure that Mia will want all three of her kids in a treehouse, or Eden or Tilly, if it comes to that. But, you know I have enough drama of my own to work out, so I'm minding my own business.

BS walks into the kitchen, quickly heading to Kya where he gives her a kiss which leaves her misty-eyed. Sighing because I want to get to that point where I can kiss my woman whenever I feel like it.

"Okay, Mav, let's go. We are going to do some recon." BS nods for me to follow him outside and he leads me to the club's van, where Wings, Chaos, Garth and Graham are waiting. "We are going to check out the shop, and yeah, I know we were going to do it before, but things happen and we didn't get it done, so here we are. Now you are with Garth, so stick together, Mav. We need to check what the fuck is going on, as I've had more intel that young girls are being taken inside."

Ninety minutes later, I'm standing with Garth across the street from the shop we are watching. We are lounging on a bench that has seen better days. But, it is giving us some cover and as we've no colors showing for the club. We relax back on the bench, watching from behind our shades.

"You noticed the same four teenagers that have been going in with bags of what looks like groceries?" Garth asks.

"Yeah, it's odd, isn't it? They've had something from that fried chicken place, too. You think they are making it headquarters for themselves? You know, for their baby gang?" I chuckle at my own description and see Garth smirk, too.

Seeing BS pop his head around one of the buildings opposite I give him a thumbs-up sign and we cross the street. Heading to the back of the shop where we can hear soft speaking through the slightly ajar door.

"Thank you. Can we leave tonight?" Hearing a female voice, and a young female by the sound of it, I give Garth a questioning look, and a worried one I have to admit.

Garth doesn't wait for any other signal before he storms into the back of the shop, and I'm right behind him because fuckin' hell, I'm not leaving him to face whatever it is alone. A high-pitched scream rips through the air, and I stop when I see six teenage girls huddled together on a dirty mattress.

"What the fuck is going on here?" BS snarls, and I can see he's getting ready to grab one of the boys. But that boy is standing firmly in front of the girls, in a protective manner.

"Mister, you need to move out with your friends. These girls are not in danger from us. We are getting them out of the area, is all. Now, who are you? What do you want here? You are not taking the girls." One of the young boys states, keeping himself in line with the other three boys, so all four are in front of the girls.

"We are not here to hurt the girls. We are working on a case at the moment where some asshole is using a date rape drug on women in our club and bar. We are brothers from the Raging Barons MC. Now, who are you and what are you doing with these girls?" Chaos asks, and he asks in a better manner than BS had.

"Please don't hurt them. They are helping us, not hurting us." One of the girls murmurs from behind the boy that spoke to us.

Stepping forward but keeping a calming distance for the boy's sake, I squat to look at the girls behind the boy's legs. "We are trying to save women from a group of men who are, as my brother said, date-raping women. We want to drive them out of town and find Mark Milanas, who is their leader."

"We have been watching a group of men. They try to take girls, but we've seen how they pick them out. They are watching for girls whose parents don't care. They even pay them to take the girls, and now we know what to look for we speak to the girls that are targeted and if they want us to help them, we have been getting them out of town." The boy who spoke earlier speaks again. It looks like he may be the spokesperson for them all.

"Where are you taking them? Somewhere safe enough to stay away from parents and these motherfuckers I hope," Graham asks.

"Yes, we're not stupid, mister. We have a man who takes them to a safe place. They are taken out of state and placed into good homes, if that is what they want."

BS steps forward and gives the teenager a look over. "What about yourselves? Are you safe?"

"We are leaving town tomorrow. Taking these with us and none of us are coming back. You need to know that Mark Milanas is bringing in at least ten men on Tuesday and will be scouring the town for any young girls or women around twenty. He has an order to fill from what we heard, and that's why we are getting out of town while we can." One of the boys that had not spoken before tells us this and fidgets a little under the eye of the boy who had spoken.

"Empty your pockets. What cash do you have?" I ask the brothers, and we all empty our wallets of what cash we have on us. It amounts to nearly seven hundred dollars and the boys' eyes round as they watch me hand it over to the main boy. "This is what we have on us. I'm going to give it to you to do what you need to do. We have a van outside. If you can all get in without anyone seeing you we'll get you to Nell's and she'll make sure you get out of town safely."

Graham slaps my shoulder because he knows Nell will do whatever is needed to make sure all these teenagers get away safely. If she has to involve Vincenzo I know she will.

"You mean Nell out of town, the one that runs the bed and breakfast, or boarding house or whatever it is?" One of the young girls asks.

"That's the one. She's my sister, and she'll make sure you get away with no one knowing where you are going. She'll make sure you have enough to get clothes and anything else you need." Graham stands proudly as he speaks of his sister.

"Come on, let's get out of here. Garth, go bring the van around back and we'll get everyone in fast and get the fuck out of here." BS takes control once more, and I'm surprised Wings has kept quiet, although I have noticed he's been watching the door and been alert the whole time. Probably was wise as we all seemed to close off to our surroundings whilst finding out what was happening.

Two hours later and sitting in Axel's office we have told all that happened, and had our ears bent for not informing Axel of what was happening. But he is good that we got the teenagers to safety. Now he is bent on finding Mark and sorting him out once and for all, but he's got to do it before Nell finds him, and she has Tank and Richie on the trail, so time is limited if we want to get to the man first. Richie is an excellent tracker, and a prize winner on recon, so we know we are on the back foot and need to pull in every lead we can. If Nell finds him first, she's never going to let us live it down, and Axel won't be happy about that. No, he surely won't.

CHAPTER FIFTEEN

I'm not impressed at all with what happened last night with Mav, and that disgusting woman. I mean, who the hell walks up to someone sitting at a table with a woman and sits in the man's lap, then kisses him? It's low and disgusting behavior, but I am and was angry that he didn't quickly push her away from him.

With it being Sunday, I can catch up with my own chores and put last night behind me, for now, at least. Getting started, I strip the sheets from my bed and get them into the washing machine. I thoroughly clean the room and remake it with the bedding, I washed them in a new lavender detergent. It's supposed to help create soothing sleep, so we'll see if it does.

Finishing the upper floor, I head downstairs and empty the washing machine, throwing it all in the dryer because I want to get done and have all my chores finished today, so I have nothing to do during the week while I'm working.

I make a drink and take a seat at the kitchen table. Tapping my fingers on the table, I wonder if it will be helpful to the Swap Shop. I will ask when I'm passing tomorrow. It's no good trying to sell it as I don't have time with Bitty allowing me to have her table and chairs.

Rinsing my cup, I quickly get started on cleaning the living room. I know it won't take me long as I only have the TV on the wall, a two-seater couch, and a small coffee table. My lack of furniture doesn't bother me at all. I agree it looks a little empty, but at least it's easy to keep clean.

Light knocking on the front door grabs my attention, and I quickly check who it is as I don't want to open it to Yax, and have another screaming match on the doorstep. Well, she does all the screaming, but even so, it is a menace and upsetting for my neighbors.

Seeing it's the Sheriff and one of his deputies, I'm rather worried but quickly open the door. "Hello, Sheriff, Deputy, what can I do for you?"

"Can we come in and speak with you a moment, Blake? You were a witness to an incident last night and I would like to take your statement," Sheriff Forest calmly asks.

"Please come in, both of you," I step away from the door and point to the kitchen. "Would you like a drink or anything?" I ask, more with nerves than anything.

"No, we are good, but thanks for asking," Sheriff Forest states as he takes a seat at the kitchen table. "This is Deputy Francis, and he's going to be taking this case. We understand you witnessed an incident where Mav of the Raging Barons MC was sexually assaulted by a young woman."

"Well, I don't know about sexually assaulted, but she sat in his lap and kissed him," I snip and realize my tone is sharp, so give a sorry look before continuing. "We were on a date night, our first date night actually, when from behind Mav where we were sitting at a table this woman walked up and threw herself into his lap."

"You mean Mav's lap?" Deputy Francis asks.

"Yes, she threw herself into his lap, or onto, whichever way you see it," again grimacing. "Then she wrapped her arms around his neck and kissed him. That's when I left the table and the club."

"So, he did not instigate any of that behavior?" Sheriff Forest asks, as he's writing everything I'm saying on a small notepad with the smallest pencil I've ever seen.

"No, he didn't even see her coming." Now, I'm feeling bad that I stormed out without waiting to see what would happen. But I'm so edgy about relationships now that I didn't want to see any betrayal.

"Okay...so, the woman walked up and threw herself at him, then kissed him, and he had no say in the matter? Now, I can see you are not realizing this is serious. But think about it, if it had been a man walking up to a woman and doing that, it would have been seen as assault, wouldn't it?" Sheriff Forest asks me and I consider it a moment, and have to admit he's right.

"Yes, I suppose you are right." I give a sheepish look to them both.

"I hope you won't hold this against Mav 'cause he's a good guy. One that would be an excellent partner for anyone that commits to him. He's been wanting to settle down for a while and I think you both would suit each other. Maybe get past this, Blake, and give him a chance," Sheriff Forest states, and gives me a pat on my hand which was resting on the table in front of me.

"I'll think about it," I respond, but the Sheriff's comment has made my anger slide.

Once they have left, I sit in the kitchen for quite some time thinking about what was said. I think it would be classed as assault if it was a woman, and just because it was a man, it isn't any less significant.

Giving myself a mental shake, I get back to cleaning and while doing so, I wonder if I can give Alf or Heather a call about the meals and my house being cleaned once Yax has gone. No, maybe it would be best to speak to one of them during work hours.

My phone rings and I pick it up and see Ed's name displayed. Now I'm surprised as I gave my number to Ed in case of an emergency. Taking the call, I quickly say, "Ed, are you okay?"

"I dropped my plate. Do you have a spare meal?" Ed sounds like he's going to go into a fit of temper any minute.

"Since I haven't had a chance to eat, how about I get some food and we can eat together?"

"Yes, that would be great, thank you." Ed has calmed a little, I can tell.

"I'll see you in around an hour. Is that good for you?"

Ed chuckles. "Yes, that is fine. I'll see you then, bye." I look at my phone because boy, did he go quickly, he never gave me the chance to say goodbye.

An hour later, I'm at Ed's carrying an order I purchased from none other than Club Whisky. They don't usually do takeout, but when I explained to Tony, the Chef, that it was for an elderly gentleman who had dropped his plate, he was more than happy to bag me some fried chicken, ribs and fries. I was more than grateful, and I'm sure he didn't charge me as much as it should have been.

Twenty minutes later, I'm wiping my chin with a paper napkin when Ed chuckles. "I don't know how you got this, Blake, but it's the best meal I've had in ages. Apart from the meal you made, of course."

I grin because he added the latter on to get himself out of deep water, but I don't care. As long as he's eaten well I'm not worried he thinks a chef cooks better than I do. "I didn't know where to get food from, to be honest Ed, then I thought about the meal last night and decided, why not just ask. They could only say no, and if that was the case, then I would have gone to the grocery store and found something to cook for us both."

"We should do this again sometime." Ed looks at me hopefully, and I grin while nodding that yes we should.

"Let me clean up, and I'll make us a drink."

"Thank you, Blake. It was good of you to do this. My hands are giving me a little pain and the plate just slipped out of my hand. I cleaned up so you wouldn't have to do that." Ed is looking at the floor in front of the stove and I can see that it's not as clean as it could be, but I'm not going to embarrass him. I will be here tomorrow anyway, and I'll make sure it's cleaned correctly then.

"Well, you did great. Thanks for doing that. Now go into the living room and I'll finish up here and come have a drink with you before I have to go home and finish my chores."

Sitting in the living room, we talk about anything and everything. I give him a little of my life's history, and he tells me a little more about his wife. It's a very relaxed moment, and I'm enjoying Ed's company more than I'd like to admit.

My phone pings and I look at it and roll my eyes when I see Bitty has sent me a message. "Excuse me, Ed, I have a message from a friend who is more of a mother these days."

Bitty: I'm coming over to speak to you.

Blake: Oh, is it important?

Bitty: Of course, it is or I wouldn't come over on a Sunday!

Blake: OK.

"Is everything okay?" Ed asks, and I look up with a puzzled look, I'm sure.

"Well, it's my adopted mother, Bitty, and she is coming over to my house to see me. Supposedly to speak to me about something important," I respond.

"Bitty? Is that the Bitty who is friends with Amelia?" Ed asks, and I look at him, surprised.

"Yes, that's the Bitty."

"Oh, my goodness. She's totally crazy. I've known her since we were teenagers. She is as crazy as you can get, and so is Amelia and that other friend..." Now, Ed is snapping his fingers against his chin trying to remember, and I'm watching those fingers and frown, because hey, I thought he was having trouble with them? My mind snaps back to him as he continues speaking, "Yeah, Sybil, that's the other one. They are like three witches, always in trouble, but always helping where they can. I have to admit that because I'd be doing them a disservice otherwise. So, you have adopted Bitty as a mother?"

"No. She adopted me a few minutes after we met. But I like her. She is rather wacky, but her heart is in the right place. The three of them are living at the clubhouse now from what Bitty has told me, and they love it. They are all selling their houses, too."

"Well, well, life is a surprise. You take care with those three. They could lead you into all sorts of trouble."

Laughing, I take our empty cups and wash them as I get ready to head home. "I'll be careful, but you know Bitty is being so kind to me. Just when I needed a fairy godmother, she appeared."

"Yeah, witches are like that." Ed snorts, and I have to giggle at him, referring to them as witches, but I see them as good witches, if that's what they are.

"Okay, Ed, I'll see you tomorrow evening. I'll speak to Alf about the food as soon as I get the opportunity, too." I kiss his leathery cheek and make my way home. I used the van and hope I don't get into trouble.

Back home, I'm only inside ten minutes before the front door opens and Bitty walks in. Taking her jacket off and hanging it on the coat rail, just as though she's done it a million times before. I shake my head and grin to myself.

"Okay, let's not mess around. This shit with Mav and that horrid woman, Sharon. I've found out he was with her once. Yeah, idiot. Men! Honestly, they think with their dicks half the time. Then when they get into trouble because of that dick, they wonder why. It's a shame God didn't give them a brain that wasn't attached to that dick, as it would have saved the world all sorts of crap." Bitty seems to be on a roll and she's only just started speaking. I remain quiet as I know that this could get tetchy if I don't react well. "So, you know Forest is charging Sharon for sexual assault. That should sort the bitch out. She's been stalking Mav for months and he's told her repeatedly he's not interested.

"Now, about last night. You didn't hang around, did you? Why not? He was on a date with you. What was wrong with you putting that bitch in her place? Now, Blake, if he's your man, he is YOUR man. You fight for him, you show him he matters, you don't run away like a little girl in kindergarten, for goodness sake. I can see I'm going to have to toughen you up some. So, what you got to say for yourself?"

"I was shocked and hurt. You know what happened with my marriage, Bitty. The last thing I want is disrespecting again."

"I can understand that, Blake, but you also have to create your own happiness and future. So, I'll organize a rerun of the date for the coming Saturday and you can try again. This time you can go to TJs. Now, I'm off, as I have things to be doing." Before I can say a word, Bitty has kissed my forehead and left slamming the front door behind her.

Shock, I'm in shock. Second date Saturday! Well, I hope it's better than the last one.

CHAPTER SIXTEEN

Axel calls his officers, Knuckles, Colton, Garth, and me into his office. It's Monday morning and unusual for this to be the start of the day. Stepping inside, I take a stand behind Wings, who is seated to one side in front of Axel's desk. Folding my arms across my chest, I wait for this meeting to unfold.

Axel walks into the office and quickly takes his seat behind the desk, wasting no time as he speaks. "I've spoken to Vincenzo Vitale early this morning. He's been watching Mark Milanas closely and has seen men leaving the area where this asshole is hiding. Now, I'm not placing us in a position where any of us could get hurt, because let's face it, Vitale has more men at hand than we have in the MC. This time I'm happy to follow Vitale's lead, but I need you out and watching the town."

"That's unusual for us to take a back seat, Pres?" Drag asks, looking as puzzled as we all feel.

"Yeah, it is, but it turns out Milanas is inside Vitale's territory, which makes him Vitale's problem more than ours. Tomorrow, if we get Milanas' men in our town, then it becomes an issue we can take in hand. I mean, grab the fuckers and get them to Nell's where Jaws can have a mighty snack." Axel gives the feral grin we all know well, and although we've all been wondering if he lost his balls to Mia of late, it seems she only borrowed them for a while! Axel continues, "Vitale wants to know when he gets his man, and he will get his man, if we want in on the interrogation."

"Not me, I don't give a shit. As long as he's dead I really don't care who did the honors." Buzz states from where he's standing with his back to the window.

BS speaks next, gaining our attention, "Me either. Let's be honest, if we are not involved, it can't come back on us at any time in the future."

Colton shuffles, and we all look at him as he shrugs his shoulders. "I suppose we can let him deal with the fucker. You know, keep our hands clean. But I have to admit I'd like to get my hands on the fucker just for a few minutes."

Knuckles smacks Colton up the back of the head while rolling his eyes, which has me smirking. Wings chuckles and rubs his chin but speaks to Colton directly, "I know where you're coming from because I'd like a piece of that fucker too. But, if we want to protect the club and the people in it, then we keep our distance. But if he gets away from Vitale, then all bets are off. I'll even use Target's sniper rifle if I have to."

Axel rubs the back of his neck and I can see he wants to be in on any action, but he's always been protective of the brothers of the club. Taking his responsibility more than a little seriously, and we all respect him for that. We've seen presidents of other clubs rush in, and then buried brothers because of ill thought-out plans. That is something Axel will never do. He weighs all the options open to him before he makes any type of decision.

Axel looks from one of us to another before he speaks. "Are you all in agreement that we leave this Milanas asshole to Vitale, unless he takes a step into our territory? If he does that or any of his men, we round them up and visit Nell?" Axel receives a resounding, 'Aye.'

An hour later I'm looking at the app on my phone where I keep all my work hours, and anything else that I need to keep track of. I love this app. It stops me from making blunders as to where I should be and when.

I'm lounging in the kitchen with a coffee and look up when I hear Sybil speak. "Mav, have you got one of those rememberals in your phone?"

"Rememberal?" What the fuck is she talking about?

"You know, it reminds you of things you need to do. Or even where you are supposed to be." Sybil has such a serious look on her face that I know she's not playing the fool.

"Yeah, if that's what you want to call it. If you go to Specs, he'll sort your phone out for you, and show you how to do it." Yeah, I'm an asshole. I just dumped Specs in the shit.

"Oh, that's what Bitty said, too. Okay, thank you, Mav." Sybil gives me such a sweet smile that I think I'm a double asshole for my last thought. But I watch her rush out of the kitchen and know Specs will be after my ass later.

Chuckling has me look up, and I give Meat a scowl. The fucker is laughing under his breath now, and I can imagine he's gonna be stirring the shit when he can. I give him a scowl back and then smirk when I think I can get him in the shit with Star. I'm sure I can devise some way of getting payback for his amusement at my predicament.

Knuckles walks into the kitchen, gives Meat and me a questioning look, but I shrug my shoulders and look back at my phone. I'm going to be free on Friday night, but I have a feeling Kenzie said Blake works evenings and Saturdays. That's on top of her stint at the coffee house. I'm thinking she's needing to let one of those jobs go because that's too much for anyone.

"Mav, what have you been up to?"

Shit, Kenzie... Now I'm going to get a ton of shit from her, I'm sure. "Not been up to anything, Kenz." Kenzie takes a seat next to me, and I'm more than happy she hasn't brought the fucking dog with her.

"Well, I heard you went on a date. Oh, and the date left you sitting at the table with a woman on your lap who was sucking your face by all accounts... hmmm..."

"I did not suck face with anyone, and if you heard the gossip you know said woman was arrested for sexual assault."

"Well, she was arrested, but she's out now and free to chase you again. You want to take BigDog with you when you go to work, you know, to ward off the evil witch?" Kenzie is smirking and doing nothing to hold it back.

I flick her nose as I used to when we were kids, and grin with her 'Ouch, Mav.' Yeah, just like when we were kids. "If she comes near me again, I'll contact Forest right away. She's been told to stay away from me, and she better or I'll take her to a visit at Nell's. Maybe I don't hurt women, but Nell has no issue with that if they are evil bitches."

"I know you wouldn't be disrespectful like that, and if I can do anything to get Blake back on side, I'll do it. You deserve to find your woman and settle down, maybe have a parcel of kids." Kenzie is grinning, but I know she means every word. She would help if she could, but I think it's wise to just let things take their own course now.

"I'll ask if I need help, but I think it's best to just let it be for now. I have a second date, thanks to Bitty. So, I'll do my best for that date to go as it should. I'll take her out of town this time." I give a small grin because I think getting away from town may be a good move for the second date.

Patting my hand, Kenzie gives me a huge smile. "I hope it works out for you. Bitty said Blake is an amazing person and she's had such a lot of bad luck, right from her cheating husband to what's happening now."

Colton walks into the kitchen, gives Kenzie a smile as he takes a seat across from me at the table. He's giving Kenzie the 'off you go' look, which has me chuckling, because Kenz will only go when she's ready and not before. But when her name is called and Jig gives her a come-on gesture, she quickly rushes over to him, where he wraps an arm around her shoulders and walks out of the kitchen's back door. Off to their little love nest, I would think, but I'm not going to let my mind go down that road.

Colton leans forward in his seat. "The fights are set for the Sunday after next. So, you have nearly two weeks to get into shape."

"What do you mean by get into shape asshole... I am in shape!"

"You know what I mean, you need to be a lean, mean, fighting machine." Colton jumps from his seat, giving me a nervous look as I slowly stand from my seat. "Okay, see you later, Mav." The little shit runs out of the kitchen, and I again look up when Meat chuckles, before nodding his head at me and grunting. "Shut your mouth. I don't need your opinion," I snap at Meat as I storm out of the kitchen. Now, I need to speak to Knuckles and get the info on this fight. I'm sure he'll know more than Colton, and he has so many underground contacts that we will know everything before the night happens.

The day runs smoothly from this point. I noticed Sybil playing with her phone, and has a huge smile on her face as she's doing it. Amelia is trying to see what's going on, but Sybil is talking about rememberals and tells her to get her nose out of her phone. It's fucking hilarious when you see those three competing against each other. But any minute one of the two is going to realize that they are not with Summer.

This morning first thing I had taken Mia to kindergarten with the boys. I waited with the SUV because nope, I wasn't getting involved with those two little shits. They were not nervous about starting somewhere new at all. They looked at it like a fresh challenge, but I pity their teacher because they have no idea, yet, what is going to come from those two. Mia cried all the way back to the clubhouse, and I wasn't sure what the fuck I was supposed to do about that, because come on, it's only school!

I check the plan of the compound and choose a position I'd like my house to be built, and put a mark on it with my name. I'm going to have to get my head together on what type of house I want. Something open plan, plenty of windows giving daylight, and modern. Maybe!

I walk the compound and I'm happy with the position I've chosen, so make my way back to the clubhouse where I inform Axel of my plot on the compound map, and my name on the list to be built. He agrees I need to know what I want before I speak to Hammer. That is how I find myself sitting in a corner of Specs' office with a laptop in front of me looking at house designs. Yeah, this is difficult and going to take some time.

Tuesday afternoon and I'm helping Knuckles build a section of bookshelves. They look good and are going to be a feature in the room where Jo likes to write. My phone vibrates at the same time as Knuckles', and we both look at each other for a second as that tells us it easily could be a mass call out from Pres for some reason. We know we're on alert for Milanas' men coming into town, so we quickly check our messages and yeah, we've been called to the clubhouse.

I hear Knuckles telling Jo we have to leave and I don't hang about for what she has to say. I run back to the clubhouse and Axel's office. Entering as the door is open and all officers are present. Specs is tapping on a laptop, but I can see he's keeping one ear on Pres.

"We have men in town. I'm sure they are Milanas' men. I need you to pair up and get into town, watch them closely and if you get a chance grab them. Nell is at the ready with Tank and Richie in their van heading to town. Graham is getting the cells ready and chomping at the bit to get these fuckers off the street. Make sure you are not seen. We don't want to give Forest any trouble. He's keeping the sheriff's department clean, and we need it to stay that way." Axel inspects all of us standing in his office. "Off you go, and make sure if you get injured, you get to Stitch. He's ready and fed up with slapping bandages on boo-boos, as he calls them." Axel grins and we all nod and head out. But I don't miss the fact Buzz and Drag walk out of the office behind me, with Axel rubbing his hands with a huge smile on his face.

CHAPTER SEVENTEEN

-:- BLAKE -:-

I'm not sure, but my life seems to be muddled as I'm dashing from one place to another. The weekend has flown past far too quickly, but I have another busy week in front of me, so I best stop wool gathering.

The morning at the coffee house passes with no incidents of any kind, and I've been working through inventory with Liam. As my boss, I find him very easy to get along with. He works just as hard as everyone else, but he works longer hours as he opens up and closes every day.

It seems Liam wants me to do the inventory check every month on the same day as he is allotting specific jobs for each of us. I'm pleased I didn't get to be the one who has to remove everything from behind the counter in the shop. They have to clean it all down, then replace it, wiping everything with cleaning wipes. Now that is a hard job to do. Fran and Millie will do that between them, so at least they can talk to each other while working.

Now it's my lunch break I dash over to the swap shop as I want to get the table and chairs out of the house, so I can replace it with the one that Bitty has given me.

Walking into the shop, I give the lady behind the counter a smile, and she returns it with a, "Hello, can I help you?"

"Hi. I have a dining set that I would like to donate. They are not perfect but they are better than no table and chairs at all. I have been given a dining set by a friend and I felt that someone could also benefit from mine. I don't know if you would be interested in taking it?" I ask, and the lady shows surprise, but then gives me a beaming smile.

"Oh, yes. We don't get a lot of furniture, but it never stays here long. Does it need picking up? Oh, I'm Hannah, by the way."

"Hi, Hannah, I'm Blake, and if it could be arranged, that would be good. I have some photographs of it to show you, then you can decide if you want to pick it up." I take out my phone and scroll through the last few photographs and show Hannah the table and chairs.

"Yeah, they are good. As you say, not perfect, but they are far from bad too. They will be scooped up in no time, I'm sure. Okay, let me see when we could pick it up!" I wait while Hannah types out a text to someone. We wait only a few minutes before she receives a responding text. "How about Friday around three?"

"I will try to organize someone to be at the house. Can I have a contact number? Then if I can't arrange that, we can schedule another pickup time. I am at work you see, so obviously won't be home myself."

Hannah hands me a card with contact details and I give her a smile as I start to walk out of the shop, but I turn and thank her for her help before rushing back to work.

I'm going to have to speak to Bitty about getting the dining set from her before Sunday or my guests will be perched with plates in their laps and I can just imagine Ed's reaction to that.

I work the rest of the day and make my way home, but take a detour to the grocery store to pick up a few things, as I want to make everyone a salad that I can leave in their fridges. That way, they can nibble on something healthy if they want, come Wednesday when I return to work.

Spending money on my clients isn't something I should do, but as I'm going to sell my house Yax lives in I am not going to worry about a grocery bill every now and again. I enjoy seeing the delight on their faces when I do something for them.

Once home, I eat some Ramen noodles, then shower and wear my cleaning clothing ready for work. I'm going to get out of the house quickly tonight, as I want to speak to Alf before he goes home.

Half an hour later, I walk into the office and give Alf a smile. "Hi, can I have a word with you, please?"

Alf leans back in his chair and gives me a questioning look before nodding at the chair near his desk to take a seat. "What can I do for you, Blake? And don't be telling me you want to hand in your notice because I won't accept it."

"Oh, it's nothing like that. I love my job and my clients. They are all such sweethearts and Ed is just adorable," I gush before I can hold it back.

Alf throws his head back with laughter, and it takes a minute for him to get himself under control before he chuckles as he states, "Ed! Adorable...Oh. My. Goodness. I've heard some things in my time, but that beats the biscuit."

"Well, he is a sweetie, and I'm not retracting that statement." I'm grinning at Alf as I respond, and he is shaking his head at me as he wipes the tears of laughter from his face. I can understand why he has that reaction because when I first met Ed I thought he was going to be a miserable grizzly bear type.

"Okay, let's get down to it. What can I do for you?" Alf asks still smirking.

"It seems the meals that are being sent are the same thing every Monday or Wednesday. They are not getting a variety of meals. I have been making meals for them as a change…" I hold my hand out to gesture he allows me to finish, "I did that because I noticed in the trash when I emptied them they were throwing away the meals. It's not the quality of the meal, it's the fact there is no variety."

"I see. Let me look into it and I'll see what I can do. Who has paid for the meals you have made?"

"I paid for them so you don't have to worry about it. I was more than happy to provide something for them as a change. I have not done it every day, just once or twice a week." I'm not going to feel embarrassed that I helped my clients. I think they are wonderful and the look on their faces when I do something for them is all the payment that I need.

"Okay, okay. But I'm going to put you a little extra in your salary at the end of the month to cover some or all of that cost. I know you are working at the Coffee House during the day, and doing this in the evening. That tells me you are having some financial difficulties and the last thing you need is spending money on other people's food."

"I also have something else I'd like to ask you. If that is okay?" I know Alf would normally have gone home by now, so I'm aware I'm encroaching on his personal time.

"Of course, ask away."

"I'm evicting the people that are in the house I own and am paying a mortgage on. As soon as they are out can someone from here go in and clean it out? I think all the furniture can either go to the Swap Shop or we can get rid of it. I don't want or need it. The house is going on the market and once it's sold I can pay the bill to you for the cleanup, if it's okay to do it that way?"

"I don't see a problem with that, Blake. You are employed by us and we assist any of our team if we can. Heather has always been onboard with helping, and she'll have no issue with this, and neither do I. You let me know when they will leave the house and I'll get a team together as quickly as I can to go in and clear and clean it out." Alf stands from behind his desk and steps around, holding his hand out to shake. "Deal?"

"Deal," I reply as I shake his hand with a smile on my face.

The rest of the evening passes well, and as I don't work Monday and Tuesday evenings, I'm going to make some cookies for my seniors. I can take them on Wednesday when I go to work.

Wednesday came around fast, and I know my seniors are going to like the baking I'm bringing for them. After cleaning and feeding Audrey, Prue and Robert, I smile as they all had enjoyed the cookies and stored the ones they didn't eat for later. I make my way to Ed where I am sure he'll be waiting eagerly to see what I have tonight.

Opening the front door of Ed's house, I shout, "Evening, Ed."

"You're late..." Oh, my, he's grumpy tonight, I think to myself, but don't reply to him as I make my way to the kitchen, and unload the groceries I brought along with me.

I don't respond to that, but place the cookies on the counter and the salad in the fridge, leaving a nosey Ed along with them. It doesn't take long before I hear him mumbling about cookies and hear the cookie tin being opened and closed.

I quickly get into cleaning mode and ignore Ed, who is following me from room to room, but not speaking a word. Well, he will find two can play at this game, and I hum under my breath as I work. I can see it's annoying him that I'm not speaking, but he'll get over it in a minute. He's not going to be able to keep quiet much longer, I'm thinking to myself when he blurts.

"Did you bring anything to eat?"

"I did, and I will get to it once I've finished making your bed. If you make sure the trash can in the living room is empty for me, that would save me some time." I don't look at him, but continue to hum as I grab the sheets I removed and take them to place in the washing machine.

In the kitchen, I take out the chicken breast I had placed in the fridge, along with the other fixings for the stir-fry I'm going to make. I can hear the washing machine on its cycle as I chop, dice and slice. Now maybe the little shit will be ready to speak, I think to myself.

"Okay, so what's eating you up and why are you being a miserable so and so?" I ask Ed, who has taken a seat at the table, to watch me cooking.

"I'm bored. I know I'm old, but I'm not dead yet. I'm bored with sitting around this house with nothing to do."

Ah, I see, he needs a purpose... "Well, you could help me out if you can, that is, as I have a slight problem that needs solving on Friday afternoon."

Ed leans forward with such eagerness to hear what I need help with that I struggle to keep the smile from my face. He looks like a young child that is excited about the next adventure they are going to be jumping into. "What do you need help with?"

"I have a dining set that the Swap Shop is going to pick up at around three in the afternoon. But I will be at work, so I need someone I can trust implicitly with my house key to wait for them to pick up and then lock up the house."

"I can do that. I'll have a cab pick me up and bring me back. I will watch them take the set and then lock up the house safely." Ed is giving me a huge grin, and I can see a sparkle in his eyes. Maybe I can do more with Ed and give him a purpose?

"Thank you, Ed, that's very kind of you. Now eat this chicken stir-fry before it goes cold or I won't make you another next week."

Before I leave for the night, I give Ed my address and tell him I'll bring the spare key for the house tomorrow when I come to work. He's all fired up about getting out of the house and I kiss his cheek before leaving, and giggle when he blushes like a teenager.

CHAPTER EIGHTEEN

-:- MAV -:-

It's only the middle of the morning and I'm on my way to kindergarten with Mia because the twins have been acting up. I knew it was a bad idea to send these two. I told Axel and Mia to have a private tutor for them so they could be at the house and not amongst other kids, causing chaos.

"I'm sorry, Mav, I know you said it was a bad idea, but they need to mix with other children. They can't spend all their lives within the compound."

Mia must have felt my annoyance at having to come to school because the two hooligans have caused chaos in the classroom. But I'm not one to say I told you so, so I keep my mouth firmly closed. After all, Mia is the First Lady of the club. I give a customary grunt because I have to respond in some way and I can't find any words to say how annoying this is without blowing up.

Walking into the school, I stay one step behind Mia, keeping my eyes peeled for any kind of trouble. I'm not sure why because come on, we're at kindergarten, what could happen? A bite on the ankle, kick in the shins, or some other minor thing?

The teacher from the twins' class greets Mia and gives me a small nod of the head, along with a smile as she leads us into a classroom where the twins are sitting near the window. They give a cheerful wave and laugh between themselves. Little fuckers, I'm thinking! But I notice they are covered in paint, bright purple paint at that. I give the teacher another look-over and shit, that's when I see the little bastards have thrown paint on the woman. I hadn't noticed as

I'd not seen the back of her. But now, as she's explaining to Mia what happened, she turns and here is the evidence.

"Oh, my goodness. I'm so sorry. I'll speak to their father and get him to do something." I give Mia a look of surprise because what the fuck is Axel going to do? Nothing, that's what. He'll laugh his ass off at the image I'm going to relay to him. But it's the very careful and calculated way Mia is speaking to the woman that has me mesmerized. Anyone would think she is well-to-do, and she's obviously been learning more shit from Star.

"We cannot have the twins causing trouble in the classroom. But they are young and boisterous, so I know it's hard to keep them well-behaved all the time. I don't mind them running around, but I can't have them throwing paint on other children."

"What?" Mia asked in a shocked voice, and I look at the twins out of the corner of my eye and those two hooligans are giggling between themselves.

The teacher relays all that happened, which basically is the twins threw paint on another kid, as he was bullying one of the girls in class when the teacher wasn't looking. Yeah, sneaky little shit is what he is. So, the twins took it in hand and poured cans of paint on his head.

The door bursts open and a woman storms into the room shouting about having the twins thrown out of school because they are not good children, and need educating how to mix with other children. Now, I fold my arms over my chest and think where's the popcorn, because Mia is a hurricane when it comes to protecting her kids, and this is going to be something to watch. In fact, thinking that I take out my phone and hit record.

"Shut your mouth about my children! Your child is a bully and if he wasn't bullying a little girl, my boys wouldn't have had to stand up for her. My boys were being little gentlemen and I'm sure proud of them," Mia shouts back at her.

The teacher is looking from one to the other, then glances at the twins who have opened their backpacks and taken out their small packed lunch that Amelia made for them, and sit eating as though this is a normal day at school.

"My son is not a bully!"

"Mrs. Granger, the truth is, Simon was bullying Abigail, but the twins put a stop to it." Calmly, the teacher addressed Mrs. Granger with an unreadable expression.

"Boys, come on, we're going home," Mia and I both watch as the twins pack up and walk towards her, both with huge smiles on their faces. Neither has said a word throughout this fiasco.

"I want them out of this school."

The woman persists, but I keep recording the incident and give the teacher a wink when she looks over at me. Turning back to the irate parent, the teacher, who I now see has a name tag, is called Mrs. Evelyn Brownlee, states firmly, "Children are children, and you need to take Simon home, clean him up and teach him about bullying. We have an anti-bullying policy at the school and it doesn't matter what age someone becomes a bully, it means they still are one. Now, if you want him to grow into a well-rounded and sensitive adult, you need to teach him that bullying is not something that is tolerated."

"Mav, come on, we are going home. I need to clean up the boys and speak to Axel." Mia stomps out of the classroom, shoulder hitting the other parent as she passes, and the twins are right behind her. But behind Mia's back, they both kick the parent in the shin, laugh and run up beside Mia, grabbing a hand on either side of her. Yeah, I got that recorded too.

We leave the screeching parent and amused teacher behind as we head outside to the SUV and head back to the compound. I look over at Mia and she's chewing her bottom lip. I know that's a sign she's thinking about what's happened and what she should do next. Me! I keep my thoughts to myself but if it wasn't a risk to my health, I'd high-five the hooligans and give them a chocolate treat.

Back at the compound, I make my way to the clubhouse kitchen after watching Mia take the boys home. I bet they are going in the bath before Mia reports what happened to Axel.

Now, speaking of Axel as I take a seat in the kitchen with a mug of coffee and a handful of cookies I nabbed from the large cookie tin, I watch as my president saunters in and takes a seat next to me. He's giving me the 'what happened' look, and I hand over my phone with the recording so he can see for himself.

"I know they are terrors, but they did right protecting a little girl from a bully. I'm not going to punish them for that. There are far worse things they could have done. As future president and VP of the club, they have to have morals, guts and be able to make good decisions. To me, this is a good decision." Axel slaps my shoulder as he stands, hands me my phone back, and walks out the back door. I'm not sure how he'll handle this with Mia, but he's not going to be hard on the twins, and he's right. I'm sure those two little fuckers will get into far worse than tipping paint on someone.

As I'm getting ready to leave the kitchen Colton walks in and seeing me, he steps over, taking a seat and clasps his hands on the table in front of him.

"You have to do some extra training, ready for the fight. I've arranged for you to fight with Garth. You don't know how he fights, so he will be a good unknown to get your mind set ready. He's a good fighter and I think you'll get a lot out of training with him before we have the fight night."

As I agree with an extra session or two before the fight I'm preparing for, I can see the sense in what he's saying. Taking Colton by surprise, I nod and simply state, "Okay. Let me know when."

Picking up my mug, I take it to the sink, rinse it out and place it in the dishwasher. Meat gives me a nod and I walk out of the kitchen right into seeing Bitty and Sybil arguing in the common room over who is going to be looking after Summer for the afternoon.

Buzz shouts for me to follow him and I stride out of the common room and out the front door, where Forest is entering the compound in his cruiser. "Forest needs to speak to you about Sharon. He is here for something concerning Pres, but he wants to speak to you too." Buzz leans against the wall of the clubhouse and I wait for Forest to step out of his cruiser and over to us.

"I need to know if you want me to continue the charges on Sharon? She's more than likely going to leave town, but if not, she'll be on my fucking watch list," Forest quickly states.

"Okay, drop the charges if you like. It was only a kiss and all this shit will have scared the piss outta her, I would imagine. I'm just sick of her following me around and I'm trying to get Blake to give me a chance, so I don't want this happening again."

"I'll be speaking to Judge Allcott and see if he can rip some strips off her. Then maybe she'll stay away or move towns," Forest rubs his chin in thought as he thinks, and shakes his head with whatever decision he came to, then asks, "Where's Axel? I need to speak to him about men I've heard are walking around town. I've been cruising the streets but not seen anything suspicious as such. But, saying that, there are unfamiliar faces out there."

Buzz responds with a massive grin, rubbing his hands together, "I can't wait to get my hands on those assholes. Axel is at his house sorting out an issue with the twins, so give him half an hour, then go over."

"Okay. I'll grab a drink while I'm here." Forest walks into the clubhouse while he and Buzz talk, and I stay where I am thinking about the bastards that have come to town, and how they need to be buried deep.

Later in the afternoon, Axel has given orders that we all be ready to roll into town as soon as the evening hits. We need the cover of darkness to get to the fuckers and if need be, take them out, or overpower them ready to take to Nell's. I heard Graham, Tank and Richie are ready and have the cells all prepared. Drag has been updating everyone, as information has been coming in from his street informants. Target and Wings informants have also given us an idea of what is going on at the old gas station, and that's where we will concentrate on starting our assault.

Sitting at the bar in the common room chilling ready for the evening, I turn my head when Axel sits beside me. "All okay, Pres?"

"Yeah, everything is fine. I calmed Mia about the boys and asked her would she rather them sit back and watch something bad happen or stand up and be men?" Axel chuckles, "She said they are not men yet."

"Honestly, women, sometimes I just don't understand them," I honestly think they are a different species at times. I watch the Ol' Ladies when they get together and they can only be described as feral at times. They are, however, very loyal to each other and yeah, they argue at times, but it never causes a problem between them. They agree to disagree.

"No, me either, Mav, but it's fun trying to work it out." Axel slaps my shoulder before walking away, whistling, and that spring in his step tells me he's going to pester Mia for a while.

Later that evening we are all slowly making our way to the gas station on foot as we've left our hogs a mile away so the engine noise doesn't alert these fuckers we are onto them, and about to take them out one way or another.

I look over at Buzz, who is buzzing to get into a fight, and Axel is smirking, so I think he's on the same wavelength. We hunker down, behind the wall that is positioned around the three sides of the station. Which only leaves the front of the station open for vehicles to drive in and out.

Axel gives a signal for us all to hang back when we hear vehicles, and they are coming in hot. The black Escalades slam to a halt in the forecourt of the station. Men all dressed in black suits pour out of the vehicles.

"You motherfucker…"

Swinging to look at Axel who's on his feet and storming toward the wall where he's about to climb and tear into none other than Vitale. Oh, fuck, now we are in for some fun, I'm thinking. Drag and Buzz are right behind Axel, with Wings and Chaos behind them. I get over the wall easily and Knuckles along with Colton, Target and Beer head to the station where we burst through the door, and find Vitale's men already have probably twelve men on the ground. Either knocked out or pissing themselves with fear.

"Aw, for fuck's sake, that means we are not going to have any fun at all," Colton snarls, then kicks the nearest man kneeling in the gut.

Hearing someone mumble, "Fuck, you seen them going at it?" we turn and head back outside where Axel and Vitale are swinging at each other.

"Go for it, Pres," Colton hoots, stomping his foot. I give him a *what the fuck* look before looking back at Pres.

Vitale snaps a punch which hits Axel on the chin, but it only has him taking one step backward before he surges forward with his own set of punches. One-two, one-two, smack... Yeah, that's a nice combination, Pres, I'm thinking.

Vitale shoots a leg out to sweep Axel down, but we work this all the time in training and Axel hops over the leg and stamps on it, causing Vitale to swear as he gets to his feet and limps a little.

Target is making bets with Chaos on who is going to win, and I am not getting involved in any of that, either. Colton now has his phone out and recording the fight. I think this has turned into one hell of a shit show.

Vitale's men are standing on one side of the forecourt. Well, the men that are not restraining the fuckers inside, that is. But they are not attempting to step into the fight. We watch as it's more than obvious Axel and Vitale are well matched, and they are doing damage to each other. Both have a bleeding nose and split lip.

"That's enough." Drag steps forward, giving Vitale's lead man a look to step in as well. "Come on, Pres. The fuckers are restrained. They will go to Nell's. Either way, it's a done deal. Let's go home and leave Vitale to clean up the mess."

"It's our territory, Drag," Axel snarls, wiping the blood from his nose and leaving a streak across his cheek. "The next time you come into my territory, I'm declaring war. We both care about Nell, but that will not be a reason to stay on friendly terms from this moment forward. You get me Vitale? You overstepped the fuckin' mark."

Vitale looks like he wants to spit nails, but he also knows he is in our territory, and he has overstepped. He gives a nod to Axel, then walks into the station, giving orders to his men.

We haul ass back to our hogs and the clubhouse. Not sure what the fuck Mia is going to say about Axel's black eye and split lip, mind you, but I'm staying well out of it. I like my balls just where they are and not in Mia's purse, where Axel keeps his, I don't want to know or care.

CHAPTER NINETEEN

-:- BLAKE -:-

Bitty is hammering at the front door, shouting, "Let me in, Blake, it's too early to be standing out here." Looking at my alarm on the bedside table, I blink as it is saying it's only 5:30 am...!

Scrambling out of bed and down the stairs, I shout, "I'm coming! Hang on, Bitty."

The door opens and in storms Bitty, looking like she needs another few hours in her bed. "Mom, momma, ma, mammy, mama...got it?"

"Wow, who upset you this morning, mama?" I grin when I see her deflate somewhat and starts the fixing for a coffee.

"I'm going to get dressed. I'll be back in a minute." I rush back up the stairs and grab my clothes for work, do my morning routine, missing out the shower, dress and run downstairs to the kitchen where Bitty is sitting calmly, now sipping coffee.

"Okay, mama, what's going on that you are here so early in the morning?"

"Well, I was speaking with Amelia and Sybil and we decided we are going to go over to speak with Yax one last time. But you need to go to speak with Sheriff Forest. Ask him to go in and remove that terrible bitch so we can get the place cleaned out and sold. Now, as your mama, I'm not going to watch some disgusting people take you for a ride, and keep living in the house you are working hard to supply. Let me do this Blake, and you get our boy Forest to move their arses."

Arses? Now, I don't think I've heard that expression before. But if it's the same as ass, then okay, I understand, and to be truthful, I'm ready to get the house gone and finished with.

"This has gotten you well riled up, mama. But we will get them out of the house and have it sold. I'll make a call to Sheriff Forest and see if he can do anything to get them removed, but we know with a child involved, a court would not make them homeless."

Bitty shot to her feet, and snarled...and I mean snarled like a frickin' Pitbull terrier in attack mode. "I'll get them out of that house within the next three days. Don't bother with Forest as I'll deal with him too. You are witness to my words."

I watch, open-mouthed in shock as Bitty throws her cup into the sink, which smashes into pieces and storms out of the house. The door slams so hard the window panes rattle and I catch a cat ornament I had on a shelf in the kitchen next to where I'm standing. 'Wow, she has one heck of a temper,' I mumble to myself, place the cat back and get ready for work.

The day sped past, and Friday evening as I'm stepping into Ed's place, I notice he is already standing waiting for me in the kitchen. "Evening Ed, how are you this evening?" I ask as I make my way to the kitchen, placing yet another zip-lock bag of cookies on his kitchen counter.

"I'm good. I went to your place, and the people came and took the table and chairs. They were great people and were very polite and courteous."

Turning to look at Ed, I can see he's just bursting to tell me more, so I pour us both a coffee from his machine and take a seat, pointing for him to sit too. Which I notice he does without a limp and takes his mug with no finger issues. Hmm, seems I am right in thinking he's a little con man.

Sitting here watching Ed, I can't help but think if I had a grandfather I'd want him to be like Ed, who is so animated at this moment by relaying what he'd gotten up to at my house.

"You listening, Blake?"

"Yeah, yeah, I'm listening." Sheesh, I best keep my wits about me!

"Okay then. I took the cab over to your place and waited until the people came for the table and chairs. They were great, as I said, and they didn't rush to leave either. I made them a drink, and we talked for quite some time. I also sweet-talked them some…"

He made them a drink…with his bad hands…and sweet-talked them! Well, I never, it gets better and better. I keep a straight face as he is telling me all this, but I want to burst out laughing because he has no idea he just outed himself. But, he continues.

"I walked over to Bitty's with them, who was thankfully home packing boxes ready for her move. Oh, she had that nosey biddy with her, you know Sybil something-or-other. Anyway, these nice people took Bitty's table and chairs to your house, so now you don't have to worry about that. They also brought the washing machine Bitty said you wanted, and they took the old one away with them." Ed folds his arms over his chest and gives me a smile so broad there is no way I'm going to ask him how he managed all that with his ailments.

"Well, that is so kind of you. I saw the table and chairs and presumed Bitty had organized it all being brought to my house. But I'm so grateful to you, that was such a lovely thing for you to do," I give it a bit of gushy thankfulness, and can see him swelling with pride in himself. "You know, Bitty has me calling her mama because she claimed me as a daughter. I would love to claim you as my grandfather if you would be willing?"

"If I would be willing? I'd be honored to have you as a granddaughter. My oh my, this is a good day. You know it'll be good to have a family. It's been a long time. But I will be a great PawPaw for you." Ed steps over from his side of the table and I stand and return the hug he gives me.

Giggling, I look at Ed. "Well, PawPaw, tell me about this issue you have with walking and your hands, hm..."

"Oh..." Ed flushes a glorious shade of red, and I throw my head back, laughing.

The rest of my evening is spent with me getting all my cleaning done and Ed following me talking about what we can do together, how he's going to be the best grandfather on the planet, and if anyone messes with me he's going to shoot holes in their asses for them as he still has his shotgun.

Back at home, I get a message from Bitty, which surprises me, as she hardly ever sends me a text message.

Mama: I've got it organized

Blake: What have you organized?

Mama: Evicting that piece of trash

Blake: Um, what have you organized?

Mama: Oh, I've got my boy onboard, and he's going to make sure that shit leaves the house

Blake: When is this going to happen? As it would be best for me to be present.

Mama: 9 on Sunday morning (smiling emoji)

Blake: I'll be there

Mama: OK.

Lying in bed, I'm thinking about having a crazy mother and a grandfather that are about the same damn age, and they are both crazy coots. But I can't hold back the smile thinking about them both. I've struck lucky, I'm thinking.

Saturday and date night again, I hope it is a better one than the last because I'm not going to keep trying again, and again. I like Mav, and I enjoyed our last date up to that awful woman turning up.

I rush through my morning chores with my clients, much to Ed's upset, but when I explain I'm going on a date, he's all ears. Of course, that meant I had to tell him all about Mav, what I know about him, anyway. I even told him about the woman and what happened, and Bitty organizing a second date. PawPaw, as I am told to think of and call him, explains he'll be checking in with Bitty to find out if this Mav, as he called him, is responsible and worth my time.

Well, I'm ready and waiting for Mav to pick me up for our date. I'm wearing a cotton summer dress with thin straps, cowboy boots and a denim jacket. I'm not making more of an effort than I need to as we're going to TJs and I fully expect to either fend off women that are looking for a biker, or storming out of our date once more.

Knocking on the door grabs my attention, and I pick up my purse before opening it. Mav is standing looking slick in his motorcycle jacket with clean jeans and polished biker boots. I look up and see the smirk on his face. "Like what you see?"

"God, I hope it's not going to be an awful night," I mumble to myself as I close and lock the front door.

"It's going to be a good night, Blake." Mav chuckles more to himself than to me, but he guides me to an SUV and opens the door, helping me climb in before quickly making his way around to the driver's side.

"So, have you had a pleasant week?" Mav asks.

"I have. Thank you for asking. I gained myself a grandfather."

"What do you mean, you gained a grandfather?"

"Well, I'm working for the cleaning company, and one of my clients is a great senior. He's bored out of his pants if I'm being honest. So, with Bitty claiming me as a daughter, I claimed Ed as a grandfather, so now I have to call him PawPaw." I can't stop the giggle that bursts out of me, because honestly calling him that seems so strange.

We continue with general chit chat until we arrive at TJs and quickly make our way inside. Mav has his hand resting on the bottom of my back, just before my butt, and he's showing I'm with him, so everyone needs to stay away from us. It's a pleasant feeling if I'm being honest with myself.

"Let's sit in that booth. I'll get us a drink and then we'll get something to eat if you're hungry?"

I take a seat and look at Mav as he's waiting for my reply, "I'm not hungry to be honest, but I'll have a Batanga, please," I've had this once previously. It's tequila, lime juice and coke. I will only have the one drink of Batanga before sticking to coke the rest of the evening.

Bringing our drinks and placing them on the table, Mav takes a seat and we talk about our jobs. Mav surprises me when he tells me he's a bouncer, come doorman, depending on what you want to call them. He also has been involved in martial arts and competitive fighting matches.

I put my drink down when a couple walk past and I'm not sure if I recognize them or not, but they are wearing costumes that are from the 1920s. The woman even has one of those long cigarette holders in her hand.

My eyes flick to Mav and he's watching my expression, which must have flicked through from surprise to amusement. I can't help but ask, "Is it theme night? If I'd known, I would have been willing to get myself one of those dresses with fringes around the bottom, or even all over them. I would have enjoyed that, would have been fun."

Mav leans over and kisses my cheek, "Next theme night I'll bring you. We'll dress to match and have a great time."

"Okay, that's a date," I grin and turn to watch how the bar staff are running around showing how capable they are. It's a delight to watch how efficiently they move from one thing to another. I notice there are a lot of men here with the same jacket as Mav and they give chin lifts as they pass our table.

The evening is relaxed and enjoyable. We even have a few dances together which surprised me how fluidly Mav dances. Honestly, he's as hot as heck and if I was an easy kind of girl, I would have jumped his bones. But, I'm not, so I don't, but it doesn't mean I can't dream about it later.

CHAPTER TWENTY

-:- MAV -:-

The date night was great, nothing untoward happened and I'm more than thankful for that fact. Blake and I talked a lot about our past, what we wanted for the moment, and for the future.

Blake has a great personality, and she is amusing once she feels comfortable with you. I like her more than a little and the more the evening went on, the more I felt she was my one.

I snagged us a booth when we arrived and it was positioned so we could watch people dancing and yet be close to the bar. Blake wasn't hungry, so we didn't bother with a meal, and she only had the one drink before sticking with coke. I had two beers and took my time with them because I did not want to get drunk.

Meat and Star were all themed up, of course. They were in 1920s garb. If I'm honest, they both looked damn good too. Blake thought it was great and asked if there was a theme night where she could dress up too. Now, that piqued my curiosity, but pleased me she would join in with the fun.

Dancing, I made sure every opportunity I got I placed my hands on her, showing everyone in this place that she was with me and mine. Ruger and Sting gave me a chin lift and a smirk when they saw me guiding Blake back to our booth. But I flicked them a middle finger when Blake wasn't looking, which had them both laughing like fools.

The best part of the evening for me was when we arrived back at Blake's. I made no effort to go inside, even when she invited me in. I told her we'd take it slow, and that I wanted to show her I'm committed to having a relationship with her.

Taking her face between my hands, I tilted her head back and slowly lowered my face until our lips met. I made sure to nip, suck and lick every part of her lips and mouth. By the time I was finished, Blake was glassy-eyed and had a gorgeous rosy-hue on her cheeks.

I told her I'd see her on the weekend as she works evenings, and I am on Club Whisky door duty all week. I also have to fit in this sparring with Garth. But I can't wait for the weekend.

Snapping to attention, I realize I'm not listening to what is being said in church. "Are you with us now, Mav? Or still got your mind on something else?"

All the brothers are looking at me and have fucking smirks on their faces. Being caught daydreaming is not going to be forgotten any time in the near future. Axel will make sure to keep this in his, *take the piss armory*.

"I'm good, Pres," is all that I manage, before noticing everyone has a tiny pencil behind their ear. My eyes flick to BS to see if he has noticed, and yeah, he has because he has his arms folded over his chest and giving everyone the stink eye.

Forest, who is sitting near me, is chuckling and points to the pencil behind his ear. "This has come in handy, BS. But it's a fucker to stay in place. Maybe you have big flapping ears, you know, to hold the pencil to your head."

Before BS can answer, Forest's pencil falls from behind his ear, which he catches with one hand, sighs and pops it back in place. But gives a look to BS that says, *what can you do!*

Everyone has a laugh over it, except for BS, of course, but Pres pulls everyone into line when he's stopped chuckling himself, mind you.

"Okay, let's get to it. BS, what do you have to report?" Axel's not wasting any time and getting right to it.

BS, after giving everyone a filthy look, takes the pencil from behind his ear which has brothers chuckling. He takes out his small notepad too and starts to speak. "I have been to every business we own and spoken to each and every employee. Some mentioned they had seen strangers in town, but they had seen nothing to spark a sense of danger, or anything to be worried about.

"But they had overheard gossip of women disappearing from town, mainly young women. Teenagers that had no solid family support. In other words, easy targets. We missed the fact that women were going missing because they were from places where no one cared. It sickens me. Oh, Lucas and his friends from the wood-yard also beat up some creep looking in a young woman's window. I'm sure the fucker won't be doing that again."

Buzz taps with his knuckles on the table in front of him, gaining everyone's attention, "I spoke with Graham, well he contacted me to give me the info on the men Vitale took over. By the way, Pres, you fought well. Vitale has a black eye, split lip and is limping by all accounts."

The room, of course, gossips about the fight between Axel and Vitale, but as I look at Axel, I shake my head because he's smirking like a fool. No wonder the twins are hellions!

"Okay, let me finish," Buzz continues, "Vitale didn't even question them once he verified they were Milanas men. He quickly gave them all a bullet between their eyes and left them for Nell to feed to the gators.

"Graham told me that the teenagers we rescued are rehoused, re-homed, or whatever, in safe places far away from here. They are going to be fine and are having counseling sessions. Graham said Nell was more than happy with where the teenagers are and how they will be looked after."

"I'm closely watching the women that frequent the club. I've all the staff onboard too. They know any sign of anything out of the ordinary they tell me, or whoever is on door duty," Silver states.

Beer follows that statement, "I've done the same at TJs, and I'm telling you if I get my hands on one of these fuckers trying to date rape drug a woman I'll have him in the back of my truck unconscious and I'll take him somewhere quiet to rip him apart. I'll even borrow Meat's cleaver to do it."

Hearing a grunt, we all turn to look at Meat who is giving Beer a nod that's saying he can have a cleaver if he wants one.

"I'll come and give you a hand, Beer. I'd be all over ripping some asshole to bits for raping women. They are not men. They are cowards and the age of some of these girls makes them pedo's too." I add to the conversation, which has everyone muttering agreement.

"Okay, keep your eyes and ears peeled. From what I understand, Vitale is close to grabbing Mark Milanas, and when he does, I'm thinking we could do a deal with Nell to swoop in and steal the fucker. We can take him out ourselves and bury him deep, after we've had our fun with him." Axel has that manic look, but it's the fact he wants to steal Vitale's prize that has me chuckling. They are becoming more competitive all the time, but I also see, even after the fight, they both have respect for each other. It's a kind of quiet alliance, I believe, and if shit hits the fan, it could be we are good allies for each other.

"Anything else?" Pres asks and Knuckles quickly speaks.

"I've heard the fighter deaths have increased. The betting on these matches has gotten out of hand, but of course it's Milanas behind all this shit. We'll take out the fuckers on the fight night as I've been speaking to my contacts and I know who's involved now. All of us involved in the fight will target a man and make sure we end them. You all in with this? If not, we need to change fighters."

"I'm up for it," I quickly respond.

Chaos is bouncing in his seat, grinning at Wings, who is sitting further away from him. "Oh, I'll take mine out, no worries. I can take Wings one out too, because you know he's squeamish."

"Squeamish, what the fuck, Chaos?" Wings snarls.

"We all know you'd rather play with your gadgets like the bee drones," Chaos continues just to annoy Wings.

"Fuck you, arsehole," Wings snaps, and when Meat chuckles we all realize he said arsehole, and not asshole.

"Organize that between yourselves," Axel states, tapping the desk to stop the squabbling that Chaos and Wings have going on.

"The fight is two weeks from today," Colton reports. "Mav is going to be sparring with Garth, and everyone else I have different brothers stepping up to help. Target has given Fist a few pointers and BS has shown Wings how to dodge a southpaw's hook. On the whole, we have everything under control, and I'm sure we can add to taking out a few assholes while we are at it."

"I'd like to bring up the subject of bringing Garth into the brotherhood. He's stepped up every time we've asked him to. I know he said originally that he wasn't interested, but I think we can get him as a brother, and he'd be a hell of a good one." I keep my eyes on Axel, because I'm sure he's thought the same as me.

"I reckon it would be a good move. He's prior military, so a good all-round man. He's jumped in as Mav has stated whenever we've asked him. He's doing door duty now at TJs and Club Whisky. I know you spoke to Sentry about that Mav, and he was okay with you having the help from Garth. He's also married and settled with his wife. Hannah I've met, and she's a good person. She fit into the Swap Shop easily. Do you have any issue with her, or Garth, Sentry?" Axel asks.

"No, they are both good people. Hannah works hard when she is at the shop. If I ask her to do extra hours, she is willing. Garth stands at the door or patrols the shop without particularly being seen. He has a hell of an ability to be a shadow when needed. He just melts into the background and I've seen women with kids come into the shop and not even notice him from the moment they walk in to the moment they walk out. I'd be happy to have him as a brother in the club."

"Mav, speak to Garth then get back to me. I don't want to put this to a vote until I know if he is interested or not. It would be a waste of time. Our bylaws also state that if anyone denies brotherhood once they are never given the opportunity a second time. Let's be sure before his name is put to the table," Axel states, then quickly plants the gavel on the table and dismisses everyone.

CHAPTER TWENTY-ONE

-:- BLAKE -:-

It's Sunday morning and I can't stop the smile that keeps appearing on my face. The date last night was good, I really do like Mav and I hope we can have more successful dates. We had talked a lot and got to know each other fairly well. Dancing had been nice too and unexpected. Who would have thought a biker could dance like that?

My phone makes a pinging noise and picking it up, I grin as I see it's a message from Mav.

Mav: Morning, beautiful. Just wanted to say hi, let you know I dreamed about you last night.

Blake: Good morning, Mav. Well, I hope it was a good dream!

Mav: Oh, it was one of the best, and I had to jump in a cold shower so I could get some relief.

Blake: OMG, you didn't just say that!

Mav: Oh, I did babe. I'll tell you now, I think I'm going to be spending a lot of time in my shower.

Blake: I'm giggling here because I'm thinking you may get a cramp in your wrist if you are not careful.

Now, even though I'm in the house alone, I can't help but blush a little at my response. I'm not normally that forward when it comes to talking about sex.

Mav: I'm sure I will and it will be all your fault.

Blake: Me? I did nothing.

Mav: No, you didn't because you don't have to. You are just perfect for me and I can't wait to eventually take our relationship further.

Blake: We'll see Lover-boy.

Mav: Lover boy, yeah, I like that. I'll see you soon, beautiful.

I better put this phone down as I'm getting everything ready for the meal I'm holding for the seniors. I have a pot roast cooking and all vegetables prepared. The house is spotless and I'm setting the table ready.

It's still early, and they won't arrive in the cab I ordered to pick them all up and bring them here for another two hours. I have plenty of time to have a nice shower and do the last chores I need to finish so I'm clear for next week when I'm back at work.

Checking the kitchen two hours later, I place the apple pie I purchased from the bakery onto a serving plate and leave it near the stove. I know they all like apple pie, as I've seen them all eating it heartily when it's been provided from the service Alf uses for them.

The door opens and in burst four seniors, all talking between themselves excitedly. Ed, of course, is leading them in as he still has a key to the house, and now I call him PawPaw he is using the title to the fullest.

"Hi, Blake," Ed rushes over and hugs me tightly, kissing my cheek. "I brought all the old coots with me, as you can see."

"Hey, look who you are calling an old coot, Ed. You are older than I am," Pru states with a touch of sass to her voice. "Now, is there anything we can do to help, Blake?"

"No, you all take a seat and I'll be serving up in a minute." I hug them all as they pass me and again they talk between themselves excitedly. It shows I did the right thing by bringing them here for this meal. They are all glowing, and it is the first time I've seen Robert smile.

Ed, of course, didn't take a seat. He's still hanging around me, trying to see what I'm doing, taking lids off the pans on the stovetop. Tapping his hand, I give him a *leave it alone look,* which I'm sure has a flush rush into his cheeks.

Quite a while later we are all eating dessert, talking about life in general when Robert asks, "Why do you work at the coffee place as well as the cleaning job, Blake?"

"It's a long story, Robert, but if you want to hear it, I'll tell you all what happened." That is how I end up giving them the story of my life and how I ended up at this point in time.

"So, are you dating that biker now?" Audrey asks.

"I suppose I am. We've been out twice. The first time wasn't so good, but last night we went to TJs and it was a great night. I really enjoyed the evening."

I watch as Ed leans forward and gives me a piercing look, but he says nothing for a minute or two. "I'll need to see this biker man of yours. As your PawPaw, I need to make sure that you'll be safe with him."

The other three at the table are all nodding in agreement, and muttering words like, 'sure,' 'unruly,' 'noisy bikes,' 'handsome,' but it's such a mixture I've no idea if they like or dislike the idea of me dating a biker.

"Okay, how about I bring him around to Ed's one day and you can all visit and meet him? But that is only after I know if it's getting serious," I ask, giving them all a *don't argue* look. They all quickly agree thankfully, and Ed puffs up that he is the one everyone will have to go to.

I've noticed more and more that Ed's hands are not bad nor is his walking. The old shit has had people blinded with this health thing. But, I'm keeping the fact I know to myself, for now at least. I see it as ammunition I can use against him in the future if need be.

I'm amazed when all four pitch in to wash dishes and clean away from our meal. We all laugh and joke along as we do so, and I am so happy to see them all enjoying themselves. I will definitely do this again. Not every week, but maybe once a month! We'll see how things go because it's an expense at the moment that I cannot do too regularly.

I really need to get Yax out of that house and get it sold. I am sick of paying for something I don't need. Bitty's man getting rid of my debts has been great and I've got some money in my account for the first time in a long time. It has me feeling safer knowing in time I'll have something if hard times come around again.

-:- BITTY -:-

"Now people, are you coming with me or not?" I ask everyone who is in the kitchen at the clubhouse.

Meat grunts, and Star jumps up and down shouting, "Me, me, I'm coming."

"Okay, dear, that's great. You and Meat can be my right-hand people." I turn to my right when I hear a snarled voice.

"I'm your right-hand person and have been for years. So, Star, you can step back, girl." Amelia is standing in front of and pointing her cane at Star, who has a huge smirk on her face, not intimidated at all.

"That's okay, Amelia. I don't mind being a left-hand person. But make sure when we get to the house we all get inside." Star once more jumps up and down, doing some sort of jig. Meat is watching her with a heated look on his face, and I have to turn away because honest to goodness, it's enough to burn anyone within the vicinity to ashes.

When I hear, "I'm coming," I turn, just in time to see Axel scoop Mia over his shoulder and slap her ass before announcing, "No, you're not," before disappearing out the door with her. Well, we all know where he's taking her, and it's a good thing Sybil and Jo offered to be on kids duty this morning.

"I'll come because Blake won't be happy if she finds out I allowed you to go on your own, without me that is." Mav grabs a cookie from the counter and stuffs it into his mouth without taking a bite, the whole damn thing disappears.

I hear a few more, 'Yeah, I'm in,' 'I'll come,' 'Me too.' And grin to myself because Yax and her man do not know what is heading their way. But as we all climb into the SUV and the van, Graham rides into the compound, leaves his bike and quickly jumps into the truck that Meat and Star are in. This could turn into a shit show, I'm thinking at this point.

Arriving at the house, we all pile out of the vehicles and I lead everyone up the garden path, hammer on the front door and wait. But after a minute nobody answers, so Meat runs toward the door and kicks it hard, which has it flying open to show the utterly disgusting mess that these people are living in.

Star steps up to the side of me and states, "What a filthy bitch she is. Who in their right mind lives in a squalor like this? I wouldn't want to take a shit in this place, because, Bitty, my shit is cleaner than this place."

Amelia laughs and I turn to look at Star, who does not know what she's just said, I'm sure. Things just fall out of her mouth as she says whatever she thinks and however she sees it, and looking around, I think I have to agree with her. I wouldn't want to drop my drawers in this place for any reason, either.

We all look up when a bang and footsteps are heard. But when Yax appears at the top of the stairs looking like she just got out of a garbage can, I sigh. I had hoped the stupid bitch had already left the place.

"What are you all doing in my house?" Yax screeches.

Mav steps forward and snarls, "Your house? You mean the one you are living in free of charge because you are a scum-sucking piece of shit that pretended to have a child with someone? We all know that your kid is not who you said he was, and you need to get the fuck out of the house before I get hold of you and throw you out. Make no mistake, bitch, I mean throw you out physically."

"I'll get the Sheriff."

"Oh, please do, that would make my day," I singsong to her, much to Star's amusement, as she now steps forward laughing and pointing at Yax.

"You are a filthy, disgusting bitch. Where are the kid and the man?" Star asks, and I'm feeling less important here than I should be feeling!

"Yeah, where are they?" Amelia joins in, tapping her cane on the filthy floor.

"You know you'll have to scrub your cane now, don't you, Amelia?" I ask.

"I'll get Meat to burn it and I'll buy a new one," to which Meat grunts and nods his head.

Graham rushes forward, bolts up the stairs, grabs Yax by the arm and bellows, 'CATCH,' as he tosses her down the stairs. Mav stops her from hitting the floor hard, but uses the momentum to toss her to Meat, who in turn tosses her out the front door and slams it behind her.

"Stop fuckin' about with her," Graham states as he storms off into the bedrooms.

Now, I'm shocked at how fast he did that, and Star is cackling like a witch, clapping her hands and shaking her hips at her man. Meat, in turn, is watching her with those smoldering eyes again. Shit, I hope they are not going to start anything before we get back to the clubhouse? But at least Knuckles and Jo are not here or they'd be getting the vibes and be at it like bunnies.

"No sign of anyone here, and no sign of the boy or the man's things. I reckon they left the bitch here on her own," Graham says as he walks back down the stairs.

Since Meat forced the lock to get in, Mav has been holding the front door closed. He then opens it and seizes Yax, who was pounding on it. "Where are your man and boy?" he asks with more than a little snarl to it.

"Gone. He up and went and took my son with him. Good riddance. They were both holding me back, anyway." Yax surprises all of us when she runs her forefinger down Mav's chest, giving him a dirty toothed smile. What she didn't expect was Mav to grab the finger and snap it back, hard, which has her screaming and holding it at the odd angle it's now sitting at.

"You have ten minutes to get your stuff and get out. I mean clothing, that's all you are taking because we all know that you supplied not a single piece of furniture or anything else in this house. Time's ticking..." I state, and give Graham, Meat and Mav a look.

Yax is pushed into the house, and Ruger, Sting, and Clay all walk inside. I'd forgotten they had even come along with us as we'd crowded the hallway just inside the front door.

"This place is disgusting. It'll need fumigating," Clay states with his nose curled up nearly enough to touch his forehead.

Ruger looks around and elbows Sting. "I don't envy anyone that has this shit to clean up."

Shaking his head in agreement, Sting walks past and into the living room, "Fuck, this place is rank."

Amelia sighs, "Heather is going to need an army to clean this place, Bitty."

"It's worse than I thought it was going to be. I don't want Blake seeing this mess. I'll speak with Heather and tell her to get everything emptied out, taken away and cleaned. Then we'll get the place up for sale." I walk into the living room, and cringe because honestly, it could not be worse. The kitchen, utility room, and the half bath are in the same filthy state. Yeah, there is going to be nothing to salvage from this place.

Two hours later, Yax has gone. Meat, along with some of the brothers, has boarded up the door. Sheriff Forest knows she's out of the house and if she returns she needs arresting for trespassing, or breaking and entering!

I open the door to Blake's house and walk inside, and hearing talking, I head to the kitchen, where Blake is speaking with Ed.

"Hi, Bitty. How are you?" Ed asks as I plop my ass onto a dining chair.

"Good, but tired. How are you?"

"Oh, I'm very good. Got a belly full of pot roast and had splendid company. I'm just waiting for my cab to take me home," Ed says before he grabs a mug and pours me a coffee from the machine, and then retakes his seat at the table.

"What's wrong?" Blake asks.

"Nothing is wrong. I took some of the boys over to Yax and evicted her. She's gone, but she's left a mess behind. I have left a message for Heather to see the place. She may need a few of the cleaners to go over once the place is emptied." I give Blake a sorry look, but she shrugs and waits for whatever else I'm going to say. "The place will more than likely take a week to clean out, if Heather can organize everyone quickly. But it's a nice place Blake, and I'm sure it will sell easily once it's ready."

"I'm not worried, Mama, it'll sell as you say when it's empty and clean. I am ready for it to be gone and that part of my life put behind me. Do you think Yax will cause more trouble?" Blake taps her fingernails on the tabletop, showing she is nervous about what's going to happen.

"No, she already has a broken finger from trying shit with Mav. So, she'll stay away knowing the MC is onboard with it." Blake has an odd look on her face, and yeah, you guessed, I had to ask. "What?"

"Mav, he broke her finger?"

"Yeah, she tried it on with him. Touched him with that finger, so he snapped that sucker back and she left him alone after that. You know he's not going to take any shit from women after the trouble with Sharon, don't you?"

Ed is grinning, but Blake is still frowning. "What?" I ask again.

"What do you mean the MC is onboard?"

"Look, you are Mav's woman, you are dating him, which makes you his, and he yours, so hey, anyone messes with you, and the MC will be onboard to sort it out."

Blake's eyes round and what she says next has me laughing so hard Ed has to catch me before I fall out of my seat.

"Is this MC a cult?"

"A cult, she says...A cult!" That is what I'm still saying and giggling about when I walk into the clubhouse an hour later.

CHAPTER TWENTY-TWO

Who would have thought on a Monday morning I'd be sporting a split lip and a sore jaw? Garth is not holding back with this sparring and I've got to speed up my dodging maneuvers or I'm going to end up black and blue.

"Come on, Mav, concentrate," Garth smirks as he jabs for my face once more. "Get your hands up...look forward...tuck in your chin."

I'm following his instructions and dodging as best I can, but he needs to know that when it's my turn to go on the attack, I'm gonna do it with as much gusto as I can muster.

Knuckles and Colton are standing on one side of the area where we are sparring. We are using the space we use on Sundays for training with the Ol' Ladies. Thankfully, most of the brothers are at work and not watching this shit show go down.

"Watch my face," I snarl. "I'm trying to stay pretty to get my woman. The last thing I need is to turn up with a black eye." Garth smirks, then chuckles, and if he smirks one more damn time, I'm really gonna pummel his ass into the ground.

"You have an ugly mug, so it's not going to be pretty at any time of the day or night," Garth replies, and that's it, I've had enough.

I go on the attack, and swing one, two, dodge, drop one leg to a knee, sweep out his legs with the other and wham, he goes down and I'm on him before he can recover.

Before I can punch him over three times, Knuckles is grabbing one of my arms and Colton the other. "That's enough, lover boy. Hannah wants her man back tonight in one piece," Knuckles laughs.

"You did well, Mav. But you have to stay alert, keep your eye on the man. You are not as zeroed in on your target as you need to be. These fuckers are not playing. They want to murder anyone that walks into that damn cage. Remember, it's not a ring anymore, it's a fucking cage that they lock you into until one of you is not breathing anymore." Garth is giving me a look that says he's worried I'm not ready for my fight.

"When are you going to become a brother, Garth? It's time. You know that, don't you?" Yeah, I'm being an asshole asking this while we are busy here.

Garth stands looking at me with a serious expression on his face, before looking at Knuckles and Colton. "If I become a brother, do I stay as I am, working doors and having time with Hannah?"

"Yeah. We are not at war with other clubs. We don't run dirty shit, or get involved in anything we shouldn't. We don't need to do any of that as we have our own businesses and they are all earning a profit and giving us all a good living." I stand with my hands on my thighs, looking up at Garth as I catch my breath.

"Okay, put my name forward and see if the other brothers want me in. I like the brotherhood I've seen, and I miss that, as most of you will relate. I want to spend time with Hannah, make a family with her, but also need a purpose in the day-to-day of things." Garth at last is giving us an insight into how he feels.

"We all roll from TJs to Club Whisky, and run any kind of body-guarding shit we need."

"Like you going to kindergarten, you mean?" Garth laughs.

"Yeah, just like that." Colton steps forward grinning right before launching himself forward, and wrapping an arm around Garth's neck, trying to take him down. But, Garth flips him and has him down on hls back, arm across his neck and tut-tutting at him. "Fuck's sake, Garth, you gotta teach me some of these moves."

Knuckles shakes his head before walking toward the clubhouse, shouting over his shoulder, "It's lunchtime."

You can bet we all scamper to the kitchen because we all saw Meat prepping his ribs this morning, and he's going to be giving them out as a lunchtime treat, I'm sure.

Sitting in the kitchen, the table has a large plate of ribs in the center and we four are all grabbing one after another. Maybe Meat is a menace around here at times, but I'd suffer him anytime, just for the fact he can cook better than anyone else I know.

I take a chunk of the crusty bread that the Three Stooges made early this morning, and bite down, enjoying the butter that is slathered on the top. Who would know that ribs and fresh bread could taste so damn good!

"Meat, do you have any spare that I can take for Hannah? She would love to try these. She does ribs for me regularly but they never taste as good as this. But don't tell her I said that," Garth gives Meat a beseeching look. We all know Meat is a sucker for the women so he's easily going to give some ribs to Garth.

Meat quickly takes a container out of a cabinet and places ribs inside. Snapping it closed, he walks over and hands it to Garth, giving him a grunt before walking back behind the kitchen island and continuing with what he was doing.

Colton tries his luck next, which has everyone in the kitchen watching. "Hey, Meat, do you have any spare ribs that I can take to my room and munch on later while I watch a movie?"

Meat slowly lifts his head, looks Colton right in the eye and flips him the middle finger. That is enough for everyone to bust out laughing and watch Colton pretending to have hurt feelings.

My mind wanders over to the Three Stooges who are sitting with Mia. Summer is sleeping in Amelia's arms while Mia eats lunch. But Bitty has everyone's attention when she states, loudly I might add, "Blake thinks this is a cult."

Colton splutters and chokes on his mouthful of ribs. Knuckles, who has Jo tucked under his arm, is frowning, so no dimple popping at the moment. Me, I'm frowning too and thinking, what the hell is she talking about.

Mia takes up the conversation. "What do you mean, she thinks this is a cult?"

"Blake thinks with everyone wearing the same clothing, you know, with the club emblazoned on that you are a cult. She knows it is a biker club, but doesn't understand what that is. So, to her, it's a cult." Bitty grins.

"Fuckin' hell, you are in for it, Mav, if she thinks we are a cult. I hope she doesn't start thinking we are like the Mansons," Colton chuckles.

"I'll put her straight. I don't want a misunderstanding about what we are and what we do. Fuckin' hell, that's all we need, isn't it, if she thinks we are a cult?" I give Bitty a sharp look.

"Oh, I'll sort her out, don't you worry, Mav. But it was so funny at the time all I could do was laugh." Bitty takes Summer and walks out of the kitchen, but she's giggling under her breath the whole time.

A while later I'm passing the kid's room and I hear Mia speaking about the girl-gang, and knowing how she likes to rope them into doing stuff they shouldn't, I wait to see what's being said.

"The meeting was okay, but the girls said no to any more bullshit at this time. As if I get into bullshit? You know that I only do what I think is right. But we had a vote that we would always be democratic, so we voted on helping get Yax out the house, before you got her out that is Bitty, and they voted to stay out of it and let the brothers sort it out, if Mav wanted them to."

Grinning as I hear Mia talking because anyone listening can hear how disappointed she is to not get involved in any shenanigans that are afoot.

Bitty speaks out, "Well, she is out now, and that man she had took off with the boy. Turned out the boy was his, so he did what was right and took him to give him a better life, away from that awful woman. We need to run her out of town, or take her to Nell's."

Shit…That was not the right thing to say, and quick as a whip, Mia takes it up. "Oh, that's a good idea. I'll speak to Nell because I want her to join the girl-gang and she'll need a bike or trike. I'll get Mav to take me over."

Damn, fuck, shit, and double-damn, I'm outta here. This is something that can only lead to trouble, and I need to warn Axel what his Ol' Lady is planning.

After informing Axel, I can see he's mulling over what he wants to do. I leave him with Wings, Buzz and Drag in the office as I head to the common room. Taking a seat, I unlock my phone and send a text.

Mav: Hey, beautiful, you having a good day?

I know it's lunch break for Blake at the moment, so I'm hoping she'll reply.

Blake: Yeah, all is good at the shop. You having a good day?

Mav: I am now.

Blake: Aw, you are such a sweetie.

Mav: Hey, I'm not a sweetie, and don't be spreading that rumor [grinning emoji]

Blake: Yes, you are, and it's why I like you so much.

Mav: Oh, you like me a lot?

Blake: Yeah, I do. But I'm worried about you being in a cult.

Mav: I'll come over tonight and explain about the club. We are not a cult and I don't want you thinking or worrying about that.

Blake: Oh, okay. Do you want to eat with me?

Mav: Yeah, but I'll bring it with me so don't bother making anything for us. I'll raid Meat's evening meal for us.

Blake: OK. I've gotta run now. CU later [heart emoji]

Oh, my, Blake sent me a heart emoji...that's damn cool, and I send her one right back. I'm thinking we are along the right lines here and I want to make her mine, but I don't want to scare the shit out of her by making my move too soon.

The Three Stooges walk past me and through to the kitchen. Mia takes Summer to the play corner of the common room and places her in a stroller that Jig had made for her and she tucks her up tight before pushing her out the front door of the clubhouse. I'm sure she'll not get far before Colton follows her either up the compound or out the front gate.

I head to the kitchen where I'm going to ask Meat about putting me up two meals to take to Blake's house tonight. But, he's not in the kitchen and neither are the Stooges. Shit, where are they now? They passed me only a minute ago!

Walking through the kitchen and out the back door, I see Garth leaning against the wall watching something intently, with Wings at the side of him. Now, I didn't see Wings pass me in the common room, but then I wasn't paying attention, as I had my eyes on my text messages.

"What are you two doing?" I can't hold back my curiosity.

Garth responds as Wings places the palm of one hand over his mouth, "Well, those three old biddies took up to the treehouse with Meat. You know he teaches all sorts of shit to the women?"

"Yeah, I know that," I respond, wondering where this is going.

"Well, he has Sybil zip lining, Amelia walking over the gangplank as I call it to the second treehouse, and Bitty, for some reason, is hanging upside down from the side of the treehouse. But I wish she wasn't because I'm not sure if I should bleach my eyeballs or vomit at the sight of her bloomers." Garth turns and walks into the kitchen of the clubhouse just as Wings hoots with laughter before following.

Slowly turning my head toward the treehouse, I see the same as they described. Sybil is at the bottom of the zip line, obviously getting ready to run back for another attempt. Amelia is now at the second treehouse, which I think is going to be an enforced nursery, and I mean locked down tight so the kids can't escape. Good luck with that if the twins are involved, is my thinking. But Bitty, now that has me quickly turning my back and storming into the kitchen.

"FUCK… I didn't need to see that, where is the bleach…" I holler much to Wings' amusement. Garth, however, is standing with his hand over his eyes mumbling, '*I can still see it.*'

CHAPTER TWENTY-THREE

-:- BLAKE -:-

It has been a great Monday. Everything ran smoothly at work and I'm learning how to serve in the front of the shop. The coffee smells are amazing and when I leave work, I take the smell along with me as it seeps into what you are wearing. It's a comforting smell if I'm being honest.

"Are you ready to leave, Blake?" Liam asks as he starts to empty the last load of the dishwasher.

"Yes, I'm done, Liam. There was only the dishwasher to empty, and that is the kitchen ready to close for the day."

"Great. Get gone, and I'll finish this. It'll only take me a few minutes, and I'll lock up the back door and set the alarm. When are you going to get yourself a vehicle, Blake?"

Sighing because I know I'll be able to afford one soon, but with the van for my cleaning job, do I really need one? "I'm not sure, Liam. I will think about it."

"You do that."

I'm not sure what look I see in Liam's eye, but I shrug and make my way out of the back door, waving as I leave. No cleaning work tonight, with it being Monday, so I'm going to make my way home and have a nice soak in the bath before Mav brings our meal. I'm looking forward to spending time with him, and I feel such a lot about him already. If I'm honest with myself, I already feel more for him than I did with Stefan. Tells me a lot about me settling instead of spreading my wings for more.

Walking along my mind is straying to things I probably shouldn't be thinking. But, I'm wondering if I should jump in, both feet together and seduce Mav, or buy myself one of those battery-operated things which I've never had before. But, the frustration I'm building has me wanting one or the other, and I know which I'd prefer if I have the bravery to go for it.

"Stay away from my man..."

On hearing a screechy voice, and the comment, I turn and see Sharon. This is all I need to spoil a perfectly good Monday. Well, it was up until this point.

"What man is that?" I ask as I take out my phone and text a message to Mav that his ex is accosting me again on the main street as I head home.

"You know what man...Mav. He's mine, I've had him and you are poaching my man. Thieving whores like you..."

Now, I'm a mild person, but nobody, and I mean nobody, calls me a whore. I also had promised Bitty I'd fight for my man, so that's exactly what I do. I step toward this awful woman and slap her with my left hand, which isn't my dominant hand. She grins at me because it was not that hard of a slap, but I follow it with a punch from my right hand and throw my shoulder behind it. Now her head does snap back and to the side, spittle flies out of her mouth as she screams in what I'm not sure may be fear, temper or pain.

Oh, she's a playground fighter. She throws herself forward and grabs my hair, but I've watched movies and YouTube and I punch her in her privates as hard as I can. She screams again and lets go of me so she can hold herself between her legs, and while she does that, I punch her again in the face and she goes down yowling like a cat in heat.

"That was damn fine," I hear and turn to see one of the cult members is standing watching with his arms folded over his chest. He holds his hand out to shake, and without thinking, I place my hand in his and give him a weak smile.

"She's a pest, and I'm fed up with it. Just because Mav stuck his... you know what in her doesn't mean she can keep being a bitch." I was going to say cock but thought better of it, but I can see by the smirk this man is giving me he realizes I stopped myself.

"My name's Chaos, and I'll wait here for Mav and Sheriff Forest to arrive. I was in the shop over there when I got a message asking if anyone was near the Coffee House. Mav got your message and wanted someone here, but, girl, you didn't need any help."

We are both watching Sharon writhing around on the ground hugging between her legs. Now, I have to admit I feel sorry, but not sorry enough to not do it again if the need arose. Turning when we hear a bike I see Mav and the Sheriff's cruiser behind him.

"Here you go, babe, Mav to the rescue," Chaos chortles as he moves to stay beside Sharon, but allowing Mav to walk over to me once he's gotten off his bike.

"Are you okay, Blake?"

"Yeah, I'm fine. It was over quickly. She isn't a fighter, she's all piss and cookies, like in the bottom of a stroller. Your cult person here came by quickly," My face flushes when I finish speaking, as it's a long time since I heard that, and it's something one of my old bosses used to say about her daughter, who was a real drama queen.

Sheriff Forest cuffs Sharon and drags her over to the cruiser, throwing her into the back and slamming the door. "Mav, I'll need you to follow me. Blake, you okay?"

"Yes thank you Sheriff, I'm good."

"Okay, Chaos, take Blake home, because I need Mav to follow me." Sheriff Forest quickly walks away to his cruiser and Mav kisses me quickly before following the Sheriff once on his bike.

"Come on, Blake, you are lucky I have the truck. I'll drop you at your house on my way back to the clubhouse."

Later that evening, Mav has brought a meal, and we sit in companionable comfort. We talk about our day and then, of course, the mention of Sharon comes up.

"Sharon won't be a problem again. She's left town already and been warned if she comes back she'll be arrested and she won't have it easy from that point. She's not a fool, well she may be, but she's gone. The Sheriff put her on a bus himself and made sure she's going three states away. He even put a tracker on her phone without her knowing so he can keep his eye on her." Mav is grinning at the thought.

"I think she's psycho, to be honest, Mav," I push my plate away and rub my full stomach. "She wasn't anywhere near prepared for me to launch myself at her. She called me a whore, and that is something I won't stand for at all."

"She's gone now, and I wish I'd never set eyes on her. But let's put that behind us and move forward. So why are you calling the MC a cult?"

Mav totally takes me by surprise by asking that, and I open and close my mouth a few times before I respond, "Well, you all wear the same jackets, and they all have the same logo thing on them. You mostly all live in the same building, too. I'm not sure what else I'm supposed to think."

"The jackets as you call them are kuttes, you can look it up on the internet, but many of us call them a cut, you know c.u.t. and not the k.u.t.t.e. Depends on each club what they call them, but they all mean the same thing. It's showing we are a member, fully paid up so to speak and you'll see we all have our names on and other things besides. A patch jacket, battle vest or cut-off are other things they can be called."

"You mean like that Sons of Anarchy thing on the television?" I ask, because now I'm getting nervous.

"Well, it's the same sort of thing, but we do nothing illegal, or get involved with clubs that are illegal. We are mostly prior military and love the brotherhood, so we find comfort and peace living amongst each other."

"Oh, that's not so bad then." I must show how relieved I feel as he chuckles and then continues explaining.

"The women at the club are mostly Ol' Ladies, and I don't mean old as in age, you know, like Bitty, Amelia and Sybil. The Ol' Ladies of the club are like, and often are the wife of a brother. Like Knuckles and Jo, Forest and Heather, Hammer and Tilly." Leaning forward, Mav picks up one of my hands and rubs his thumb slowly over it, soothing me as he speaks. "And, hopefully, one day, it'll be Mav and Blake."

Now, I sit up straight and look Mav in the eye, not sure if I heard him right, but he gives me a slow nod to say that I had and I must look like an owl because my eyes feel like they are going to pop out of my head. But Mav waits patiently while I mull over what he has said. Then, without even thinking about it, I smile, "Actually, that would be nice. But let's see where this leads, because we've only just started seeing each other."

"Hey, most of the brothers meet their woman, and that is it. We know immediately she is the one, and we don't waste time because none of us know how long on this earth we have. I think you are my one and only, and you've just got to catch up quickly." Now the smile he gives me lights up his entire face, and for the life of me, I cannot hold back the smile of appreciation that appears.

My phone rings and seeing it is Heather, I quickly take the call. "Hello, Heather."

"Blake. I've spoken with Bitty, and she said it's okay to go in and remove everything from the house Yax was living in. Then to clean every inch of the place. I just wanted to verify with you if that's what you wanted done?"

"Oh, yes, that is good. I was going to speak to you during the week. But, yes, the place needs everything removed, then cleaned before I put it up for sale. Bitty has organized a realtor for her place, so I could use them," I add to the conversation.

"Alf has a friend who sells property. He is a good realtor. Let me speak to Alf and see if we can get your place up and sold quickly, and I'll also speak to Bitty about her place." Heather speaks to someone on her end, but she must cover the speaker to her phone, as all I hear is mumbling. "Let me organize everything, Blake, and I'll get back to you, and keep you up to date."

"Okay, thank you." Before I can say more she's gone, and looking up at Mav, he is smirking so obviously knows Heather just went without saying goodbye.

The evening quickly passes, and Mav kisses me thoroughly before he leaves, but as he's leaving, I notice he has mud on his biker boots. That's odd because I don't think it has been raining.

Earlier this evening, before I came for the meal with Blake, I was standing in a farmer's field watching Sharon digging a hole. Forest is standing at the side of me and we are amused at how slowly she is digging.

"Get digging, Sharon. Because once that grave is dug you've got a huge decision to make," Forest states and folds his arms over his chest, taking an easy stance.

"What are you making me dig this for?" Sharon asks, and I roll my eyes at Forest because if anyone can't work out why they are digging a grave in the middle of nowhere, and certainly where the farmer won't see, then they're probably brain dead, anyway.

"Come on, get a move on, my woman's waiting on me at home." Forest snarls. He didn't answer her question, I noted, but I keep quiet as this is very amusing and I'm imagining any moment she's going to piss her pants.

Twenty minutes later, Forest speaks again, and I'm sure Sharon has worked out what is going on as she's crying a river and pissed her pants. But me, I keep quiet still because she caused all this herself.

"Now, you can stop digging and decide. You either fuck off out of town, where I'll drop you at the bus depot and you move at least three states away, or I put a fucking bullet in your brain now and we bury you here in the grave you just dug."

"I'll leave. I'll leave and never come back." Sharon is pissing again and you can see it running down her skinny jeans. Jesus Christ, she was brave to have words with Blake, but she is a coward when it comes down to it.

"Okay, put your legs and ass in that bag because you ain't leaving no piss on the cruiser's back seat for me or anyone else to clean up," Forest snarls and pushes her to the vehicle, watches her hop in the bag and into the back of the cruiser. Turning to look at me, he winks, "You got a hole to fill, brother."

That's exactly what I do, at double speed, as I have to get the meal and get to Blake. I try to kick off the mud that is clinging to my boots and hope it is not mud because of the piss mixed in with it.

CHAPTER TWENTY-FOUR

-:- MAV -:-

Mav: Good morning. I'll be over this evening and I'll bring food.

Blake: Morning. OK, that will be good. I'm going to be home by 6.

Mav: OK. Have a good day and stay out of trouble [winking emoji]

Blake: Wow, I don't get into trouble, it's your skank that keeps causing trouble.

Mav: She's gone never, never to return. See you later, honeybee.

Blake: Honeybee?

I don't bother replying to the last message because I'm going to be calling Blake any kind of endearment I can think of. But I'm also setting my phone to show My Blake from this point forward.

"Mav, are you ready to take the twins?"

Turning I give Mia a nod and follow her out of the clubhouse to the SUV where she has both the boys in their car seats. They look like butter wouldn't melt at the moment, but anyone that knows them, knows it'll not last. They'll be up to no good as soon as Mia turns her back.

Pulling up outside school, I help Mia get the boys out of the vehicle but I'm not going inside. I'll leave her to deal with signing them in and then leaving them, and if she cries I'm gonna be more than a little pissed because these boys are damn hooligans and she's no reason to feel bad about leaving them. They more than likely will have the place under siege in an hour.

Fifteen minutes later Mia walks out of the building and climbs into the SUV, all without a word. I jump into the driver's seat and look over at her, but for once see she's not crying and has a small smile on her face.

"What?" I ask, because something is going on.

"I bribed them," giggling more to herself than me, "I told them if they behaved and I didn't have to come over to school all week they could have their own dirt bikes. I saw them and they were called Renegade MK250's, kid's electric dirt bikes, and I showed the twins the picture so they knew what they would miss out on. That will keep them from being assholes all week. Oh, they have training wheels on them too."

"Does Pres know about these bikes?" I ask because I am not sure if he would want them on electric bikes, even if they have balancing wheels.

"No, why do I have to tell him everything? Honestly, he has enough to do without thinking about what I'm doing all the time." Mia sniffs as she looks out the side window before ignoring any of my attempts to speak to her.

Walking into the clubhouse kitchen I grab a coffee, and one for Mia who has taken a seat at her usual table. Sybil is sitting with Summer and they both get to gossiping. I leave them to it because I don't want to be involved in anything that any of the women may get up to.

Taking a seat at a table a few away I take out my phone and send a text to Blake.

Mav: Hope you are not too busy, and having a good day.

I don't expect a reply, so I'm surprised when my phone pings and I see a message.

My Blake: I'm having my break. It's been busy but I've been in the shop serving customers. [smiling emoji]

Mav: Oh, is that good then?

My Blake: Better than emptying the dishwasher all day.

Mav: Yeah, I suppose it would be. You have any preference to what you want to eat tonight?

My Blake: No, anything is fine.

Mav: Anything?

My Blake: I have to go, CUL8R [heart emoji]

"What are you grinning about?"

Looking up I shrug my shoulders because I'm not telling any of the brothers what I'm saying to my woman. Wings takes a seat and gives me another questioning look but doesn't follow through with the question itself.

"Why are you not busy?" I ask as I change the subject.

"Pres is wanting everyone out of his office while he speaks to one of his informants. I reckon something is about to go down with that Milanas. I hope Vitale catches him, then we can sneak in and grab the fucker right from under his nose."

"That's what he wants, teach this fucker he has to pay for his crimes, and to piss off Vitale of course." Both of us chuckle but turn when we hear a female voice.

"Oh, we can piss off Vitale don't you worry about that."

"Hi, Nell, follow me and we'll go somewhere private to talk," Mia quickly says, taking Summer from Sybil and speaking over her shoulder to Amelia behind the kitchen island," Can you bring us refreshments please, Amelia?"

Amelia's eyebrows shoot up to her hairline in surprise, and I'm waiting for the sassy response, but she smiles sweetly and replies, "Yes of course I can, I'll be along in a few minutes."

Sybil gives Amelia a small nod as she follows Mia and Nell out of the kitchen. I turn and look at Graham who was behind Nell, but he throws himself into a seat grinning.

"What the fuck is going on?" Wings asks.

"You don't know anything about women do you?" Graham smirks at Wings.

Wings snaps back at Graham, and I keep my mouth firmly closed as I hear. "What's that supposed to mean?"

"Well, anyone can tell Amelia is going to make a tray of drinks and snacks. Then she's going to take them into Mia and Nell. Once in with them Sybil will appear to look after Summer while Nell and Mia have some peace. But that places Amelia and Sybil in the mix knowing exactly what is going on." Graham stands from his seat and walks into the kitchen, serves himself a coffee before coming back and looking at Wings, who is sitting with a stunned look on his face.

Wings doesn't say a word before walking away from the table, out of the kitchen. I wait to see if he's coming back, but when he doesn't reappear in a few minutes I shrug and give Graham my attention.

"So, what's going on with Nell and Mia?"

"Mia wants Nell to be in her girl gang although she isn't a club member. Nell is a good one to have in any gang if you need your back covered, but more than that they both get on well, and Nell needs female friends. She never leaves the property, but needs more than what she is doing. Too much goes on at times and I know she's a tough cookie but she is a woman, and needs some softness in her life." Graham places his chin in the palm of his hand while he rests his elbow on the table.

"Not sure you can say Mia brings softness, Graham. She's a tough one all of her own." I watch Amelia carry a tray out of the kitchen, and think Graham had it right from the look on Amelia's face.

Wings walks back into the kitchen with a laptop. Taking a seat at the table next to us he opens it and taps in commands. I lean over and see his monitor is showing the inside of the playroom where Mia, Nell, Amelia, Sybil and Summer are situated.

"Yeah, yeah, shut it," Wings snaps.

"Oh, are you using one of your bugs? I want to learn this shit, you gotta teach me Wings," Graham all but whines.

"I'll teach you. I'll come over to you to do it. Will give me a break from here, but I want to give the cells a check over while I'm there."

"Why do you want to check the cells, Wings?" Graham gives him a shocked look.

"Last time I was in the cells I thought they could do with extra cameras to monitor them, and the hallway. They could do with auto lockdown too. That way if anybody like the FBI tried to get in they'd lockdown tight and do it with a flick of a button from the office, your phone, tablet or laptop."

"Come over, and we'll discuss it with Nell, Tank and Richie. I think it's a good idea, but I know Nell has never agreed to have anyone outside of us know our security measures."

"I'll come over. Show you all what I have in mind. So, tell us what happened with Nell and the Mafia evening." Wings eyes are sparkling with anticipation.

Axel walks into the kitchen and heads right to our table, taking a seat and waiting for whatever we are talking about. Shrugging, Graham starts the story.

"Well, Nell looked awesome even though she is my sister, I have to admit she looked outstanding. I gave Vitale the dressing down to keep his hands to himself or I'd chop the fuckers off. He was amused, rather than upset mind you, which pissed me, Tank and Richie off. Nell however, lifted the split in her long dress and guess what we saw?" We all shake our heads that we don't know what they saw, and he chuckles continuing, "She has a holster and a gun strapped to her thigh. I know she's not going to be taken by surprise, and she'll take no shit no matter who tries to dish it out.

"Well, we all get a call from herself saying pick her up, and we'd all been waiting for it, because you know this is Nell we are talking about. She didn't want to go to this fancy-ass shindig anyway, well that's what she called it."

"Wait, you all were waiting for her to call you, to pick her up? Rather than Vitale bringing her back?" Wings looks astonished. Me, I'm not sure much surprises me anymore, especially when a female is involved. I've come to the conclusion they are far more versatile than us men.

"Yeah, we knew she'd either get pissed off by someone, or she'd piss them off. Turned out a bit of both. Seems Vitale has had a woman on the side for quite some time, and she thought she was going to be the Donna to his Don, well seems not! But, of course, that didn't go down well when Vitale walked in with Nell on his arm, and her looking a million bucks too."

"Oh, please say the bitch had the nerve to say something to Nell…" Wings grins and lets out a chuckle, along with Axel I might add. Axel has one shit-eating grin on his face anticipating what happened next.

"Well, the stupid bitch strutted up to Nell and asked if she was Vitale's new whore. Now, you all know Nell and that she has a short fuse at times. It seemed her fuse was extra short with her not even wanting to be at this shindig to start with. She from somewhere whipped out a knife and held it to the bitch's throat before anyone could do jackshit, and purred, *'You wanna die? Nobody speaks to me like that and lives, so you want to apologize quickly or should I shove this knife into your throat and end you now?'* I would have given anything to have been there and seen that," Graham chuckles.

"What did Vitale do?" I ask, because what the fuck do you do with a date that makes an entrance like that?

"He grinned and stated so everyone could hear, *'This is what my woman looks like, and don't you all forget it. She'll gut you like a fish she's about to cook and then lick her fingers.'* Now, Nell wasn't so happy with that description, she shoves the woman hard, who falls on her ass screaming. People rush forward, and Vitale puts himself between Nell and everyone else. While his back is turned Nell does her disappearing act and we eventually find her walking home in her heels and evening gown."

"Fuck me," Axel mumbles, but he still has that damn grin on his face, "So what happened after?"

"Well, Nell told Vitale to fuck off to his whore of the month and she hasn't spoken to him since. He however, keeps sending flowers, chocolates, jewelry and other shit, which Nell immediately sends back with a notelet she had Tank make that has a photograph of her holding up her middle finger."

Now, we all break down into hysterical laughter but if anyone knows Nell, they know this story is as true as the sun will rise in the morning. I can't wait to see what happens eventually between Vitale and Nell. But, if Nell ever becomes the Donna of the Mafia they will know they've got her, and she'll rule with an iron fist and a cellar full of gators.

CHAPTER TWENTY-FIVE

I'm leaning on the wall of the clubhouse watching Knuckles and Colton go through their paces. They don't hold back punches, and I'm sure Colton is going to have a shiner when they've finished.

Mia is sitting on the bench in front of me watching them, and speaking with Jo, who it seems is having a week off from her writing as she has what she calls writer's block. No idea what that is, but I don't hold back the smirk as I consider if it is Knuckles not performing his duties as well as he could, or should.

"Did I tell you Nell is joining the girl gang? She is such a sweetheart, and you would never know she can chop someone up and not bat an eye. She helps anyone she can, and she jumped at the chance of joining in any fun and games we may have. Oh, she's going to get a trike and get her men, as she calls them, to teach her to ride it, and get her license. She said Graham would be up for it as he's been trying to get her to ride his hog for quite a while." As usual Mia is talking so fast she runs out of steam and has to take a large gulp of air before she continues, "I'm thinking of having a girl gang meeting once every month, just so we can have a get together and make sure everyone is alright? What do you think, Jo?"

Jo, turns and looks at Mia, but from her expression, I'm not sure she heard what was being said, "Yeah, that's good."

Yeah, I don't think she is hearing what is being said to her from her bland reaction, but Mia seems okay with it. I can't stop the tip of my lip curling up, but I stop the smile from forming.

Axel appears at my side and also leans against the wall. Both Jo and Mia don't register that he is here, and I hold my breath for a moment when the subject changes and Mia speaks about the boys and Summer.

"I love my boys, but shit, they are hard work. I hope Summer is going to be a little ray of sunshine and not cause any trouble. The twins have already had the teacher calling to say they are acting up today and I'm half expecting them to tell me to fetch them home," sighing, more to herself than Jo.

I quickly take a peek at Axel, who I have to say is smirking as he loves that his boys have spirit. We all know he wants a passel of kids, so three isn't going to be where he wants to stop either.

Mia continues, "I'm going to get fixed. I don't want a dozen kids. I'm struggling to look after the three I have. I know if it wasn't for Amelia..."

Now, before she can say another word, Axel is on her, picking her up, throwing her over his shoulder and he slaps her ass, and I mean slaps it. She's gonna have a red handprint on that butt cheek, I'm sure.

"We discussed this, and you agreed we'd have six. Now you can't go back on a promise..." Jo and I hear no more because Axel is storming back into the clubhouse, and I'm sure his room. Why he didn't go to their house on the compound I don't know, and I'm not asking.

Taking out my phone, I send a message to Blake.

Mav: How many kids would you like?

Only a few minutes pass before Blake responds, and as the time is her lunch break, I can imagine she's sitting outside on the bench behind the coffee house relaxing.

My Blake: I always thought I would like two, one of each, you know, a little girl to pretty up and a boy to rough around with.

Mav: That suits me fine. The sooner we get started on that, the better.

My Blake: Get started? What?

Mav: Well, we are not getting any younger, are we?

I can imagine her screwing her nose up, and getting that serious look on her face when I say this, but it's getting her thinking about the idea more than anything.

My Blake: OK, but you know we've not even tested if we are compatible–in the sex department yet.

Mav: That's okay, I'll come over tonight and we'll test it out.

To my utter surprise, the reply is: Yeah, OK.

The day passes quickly and before I know it I'm carrying a carton of Meat's ribs and a salad into Blake's house. I carefully put them down on the kitchen counter and walk over to where she is watching me, while leaning her hip on the kitchen table.

"You hungry, Blake?"

"Yeah, but not for food, Mav." She is giving me a bit of sass here, and I love it. I grin and step up to the front of her, placing one hand on each side of her, boxing her in.

"I need to know if you are all-in with this relationship, Blake, because I'm not wanting a one-nighter, or a casual hook-up type relationship. I'm after the full on, for life relationship. Being my Ol' Lady, and possibly wife, if that's what you want. I have a house being built on the compound, where we'll live, bring up our kids and be part of the MC brotherhood and sisterhood because Mia ain't gonna have any woman on the compound who isn't in the girl gang. Now, you in for all that, Blake?" I wait calmly for her response, but she doesn't hang around thinking. She gives me the most beautiful smile I think I've ever seen before speaking.

"I'm up for it, Mav. I know we haven't known each other long, but I think you are my one. You know, the one who will own my heart until it stops beating. I see you and my heart lurches and speeds up until I feel slightly breathless, and the anticipation of you being mine is nearly impossible to bear. Yeah, I want all that with you, but as I said, we don't know if we have the chemistry yet."

Oh, that's like waving a red flag to a bull. I slam my mouth over hers and take command of a kiss I hope she'll never forget. My tongue tastes every piece of her mouth, and I nibble, lick, and suck her lips.

Sliding my hands down, I cup her butt and lift her until she's sitting on the counter in front of me, but I don't stop the assault on her mouth as my hands slide up and down her bare legs. Lucky me, she's been home long enough to shower and change into a summer dress.

Blake runs her hands up and down the back of my neck, and I have no doubt if I'd had longer hair she'd have had her fingers in it, pulling and tugging. But she'll have to be satisfied with my short hair, and my ball cap because I love that thing. I left it at the compound tonight, mind you, as I had hoped our evening would move the relationship forward.

Blake makes little noises of appreciation as I kiss her, and my hand reaches the top of her thigh, over her hip and tucks into the top of her small lace panties.

"You sure you want this, Blake?" I ask because I want her to be sure this is how she wants to move forward. After we've done this, she'll be mine and I keep what's mine, close and safe. "If we do this, you'll be mine and I'll claim you in church with my patch."

"Yeah, I'm sure Mav."

But that is as much as she says because I have her off the counter, panties off, and turned with her hands on the counter before she can change her mind.

My jeans are undone and I'm well ready to claim her, but I test using two fingers before I go further as the last thing I want to do is hurt her. But she is hot, wet and wanting, and I don't wait any longer. I spear her with one long, easy stroke, not aggressively, but I'm totally in control.

Blake gasps, but gives a long moan of pleasure alongside whispering my name so reverently that I'll never forget it, even if I live to a hundred.

I slide my hands up the inside of her dress and pull her bra down, freeing her breasts so I can cup one. Pulling her nipple that is beaded gently, gaining another moan from her sweet lips.

As Blake pushes back onto me, I pick up my pace and with my free hand I slide it around to the front of her and pinch her clit, which has her jump and push back onto me even harder.

The pace increases and it's not long before I'm holding both her hips and I'm pounding into her, gaining what can only be described as a euphoric reaction. Blake gently screams with her release, and I see white spots before my eyes as my orgasm rolls through me.

I slow my pace and hold us both still as the pleasure rolls over us both. I can hear Blake panting and can feel her body shaking as she's breathing heavily. I'm not much better myself. At that moment, I know I'm never going to let her go, not willingly, anyway. She is my everything. She's the one I have been waiting for.

"I think we can say we are compatible now, Mav," Blake giggles, and I slap her sassy ass gently before rubbing the sting away.

"Maybe we should be sure?" I state, and that's exactly what we do. We test out our compatibility on the kitchen table, living room couch, halfway up the stairs, and the bed. To say we are both sated and exhausted would be an understatement, and my dick hasn't seen so much action in its entire life. Holding Blake while she gives puffing little snores, I can't help but be thankful for where I am right now. I feel like the luckiest fucker alive.

After a couple of hours of sleep, I'm awake and still holding Blake, but she is now awake and looking right back at me. I kiss her nose before taking her lips with a gentle kiss. "Good morning," I murmur against her lips, and feeling her smile against me has me smiling right back.

"Morning. I've got to get to work, Mav. Let me up and shower." Blake wiggles out of my grasp and heads to the bathroom, but I follow her and right into the shower.

"I'll drop you off at work, then make my way over to the clubhouse. I have some training to do this morning."

"What training?" Blake rinses the soap from my back as she asks.

"I've a fight on the weekend, so I'm getting some extra training in, you know, make sure I'm sharp." Now, I'm not sure how she'll react to fighting, but she knows I'm a doorman at the club and bar, so she should expect I can fight!

"Okay, but don't get lots of bruises. Can I come to the fight and watch at the weekend?"

"No, but you can stay at the clubhouse with the others while we are at the fight. I'll explain it all later, then you'll understand what's going on and why you need to stay out of the way and safe while the brothers are at this fight night."

"Oh, alright. I'll talk to you about it later. But come on, Mav, I'm going to be late and Liam will kick my ass."

"If Liam touches your ass, he'll be in a body bag," I mumble.

"What's that?" Blake asks, and I quickly reply, "Nothing, let's go."

CHAPTER TWENTY-SIX

-:- BLAKE -:-

Friday and it's been busy. I know that the other new lady is wanting a few extra hours as she has a young son to provide for. I'm sure I'm going to want to work less hours now that the house Yax was living in will be sold. I want to spend time with Mav too, I love being with him, and I don't want to get into that awful place I had with Stefan where we hardly saw each other. Mind you, my feelings for Mav are far different to any I had with Stefan so I can't see that happening.

Liam walks into the kitchen as I finish stacking the clean dishes I've taken out of the dishwasher. "Time for your break, Blake."

"Can I have a quick word, Liam?"

"Of course, what's up?" He stops from where he was heading upstairs to his apartment.

"I'd like to drop my hours down as I'm getting very tired working the two jobs. Elaine needs more hours to help with her family, so she could take the days I drop. If it's possible I'd like to remain working Monday, Tuesday and Wednesday."

Liam rubs his chin, and I wait for whatever he's going to decide. I don't want to lose my job but I can't keep working all these hours, I'm tired out now, so what will I be like in another month!

"Yeah, you can do that. I'll speak to Elaine. She did ask me about more hours, but I didn't have any to spare for her, but if you only want three days I'll offer her the others. You're sure now?"

"Yes, I'm sure. I love working here, and my second job with the seniors, but I'm sure I can't keep doing both with all these hours."

"Okay, starting next week then. But if I need you to come in for any coffee mornings, and the like, I want you to be available for those." Liam frowns, but I don't have a problem with that.

"That's fine, Liam, I can be available for any events you hold."

Later Elaine gives me a hug and thanks me, but I thank her in return because I'd not be able to keep up all those hours indefinitely, but I sure wouldn't want to leave anyone in the lurch either.

During my afternoon break my phone pings and a message catches my eye.

Mav: Fancy a night at the clubhouse tomorrow? So you can meet all the ladies.

My Blake: I've met them at the Coffee House, when they had the morning drinking, gossiping and looking after the kids. [smiling emoji]

Mav: Oh, I forgot about that. Well, we can have a chill night, because Sunday I'm fighting.

My Blake: What about you move into my house and we have a movie night instead, just the two of us.

Mav: Yeah, I can do that, and I was going to ask you about moving in. Do I have to speak to Bitty for permission [Laughing emoji]

My Blake: No, I'll tell her and PawPaw.

Mav: Oh, I forgot about Ed, and being PawPaw. Well, the old fucker will have to live with it.

My Blake: He will be okay with it, but I do need to tell him.

Mav: OK. Catch you later, sweet cake. I'll be around when you get home from work tonight.

My Blake: OK.

I can't stop the smile when I see he'd put me down as My Blake, and now he's calling me beautiful, sweet cake and other silly stuff. But I love it if truth is told.

Leaving work, I double timed it home, get changed and grab the work van, as I want to catch Alf before he leaves for the evening. I walk into Alf's office with what I know is a flushed face from racing around. Smirking at me Alf points to a seat in front of his desk.

"What can I do for you, Blake?"

"Well, I'm sorry to dash in at the last minute, but I wanted to catch you before you left for the day. First, Ed mentioned the meals have been better. Pru was impressed with a seafood thing she had. She didn't know what it was called but she ate it all." I grin at Alf who is showing how amused he is at that comment regarding Pru.

"I did speak to the caterers and they admitted they were not doing much of a variety, and I understand that they have more than my people but, if they wanted to keep the contract they had to do better. I'm pleased to hear that they have done that, but I will be keeping my eye on them." Alf is one of those people who doesn't miss a trick, and he knows I have more to discuss, so he inevitably lifts an eyebrow questioningly.

"I wanted to talk to you about the house too. I don't want to keep a single thing that was in the place. Sell, donate, or ditch everything, I don't care. If you sell give the money to a charity or use it to give the seniors a treat. I don't want anything from what was in the place. Once it's done do you think it'll take long to sell?"

Alf leans forward and clasps his hands together as he places his forearms on his desk. "I've employed four workers, two men and two women. They are going through the house, and anything they can clean and keep I'll get them to put on one side and I'll see about selling it. But on the whole I'll sort it, Blake, the men are doing the heavy lifting and the women are starting the clean-up. I have a decorator at the ready, and if it needs sprucing up a little then I'll get that done. Heather said she'd ask the MC about cutting the lawn and tidying the outside of the place. Once it's sold, and my realtor thinks it'll sell quickly at the right price, we'll get the mortgage gone and anything left after you've paid the business here, I'll get put into your personal account. It's made it easier that you signed over everything for me to do as your agent, so sit back, and enjoy the fact the bitch has gone."

"Well, I hope she's gone. Nobody has seen her that I know of, but she's like a bad dream, she haunts you." I mumble more to myself than Alf, but he hears me anyway and cocks his head to one side.

"If she comes back you need to speak to Bitty, she'll get the MC to move her on for good."

Nodding, because if she comes back I'll let Mav deal with her. I've had more than enough of the terrible woman. I hope the MC dragging her out of the house is enough of a warning for her to disappear and never come back.

Walking into Ed's house later that evening I give him a kiss on the cheek and stop myself from smiling as he follows me into the kitchen.

"What have you got in that bag?" Ed asks just like a little boy following his Momma into the kitchen after she comes back from shopping.

"Well, I made cookie dough and froze it, so I have some to put into your freezer. It's two batches, so you take out one, remember you flatten it out and cut it, then put it onto a baking sheet. I've written all the instructions on a sheet, and will pop it onto the fridge. When you take out the second batch let me know and I'll bring you some more."

"Oh, let me see." Ed takes the instructions, reads them and then uses a magnet to keep on the fridge door. "I can do that."

"I know you can as you're not helpless, PawPaw," now I give him an innocent smile as I get started on the cleaning chores I'm here to do. But of course, he follows me from room-to-room, talking about how bored he is and what can he do with himself.

"I feel like I've already got one foot in the grave. I'm bored, what the hell am I going to do with myself? I'm sick to death of sitting in the chair watching people walk past."

Oh, he's really feeling sorry for himself tonight. Maybe I can think of something he can do, but he's not a young man so he's going to need to do something where he supervises rather than is physically doing…!

"Do you think you could visit the house that Yax was living in. Just pop in, see if everything is running smoothly. Maybe look at my own house's front yard, and find me a company that would clear it all and make it presentable. I've not had time to do the yard and it's looking decidedly bad." I give Ed what I hope is my helpless look, and I blink a few times along with it.

"Oh, I can do that. I know where that house is too. I'll go over and see what's happening, and I'll speak to some of my friends about a company for your yard. Do you want bushes and stuff?" Ed is looking excited now that he has something to occupy his mind.

"I'm not sure, but I think I would like you to design the front yard and surprise me. When I have the house sold, I should have enough money to pay for the company to do the work, too."

"I have plenty of savings, Blake, I'll get it done for you."

"No, you will not. You are not spending your savings on me. Not ever, Ed. You may be my PawPaw now, but that doesn't mean I'll take what you worked hard for, oh no, not on your life." I know he's going to argue so I quickly change the subject, "Now, while I remember Mav is moving into my house with me today, so when you come over don't be shocked to see him."

"You've moved him into your house? You going to marry this guy?"

"I may marry him, but not yet. He's the one for me I'm sure, PawPaw," yeah, I shamelessly use his title. "Mav is having a house built on the land where the clubhouse is, and when we move into that I'm thinking of leasing my place rather than selling it. If I did that would you be the landlord and watch over it?"

"Of course I would. I wouldn't allow anyone to mess up the place. I'll keep my eye on them, no problem on that score. Now, I want to meet Mav over a meal, and make sure he's legit, because if he's not I'll find my old revolver and shoot his pecker off for him."

I stare at Ed who is ranting and raving about peckers being shot, liars, and cheats and if Mav is either of those things he'll not be needing a pecker as he'll be six feet under, and he'll get his pals to help him dig the hole.

I'm not sure what the heck is going on here but I keep nodding and agreeing, but I'm thinking I'm going to have to warn Mav that Ed is after him.

CHAPTER TWENTY-SEVEN

-:- ED -:-

I may be old, but I've still got some life left in me. Maybe not the sexual kind, but plenty of ass kicking and talking smack to folks. Grinning, I step out of the cab that I've hired to check what they are doing here at the house Blake evicted Yax from. It's a nice-looking place but I can understand why she wants to get rid of it.

"Can you come back in thirty minutes?" I ask the driver and he gives me a nod before taking the cash and driving away.

Walking the garden path to the front door, I'm thinking the yard needs an overhaul. Seems my Blake isn't so good with the outside of houses, but she sure makes the inside cozy and welcoming.

Stepping inside the front door, a woman walks up and gives me a smile. "Can I help you?"

"Well, I'm here on behalf of the owner. I'm just checking that things are running along smoothly."

The woman steps a little closer and holds her hand out to shake. "I'm Glorianna. I'm here to clean out this place along with Scarlett and the two men who are here to do all the lifting and taking things away. Either to the charity place or the recycle center. There's not much for you to see, as we're just starting to clean out the upstairs bathroom. Whoever was living here didn't clean a thing at all. It's disgusting."

"It was a woman, along with her man and son. Not sure if they were married or anything, but they had that kid together. He's gone and left her now, took the kid with him," I inform Glorianna, "Your name's a bit of a mouthful, isn't it?" I ask without thinking.

"Yeah, it is," giggling, she continues, "Just call me Glo, that's what my friends call me."

"Well, Glo, I'm not here to interfere. Just to check everything that is running smoothly. I'll come back in a couple of days, but if you need me, here's my number." I rattle off my mobile number and pat myself on the back mentally, because I can remember the damn thing.

"Okay then, I'll do that. What was your name again?" Glo asks, and then I realize I'd never told her.

"Oh, I'm sorry, that was so ignorant of me. My names Ed. I'm the owner's PawPaw." Now, I said that last with a puffed chest and more than a little pride. Maybe Blake has only just become mine, but I'm gonna keep her.

"Well, Ed, I'll give you a call if anything untoward crops up. How's that?" Glo gives me a smile and picks up a bucket filled with cleaning bottles.

"Okay, thank you, Glo." I make my way out of the house and back up the path, thankfully just in time for the cab to arrive.

Back home, I give my pal a call and get the name and number for a company that maintains yards. I quickly contact and make arrangements for them to look at Blake's place. But I will hang fire on the other house in case something is already organized for that.

I overheard Blake speaking with Bitty the other night. She was telling her she was having a movie night tonight with Mav and a meal, too. Well, guess who is going to turn up for a movie night? Yeah, you got it. I make sure I'm showered, changed into my best pants and button up and throw on my jacket before heading out to Blake's house. I can't help but whistle, knowing I'm going to be putting a spoiler on this guy Mav's evening.

In the cab, I take out my phone and send a message to Bitty. Now, I've known Bitty and her other two witches for years, so this won't be a surprise. I'm positive Blake would have filled Bitty in on my being her PawPaw now too. Grinning, I type out my message.

Ed: Bitty, it's Ed. You want to mess with Blake's man for a while?

Bitty: What do you mean?

Ed: I'm on my way to Blake's house. They are having a movie night with a meal. But guess who is going to crash that night? Oh, I've got popcorn.

Bitty: Oh, I love popcorn.

Ed: OK, see you later.

Grinning broadly, I walk into Blake's house, and she gives me a startled look. "Evening, Blake. I thought I'd come and spend the evening with you. It's Saturday night after all. Do you fancy watching a movie? I brought popcorn."

I think Blake is amazing, because I know she had plans, but she doesn't bat an eye. Stepping over to me, she gives me a hug and a kiss on the cheek before smiling, "I've got finger snacks if you fancy eating? Mav will be here soon, he's moved in with me today, so you be nice, PawPaw."

The door opens, and the man called Mav walks inside, giving me a frown before zeroing in on Blake. Wrapping her in his arms, he kisses her gently before wrapping an arm around her shoulders and looking at me once more.

"You Ed?" Mav asks, and I nod, but give him my best *'don't fuck with me,'* look. "Well, it's great to meet you. Blake has told me a lot about you, and you adopting her as a granddaughter, or the other way around. I'm not sure since Bitty adopted her as a daughter, too."

"Don't matter which, she's my granddaughter now, so you better be on your best behavior."

"Oh, I'll behave, don't you worry none about that."

The asshole kisses Blake on her forehead, then grabs the bag he'd dropped at the door and heads upstairs. I turn to look at Blake, who is now heading into the kitchen.

"It's all good, PawPaw. Mav is moving in as I told you, but if he does me wrong, I'll let you shoot his ass. How about that?"

Grunting, I grab a plate on the side that is made up of different finger snacks and head into the living room, where I plant my ass into the easy chair. From this position I can see the TV and keep my eye on the pair of them. Yep, that's a good move for me. Once comfortable I take out my phone and text Bitty again.

Ed: You coming?

Bitty: I'm on my way, and I've got popcorn.

Blake enters the living room, with Mav right behind her. A plate of snacks is in their hands and they take a seat. Mav messes with the remote and the movie starts. I stuff a piece of one of the snacks in my mouth and give Mav a stare down. Well, it would be if the fucker would look my way.

The front door opens and I grin, knowing full well who is joining this lovely movie night.

"Yoo-hoo, I thought I'd come watch the movie with you. I've brought popcorn." Bitty saunters into the living room, throws her jacket on the back of the spare chair and takes a seat. Giving Mav a shit-eating grin as she does.

Both myself and Bitty keep giving Mav looks that I'm sure he's ignoring, and he cuddles up to Blake watching the TV. Not once does the fucker look at Bitty or me, but from the tip of his lip, I can tell he knows we've appeared for movie night on purpose.

"You okay there, Ed?" Mav asks.

"I'm fine. You okay?" I respond, but give Bitty a look that tells her I know what he's up to.

Bitty giggles, "We're all fine, Mav. What about you Blake, are you fine?"

"Oh, I'm good, thank you, Mama." Blake is blind to the tension in the room, and looks happy to have all three of us here. She is a darling and I'm sure she has to be the kindest person I've met.

"Tomorrow you've got to come to the clubhouse, Blake. Something is happening, and the girl gang is all going to be battening down the hatches, so to speak. Now you are Mav's girl, you need to come too, and be added to the gang," Bitty states, and I give her a sharp look because what the hell is a girl gang? I'm not sure I like the sound of that.

Mav kisses Blake on her cheek before speaking, "Yeah, you need to be at the clubhouse tomorrow. What about you, Ed? Do you think you could go along with Blake, you know, make sure she's okay?"

Now, I puff my chest out because I'm a PawPaw and anyone messes with my girl and they mess with me. I don't care that I can't run anymore, I'll do damage anyway I can. "Of course I can go with her. Just need the time and I'll be here ready."

"What is going on that I need to go there?" Blake asks while giving Mav a frown on her face.

"It's fight night, and I'm going to be fighting, but don't you go worrying. I'll be fine. It's the other one that needs to worry," Mav grins, but the frown on Blake's face hasn't disappeared. "We just need to know all the women will be safe while we are working, and we'll be leaving Specs and Sting at the clubhouse with you. But the girl gang are quite capable of keeping themselves and the clubhouse safe. Remember, I told you Winter is a sniper, and she's been teaching some of the others how to use a weapon. We don't envisage trouble at the clubhouse, so it's a precaution only. But if Ed will go along with you, I'll feel easier."

"I'll go along and make sure everyone is safe. Oh, I've someone coming to check out the yard, Blake. Sorry for the change in topic, but you know my memory isn't as good as it was." That took the frown from Blake's face and was my intention.

"Watch the movie or it'll be over before we know it," Bitty snaps, and fills her face with more popcorn.

CHAPTER TWENTY-EIGHT

-:- MAV -:-

I knew what Ed and Bitty were up to last night, and not reacting to their staring was the best way to handle it. They deflated fast when they realized they were not getting anywhere with their antics. Giving Ed responsibility for Blake tonight softened his attitude and I know I can win him over, given a little time.

"Everyone in church now," BS shouts as he passes through the common room. We all follow behind and take our usual seats while waiting for Axel, Buzz and Drag to appear.

Knuckles is sitting quietly next to me, lazily leaning back in his seat with his arms folded over his massive chest. But it's the look of peace on his face that attracts my attention. "You okay, Knuckles?"

"I'm more than okay. I have my woman, my club brothers, the best food in America thanks to Meat, and tonight I'm gonna pound some asshole's head into the ground. What better way of spending my life!"

"Well, I suppose when you put it like that, it is a good way to spend your life," I respond with a chuckle. "I like the way you added Meat's cooking into your good life."

Hearing grunting, I look to my left and see Meat with a smug grin on his face. He obviously overheard our conversation, but Wings joins with his own comment. "Well, I only came here for Meat's cooking, and nothing and nobody is going to have me move from the brotherhood at this point."

"Me either," Chaos adds, "We were a brotherhood before, and we will stay as one until we are six feet under."

Target, BS and Stitch were all brothers together in the military, and they'll certainly stay brothers until their time on earth ends. That is a given, and every brother in this room knows it.

Axel, Drag and Buzz walk into church and take their seats. Axel quickly opens the meeting and gets right to it. "Okay brothers, we have our mission tonight to take down the fuckers who are murdering innocent fighters. You all know what you have to do, and I've spoken to you all about your role tonight. Mav, you make sure you get your man down fast. Don't kill him, just get him down and out so we can get you out of that cage.

"Knuckles, you watch Mav's back, and Colton, you strut around like a pimp on his best day at the brothel. Keep as many eyes on you as you can and that'll give us the chance to get fuckers that have their backs to us."

"I can do that, Pres." Colton grins, rubbing his hands together. But it's the fuckin' twinkle in his eye I'm worried about.

"Any questions about this evening?" Axel asks and nobody has an issue because we all know what is going to happen and how. Axel, Buzz and Drag have spoken with all of us, making sure we know our position and what we have to do.

"Any other business?" Axel asks.

"Yeah," I quickly say, "I'd like to nominate Garth as a brother. I've spoken to him and he'd be honored to be a brother, now that he knows us all and how the MC works. He was worried we were like Sons of Anarchy bikers."

The room bursts into laughter, and comments fly about the program being a hindrance rather than a help to MCs that are legitimate.

"I'll second that nomination." Hammer taps on the table in front of him, gaining attention.

"Okay, show of hands for Garth as a brother, and I need a unanimous vote." Axel counts heads as he looks around, and he has the full vote. We have a new brother. "What about a name?"

"Well, Garth likes the name his momma gave him, so let's just leave it. But if he does anything that gets him a name, so be it," I add. Everyone quickly agrees and PT will arrange his patch.

"I also want to put out that Blake is my Ol' Lady. I've ordered her property patch from PT, and it'll be here next week. I just need the brothers to give me the go and it'll be done." I quickly throw that into the mix.

"We all want our woman, Mav. I can't find my fucker. She must be living abroad or she's found someone else. Fuckin' sick of looking and waiting if I'm honest," Dice states and we all give him a shocked look because I don't think any of us realized he was keen to have an Ol' Lady.

Clay laughs sourly as he responds, "She's probably with mine, living under a fucking rock somewhere."

Now that is interesting, I'm thinking, and by the looks on some of the brothers' faces, they are feeling the same. Well, except for Chaos, who has a shit-eating grin on his face. Before he can say whatever was about to come out of his mouth, Target slams his hand over it and shakes his head to be quiet.

Axel takes up the call after he stops smirking at Chaos. "Okay, show of hands, let me see them for Mav to claim his lady Blake." It's simple, every hand raises and as I've gone around speaking to all the brothers, it is exactly what I expected.

"Anything else?" Axel asks, and we can all see he's getting ready to leave church, and we all know why... He always makes sure he and Mia have some loving before he goes off on what he calls a mission.

Forest speaks out, but surprises me with what he says. "Heather asked me to bring up that Hammer and his team, or he has a team go over to the house that Blake is going to be selling. Yeah, Blake who is now Mav's Ol' Lady. The yard is a mess and needs some designing, plus a new path to the front door. The people that were in it have left a fuck of a mess to be cleaned inside and out. Heather said if you can do it Hammer, or arrange it, then she'll pay through the business as they are doing the cleanup job."

Hammer nods. "I'll take a look and give you a quote for the work. I'll keep the price down, but it will be an outside team I use because we are starting Mav's house this week."

Now, I'm excited to hear they are building my place, and I've given the plans of how I see the house to Hammer, so it's all in his hands now.

Meat taps the table, gaining everyone's attention. "Theme night soon, be ready."

Nobody responds, as we all know it's mandatory to attend theme night or we have the worst meals you can imagine afterward. Brag didn't attend the last one, and he was given separate meals for a month. They were disgusting, and he vowed never to miss another. Meat didn't say what the theme was, but we all know we'll be told, and we'll all be going to the costume shop to get rigged out.

Later that evening we are all ready to depart, and I walk over to Blake, who is sitting happily with Ed on one side of her and Bitty on the other, talking animatedly with Raven and Destiny.

Leaning down, I take her face between my hands and lower my face to hers, placing my forehead gently onto hers as I murmur, "See you later. Have a good evening and stay out of trouble." I don't wait for her response. I slam my mouth over hers and kiss her thoroughly.

"Hmmm, that's enough now. We have children in the room."

I look up and grin at Ed who is the one mentioning kids, but as we all know the twins have seen far worse and the other kids are too young to notice I give Ed a cheeky wink before walking away and joining Knuckles and the others who are my team for the night.

Walking into the warehouse behind Colton and Knuckles, myself, Wings, Chaos and Fist give off the impression of not having a care in the world. What we are doing, in fact, is scanning the place, and making sure we have noted all of Milanas' men. They are fairly easy to detect, as they are all jittery and look like they need a good meal and a bath. That's what drug taking does for you and it makes you very easy to spot, even in a room with hundreds of other people.

I flip my baseball cap so the peak is over my eyes, giving me the option to flick my eyes over the room without it being obvious. Fist, however, is hopping from one foot to the other. I'm thinking it's probably a good thing he'll be the first of us to fight.

Colton disappears to a side room, which at one time was an office, I'm sure. Knuckles leads us all to an area where a bench has been placed and a dirty blanket strung up to give the illusion of privacy.

Chaos sarcastically comments, "Very professional." I have to admit, we all chortle at that one.

The cage is ready, and by the look of it, we won't be long before the fighting starts. I scan the room from where I'm standing in front of the filthy blanket and see brothers scattered around the room.

Axel has on a ball cap, his hair tucked under, probably in the man bun that Mia likes so much. Buzz is doing his best to not look intimidating, but I'm not sure he's going to get away with that, as people are giving him a wide berth.

"Fuck..." I quickly turn and speak to Chaos, Wings and Fist, who are all ready to start this night's massacre. "Fucking Vitale is here, and shit, he looks like he's not going to wait for us to do any fighting. Well, inside that cage anyway."

Colton rushes from between a group of spectators and waves his arm around like a windmill. Honestly, what is he trying to say?

"What's wrong with Colton?" Chaos asks nobody in particular.

"No idea, but look over there." I point to our left and we see Vitale storm into a room, which sets off a chain reaction. Vitale's men zero in on a man each, and I glance up at Axel, who throws his arm out and punches some sucker who is near enough for him to target.

"Yeah, let's roll," Wings hollers, and not waiting for anyone, he runs into the crowd and targets a man.

Well, we have to follow, of course, and that means the fight is on. We all know who we have to target, and that's exactly what we do.

I run for one of Milanas' men who is trying to get to the back of the room and escape. I grab the fucker and slam his head against the wall, making his ears ring, I'm sure. This is one of the fuckers that was organizing the death fights. He was on our radar to take out, and he's going to be going to Nell's and meet Jaws. Just to be sure, I slam him against the wall once more and as he slumps to the ground. I kick him in the head to make sure he's out for the count. Just for the hell of it I kick him a few times in his gut, and that has me feeling a little better.

I grab his collar and drag him out of the building and to the van where I throw him in and leave him with Ruger, who quickly has him hogtied and gagged.

That is the momentum we get going. Take out a man, drag him to Ruger. Go back for the next. Passing Fist, I hold up my hand, showing four fingers. Frowning, Fist snarls, "Fuck, I'm gonna beat you this time." I chuckle as Fist runs back into the room and pummels his fists into the nearest Milanas man he can find before dragging him to the van and running right back inside.

"What's up with, Fist?" Wings asks as he passes by me.

"He was behind my body count, so he's hurrying to catch up and bypass. You know how competitive he is."

"How many has he got?"

"He's got four now, drawing level, so I best get a move on." I hear Wings laughing as I run back in and pick my next victim, which isn't easy with the screaming, fighting and fleeing going on.

It can only take around thirty minutes, and it's all done. Everyone that could be was out the door and disappeared faster than you could say 'motherfucker'.

Vitale had Milanas out the door and into an armored vehicle before Axel could get to him, but we all know that our Pres isn't going to let that stop him. We have plans already in place to steal the fucker away from Nell's, with Graham and Nell's help, of course.

Standing with my brothers waiting for orders to get the hell out of here and back to the clubhouse, I look at Fist, who is holding up eight fingers, I give him a smirk and hold up seven which has him dancing around like a fool.

Wings nudges me and murmurs, "You took down nine. Why are you telling him seven?"

"Look at our brother, brother, he's ecstatic. How could I take that away from him?"

"Yeah, I see that," Wings mumbles under his breath but I can't tell what he's saying, but he walks away and I lean on the side of the van while waiting for orders. My mind is already thinking about Blake and hope she's had a nice evening with the other Ol' Ladies.

CHAPTER TWENTY-NINE

-:- BLAKE -:-

Ed follows me into the clubhouse front door, and we are greeted by Bitty who rushed over and wrapped me into a hug. "It's going to be a fun night, Blake. Come on, and we'll grab a seat. Evening Ed, come on, you too."

Now, Bitty is always a bundle of energy, so it's no surprise when she drags us both over to a table where Amelia and Sybil are sitting. "Raven, Destiny, this is Blake and Ed. Ed is Blake's PawPaw." Introductions done apparently and Bitty bustles away leaving me and Ed to take a seat.

"Did you see the stripper pole?" Raven asks the table in general.

Destiny replies, while grinning. "Yeah, but you know I've never done that and never wanted to, but did you see Bitty's smile when she said she'd got one organized and fitted for the evening."

Amelia smiles, "Well, I'm too old so that rules me out, and Sybil of course. But you three young'uns should be fine to give it a try."

Ed chortles, but keeps his comments to himself. He's obviously a man that has learned not to piss off women. But I reach to my side and take his hand and give it a squeeze. My way of letting him know I'm as amused with this conversation as he is.

Mav comes over, kisses me and heads out with the other men, and I'm not sure if I should be worried or not, but the others at the table seem chilled out, so I shrug and go with it.

Bitty comes back with a large tray which she places on the table in front of us. There are an assortment of sandwiches and around the edges pieces of carrot, celery and other vegetables to munch on. But the large bowl of dip in the center of the tray looks wonderful.

"Dig in when you are ready. Meat did this for us, he's a good one and Star, you keep him sweet." Bitty giggles to herself mostly, turns and heads back into what I assume is the kitchen.

"I'll help Bitty," Sybil stands and quickly walks away, but Amelia grabs herself a sandwich and takes a huge bite, not worried at all about anything else going on.

"I'm not eating yet, I'm going to have a go on that pole." Raven walks over to the stripper pole, and is joined by some of the other women, who are all saying how they think you should twirl on it, around it, or even climb up it. But I'm thinking I don't want anything to do with it, because I'm liable to break my neck.

I take a sandwich and as I'm munching I watch Raven on the pole, wincing as she keeps slipping off it and sliding to the bottom. But she giggles and gets back up for another try.

Mia walks over and takes a seat next to mine, taking me by surprise when she announces, loudly I might add, "Blake is Mav's Ol' Lady, so a show of hands for her as a girl gang member."

Every hand in the room goes up apart from Ed's and the two men that have been walking in and out of the front door. Noticing me watching, Amelia catches my attention. "That's Sting and Specs. Specs is usually in his office but if you look closely you can see he has one of those things in his ear, so he's still technically in charge and connected to his office."

I'm not sure what the heck she is talking about but I nod as though I understand and quickly turn my attention back to Mia, "I'm not an Ol' Lady, Mia, I'm only..."

Now before I can finish, Mia laughs, "We all thought the same thing, but it just means you are Mav's woman now, and you've just been voted in with the girl gang, so what's your poison...hog or trike?"

My eyes flick to Ed, who is sitting with his mouth open. I place a finger under his chin and gently push upward to close it, and he snaps out of it, shaking his head to clear what can only be the confusion I'm feeling.

"What do you mean hog or trike?" Ed asks, and I look back at Mia because I'm not following this topic of conversation either.

"Well, Blake is officially a girl gang member now, so she needs to ride her own hog, you know Harley Davidson motorcycle, or trike, which is a three wheeled HD." Mia explains, looking like she's doing her best to stay calm and patient.

"Um, I'm not sure about that because I've never thought about riding or owning a motorcycle." I reply, giving everyone what must be a panicked look. Destiny who has been watching all this drops in a comment. "I don't have one because girl, I'm a lethal weapon if I climb on one of those things. I have my pickup and I ride bitch with any of the others. Believe me it's safest for everyone that way."

"Hm, I'll speak to Mav about it at another time. I'm not at a stage where I can afford one right now anyway." I grimace as I throw that out, because it's not nice letting people know you are about dollarless.

A squeal has us quickly looking towards the pole, and see everyone helping Raven to her feet. Now, I'm not sure what has happened but she is wobbly on her legs and Star helps her back to her seat with us.

"What happened?" Destiny asks.

"Fell on my head, but don't worry, it'll be fine. If I keep getting blurred vision tomorrow I'll get Stitch to take a look at me." Raven gives a very lopsided grin as she sits with her eyes closed.

"Open your eyes, you don't want to be passing out. I'm going to get Stitch to come back early in case you have a concussion." Mia takes out her phone from under the neck of her tee, and out of her bra.

I'm watching it all with a sense of wonder, because it's like I've dropped down Alice's rabbit hole. Everyone is doing something different by the look of it. Nobody is worried about the danger that pole could bring, and Mia is demanding someone called Stitch get his arse back to the clubhouse pronto, and yes, she said arse!

Ed pushes another sandwich in his mouth, and keeps looking around the room as he does. I think he's as shocked at how this evening is going as I am. Turning my eyes to the side I see Ed doing the same to me, and I let out a little giggle, not able to hold it back. I think it's called hysteria, but I'm not sure.

Ed pats my hand before gripping it as though he is holding onto a lifeline as much as I am. "It'll be okay, Blake, I'm here with you for this whackadoodle journey."

Now, Ed saying that is the last straw and I bust out laughing. I laugh so long and so hard I'm holding my stomach while tears are freely flowing down my cheeks. The whole room is watching my display, but every single person is smiling at me, obviously enjoying the show I'm putting on.

From that point the evening flows nicely, and Jo surprises everyone when she has some nice stripper pole moves. She can climb that thing and flip upside down, without falling on her head. Turns out she's done some pole lessons so she could write about it accurately in one of her books. Seems her character had sex while with a pole too, but I cover Ed's ears when the nitty gritty details start flying. Ed however is very amused with it all, and keeps wiggling his ears under my hands.

Sting runs into the common room, and shouts, "Everyone take notice. We have intruders coming in from the south. They'll make their way to the front door in about six minutes."

"Okay, so how many?" Star asks, while Winter takes a step to the side of her.

"I think three, and they look like Milanas men." Sting turns to leave, but Star grabs his arm and stops him.

"What if we entice the fuckers in, then take them out?"

"How?" Sting asks.

"Well, if one of us ladies entice them from a distance through the door, then as soon as they clear the entrance we jump the fuckers." Star is looking around as though this is the best idea she ever had, but damn everyone is nodding agreement. Even Ed is agreeing, I'm gonna kill him later.

"I'll entice." The woman named Gemmy states, and wiggles her hips as she offers to be the guinea pig to slaughter.

"Okay, take your places ladies, and grab something to use as a weapon." Mia states, but yanks up her pants leg to show she has an ankle holster with a small pistol of some kind in it.

Holy mother of God, what do we have here? Weapons, and I mean weapons because more of the women are showing they have a weapon hidden somewhere on their body. I grab Ed's hand and drag us to the back of the room, well away from all these psychotic women.

"It's okay, Blake. We all have our permit to carry." Mia grins what can only be described as gleeful. Then she shouts to Amelia, "Meli, take the kids to the playroom, and I'll come in a few when this shit show is over."

"No problem, Mia." Amelia picks up Summer from a stroller on one side of the room, while Sybil and Bitty grab a child each and force the twins to go with them.

We, meaning Ed and I stand back and watch Gemmy do this enticing act, and she spouts some bullcrap to whoever is outside. But unbeknown to them outside the walls, inside the room here is lined with women who have guns, knives and even a cane. Now I think I recognize that...isn't it the one Amelia uses?

A man saunters into the room with two men behind him, and I'm telling you I didn't have time to spit before they were on the ground, with a woman kneeling on their back holding them down while others are tying them up and stuffing something in their mouths.

The man named Sting is throwing out orders, and before we know what's happening the three men are dragged away out the front door. I side-eye Ed and he shakes his head, mumbling, "Don't ask, Blake, don't ask."

"Can we go home now, PawPaw?" I ask and just as he opens his mouth to reply a woman runs into the room screaming about how dare the MC people ruin her life.

"Oh, fuck me," Ed states and as I take a closer look at the dirty, disheveled woman I realize it's Yax. What the hell is she doing here screaming about the MC ruining her life?

"It's all your fault," Yax screams as she sees me standing in the room. "You had these people come to the house and cause trouble. Now my man and my son are gone."

Before Yax reaches me waving a large knife in her hand, one of the ladies walks up behind her and smacks the back of her head hard with Amelia's cane. "Take that bitch." I hear, and I look up into the grinning face of Kenzie. Now, I know who this is as she works at the vet's and I saw her when I rescued a kitten and took it there for treatment. I didn't keep the kitten, but I made sure it was alright before they kept it for the rescue people to pick up.

Bitty is standing with her hands on her hips, smiling. "Well, that was a good evening, wasn't it ladies? We got ourselves three pricks and an asshole."

I'm saying nothing, not a word. I look at Ed, he looks at me, and I take a seat waiting for time to go home. It's safe at home!

CHAPTER THIRTY

-:- MAV -:-

Back at the clubhouse I look for Blake but she's not here, which is strange as I expected to find her here waiting for me. Hearing my name, I turn and spot Mia rushing over to me.

"Mav, we had a bit of an incident and have three men in custody, you know in the shed," which she says with a conspiratorial whisper, why I don't know because everyone here knows what the shed is for. "Anyway, Yax turned up too and tried to attack Blake, but we sorted the bitch out and she's in the shed too. Blake went home with Ed. He thought it would be best for them both to go home and rest."

"Okay, thanks. I wondered where they were. She wasn't hurt, was she?"

"No, Kenzie knocked out Yax before she could get near her. You know we are all good with Amelia's cane now. It was great when she gave us all lessons on how to use it," Mia grins then walks away with a spring in her step, straight to Axel, and jumps into his arms, kissing the ever loving shit outta him. Sighing, I can't help but think, 'I wish that was me.'

Walking over to Meat, who is the nearest to me, I ask, "Can you let me know if anything untoward happens? I'll come back in the morning and sort that bitch Yax out one way or another. I know of a nice spot I can bury the bitch if need be."

Meat grunts and nods, but Chaos had to have overheard with those big ears of his, because believe me he misses nothing. "I'm in. I'll bring the fuckin' shovel, spade, or anything else that's needed."

Nodding, I arrange to meet them mid-morning tomorrow to take out the trash. We'll be removing the three assholes to Nell's tomorrow, I'm sure, but that'll more than likely be after lunch. When Axel appears once more from their house and the love-in they'll probably be having.

I'm going to make sure I'm not the one who takes the twins to school, because those little fuckers are already known as the two Johnny's for their antics in class. The last incident had two other kids painted blue, green and yellow. I have no idea why and I didn't ask, but the teacher said their 'Fuck you,' comment was heard by all. Mia was mortified, Axel was amused, and the Three Stooges gave them cookies!

Home at last. I double check everywhere is locked up tight before climbing upstairs and checking Blake is asleep. Not wanting to wake her, I quietly enter the bathroom and close the door, turning on the shower and stripping out of my clothes. I make sure everything goes inside the laundry basket because I'm not going to have my Ol' Lady berate my ass for dropping shit on the floor next to the basket.

Stepping into the shower, I place my hands on the tiles and drop my head so the water runs over my head, shoulders, and down my back. Enjoying the warmth, I close my eyes and breath slowly, easing away the tensions of the night. Not one of us had an injury and for that, I'm grateful. We all took down our target with the minimum of fuss, and that's all down to the training we do with Meat, Wings, and Target. They are tough on our training, but it pays dividends when we need to fight.

The shower door opens and Blake steps in, closing it behind her before she takes the shower gel and lathers up her hands. The feel of her running her hands up and down my back and shoulders feels amazing, and eases my tension even more, plus helping my muscles relax.

When I release a small groan of appreciation, Blake massages my shoulders, back, arms, and buttocks. But when she runs her hands down and around to my abs, I can't help but tense with the anticipation of what she's going to do next.

Sliding her hands up my body, she soaps my pecs, then down again, over my abs and to my engorged dick. Which I have to say is standing at full attention at this point.

Wrapping a hand around my dick, Blake squeezes just hard enough for it to twitch in welcome, which has her giggle under her breath. But when she starts to stroke steadily up and down, using the suds as lubricant, I have to grit my teeth or I'll blow like a whale, or a teenager having his first experience.

Blake kisses between my shoulder blades, and murmurs something I can't quite hear. But her hand works wonders on my dick and she perfectly works it until my legs start to shake and goosebumps rise along my legs and over my butt.

With an extra squeeze and twist, Blake has me shoot my load all over the shower's tiles, and my call of release echoes around the bathroom for a moment.

"You okay, Mav?" Blake asks, but I can tell she is amused by her own question.

"Never better," I rinse quickly, making sure the shower hits the tiles too, before turning and grabbing Blake in a tight hold before heading out of the shower, dry us both and climb into bed, where I thoroughly show Blake how much the shower moment was appreciated.

Once we've had yet another shower, and a quick one, I might add, I wrap myself around Blake and whisper. "You okay about what happened tonight at the clubhouse?"

Blake sighs, "Yeah, I'm good. PawPaw was nervous about all the weaponry the women have about their person, but he was happy that they can protect themselves. He got us both here safely, before he took himself home, where he said he needed a good shot of Jack Daniels."

I chuckle at the thought of Ed taking a good drink because he's met all the Ol' Ladies. Honestly, it's nothing to be embarrassed about because they are all damn awesome and a little on the frightening side if truth be told.

"I'll deal with Yax from this point. She needs to know this is her last warning, the same as Sharon had hers. We are not fucking around with her any longer. She messed with your husband, and has messed with you. That, for me, is the end of this shit. I'll speak with Ed about the house she was in too, see if he'll allow me to get it done and push the realtor to get it sold. Will that be okay with you?"

Hu-hm is all I hear before I listen to her small snores. Yeah, my girl is gone. She's out cold. I kiss the top of her head before making sure I'm tightly wrapped around her, and sleep takes me.

I'm up bright and early, and considering the late night I had, it's a wonder. But I leave a note on the table before heading out. I quickly make my way to the Coffee House, and fill Liam in on why Blake will be late to work, and yeah I'm sure she's gonna be pissed, but it is what it is.

Walking into the clubhouse, I wave to Wings, who follows me from the common room into the kitchen. I grab a mug of coffee and after taking a large swig I check who is near to us before asking, "You up for getting Yax out of here, and I mean, this will be the last time she's seen one way or another. I don't care which way, either."

"Yeah, I'm in. Chaos slept here last night, so he'll be up for it, too." Wings turns at the same time as me when we hear a loud grunt. "You in too, Meat?" Wings asks, and with another grunt and chin lift, we know he's up for it. When he grabs two cleavers from his 'Meat Only' cabinet we high-five each other and I finish my coffee while Wings goes to find Chaos.

Chaos arrives fifteen minutes later, and just as we are heading out, Axel shouts, "You four. Don't think I don't know what you are up to. Take the bitch and get rid of her. But be back to take the three assholes to Nell's and be ready to do a retrieval mission. I want Milanas in the shed before evening meal."

Meat grunts. Chaos chuckles. Wings states, 'Yes Pres.' Me, I keep quiet as I know that we have no option but to do as our President tells us. Now taking those three to Nell is our pleasure, because whoever wants to traffic, rape, or any other nasty shit to a young woman deserves no leniency in my book.

After retrieving Yax, who is tied up like a turkey for Thanksgiving we head out of town. The truck bed has Yax bouncing around over every pot hole or bump we can find in the road. She can't climb out as she's so tied up she can't even turn onto her side. She's sure gonna have a sore back when this is over.

We travel an hour before pulling over and into a field. One that has more than enough trees to cover what will happen if this bitch refuses to leave and never be seen again.

Dragging her out of the truck bed, we untie her and take the gag out of her mouth, but before she can start spouting bullshit, Chaos is in her face. Now, I mean nearly nose-to-nose, and he looks vicious.

"Now, you listen up, bitch. You have two choices and two only. One, you take your skanky, nasty ass out of our state and stay out, because if this is your choice and you come back, you are dead. Two, you die here and now and we bury you. Those are your choices, so what's it to be?" Chaos isn't fooling around.

When she opens her mouth to spout crap, Meat slams his cleaver down. Right through her shoe and takes off her littlest toe. She screams like a banshee for sure, but what has me smirking is Wings who steps forward and hands Chaos the cigarette lighter from the truck, glowing nice and red.

She howls even louder when Chaos plants that sucker on her toe stub to cauterize the bleeding. "You making your choice yet?" He asks, and we all wait for the reply we know she'll give.

"Yes, I'll leave." She's still whimpering, but not one of us gives a shit.

"And?" Chaos pushes.

Yax looks him right in the eye, but it's not with any form of challenge. She's letting him see her sincerity. "Yes, I'll leave and never come back."

Meat grunts, which has Yax jump nearly out of her skin, much to Wings amusement. We three turn back to the truck, and Chaos throws her back into the truck bed, points at her and snarls, "We'll drop you at the bus depot, then you are gone."

We don't hang around once Chaos jumps into the truck. We head right to the nearest bus depot, and watch her limp onto it, ready for departure. We wait the thirty-five minutes after we've purchased her ticket for the bus to leave, then we hightail it back to town and the clubhouse feeling more than a little pleased with ourselves.

Pushing the last of a toasted cheese into my mouth, I look at my phone as it vibrates on the table. Seeing Ed's name, I look quickly in case something is wrong with Blake.

Ed: Can you make sure the house Yax was living in is finished being cleaned, and check the realtor has a buyer. We need this place gone before it stresses Blake out.

Mav: Yeah, I can do that, PawPaw.

Ed: I'm not your fucking PawPaw, asshole.

Chuckling to myself because I knew that would get the old goat going. I'll call him that in the future just to get a reaction out of him. But as long as he watches out for Blake, I'm more than happy with him not liking me much.

Finding Heather's number, I hit the call button and wait.

"Hi, Mav, what's up?" Heather asks quickly as she takes my call.

"Will Blake's house be ready for the realtor this week?"

Heather sighs but replies, "It will be cleared and clean by Friday, and the realtor already has someone interested in the place. But you need to get the yard tidied up. My people have removed all the garbage, it just needs to be made respectable. I asked Hammer, but he's not sent anyone yet."

"Okay, I'll chase up Hammer, and you get the place done and sold if you can. I want it gone so Blake can step away from it."

"I'll do my best, Mav." Heather has left the conversation before I can say thanks, but I shrug and grab another toasted cheese.

Mav: Can you make sure the yard is done by the weekend at Blake's place, Hammer? I want it done so we can get it sold and off our hands.

Hammer: I'm on it, Mav. The crew will be there tomorrow and clean the borders and the lawn. It'll be tidy, but that's the best we can do. The fresh path I can't get done in time, but that's up to the new owner anyway, if you ask me.

Mav: OK. I'll leave the path alone, let's just get it sold and gone. Let me know when your team is done and I'll get the realtor to check it out. Heather's dealing with it all, so I'll just nudge her.

Hammer: OK, unless you want me to keep liaising with Heather?

Mav: OK, you do that.

That's another thing off my list of to-do's for this week. Okay, back to the now, and going along with Axel and the three assholes who we are delivering to Nell.

Axel walks past with Drag, Buzz and Wings behind him. I join the troupe, but notice Meat, Knuckles, Fist and Colton sneaking around the side of the clubhouse as I climb into the van next to Buzz, while everyone else has jumped into the truck.

"The assholes secure?" I ask as the door opens and Garth pushes inside the van, shoving me over toward Buzz. "Fuck's sake, Garth, what you doing?"

"I'm coming. You know I have excellent skills." Garth smirks at me, then chin lifts to Buzz, who chuckles at the antics he's watching.

Once we arrive at Nell's we get the three out of the van and down to the cells easily. Nell and Graham have a decidedly shifty look on their faces. Graham whispers something to Drag, who in turn takes off.

We have the fuckers locked down and head upstairs, and I'm thinking how the fuck we gonna get Milanas out of the building when I saw two of Vitale's men out front. But I should have known better since we are talking to Nell and her brother.

Drag is arguing with Tank out in the front of the boarding house and takes a swing at Tank. Fuck me, this is the distraction and my eyes dart to Vitale's men who have stepped closer to take a better look. One has his ear to his phone, is sounds like he's relaying what he's seeing.

I don't get time to ask what's happening when Axel storms out of the building shouting, 'Benjamin on Drag.' I see Garth heading my way just in time to dodge as he throws a punch, and shit, he only just missed me. This distraction wasn't supposed to include me, well, not that I knew of, anyway. 'Benjamin on Garth.' Axel shouts, which has me spin around and give him a nasty look, right before Garth punches me in the gut, doubling me over.

Now bedlam has erupted, Drag and Tank are going at it, with as much angst as a civil war. I spin on Garth, wipe my forehead from the sweat that's appeared, then give him my best ever evil smirk.

We throw more than a few punches. I have a fat lip and Garth has a black eye and a bloody nose. If it wasn't so painful it would be fun. Nell screeches at the top of her voice, more than a little dramatic I have to admit.

"GET THE FUCK OFF MY PROPERTY AND DON'T COME BE COMING BACK ANYTIME SOON!" Just the excuse we need to break this up and get out of here without Vitale's men thinking this is a set up.

I can hear Axel asking who won because he wants to collect his winnings. Fucking Axel, he's an arsehole. Yeah, I said arsehole.

We hightail it back to the clubhouse with Milanas nicely settled in the van. Mission accomplished. I high-five Garth and he smirks while wiping his face with an old rag he found in the glovebox.

"Wonder if we can do that again sometime soon?" Garth asks, and Buzz laughs along with me, because it looks like Garth is as crazy as the rest of us.

CHAPTER THIRTY-ONE

Arriving at the clubhouse this morning I know that Axel is going to be full of himself. He's going to be giving this asshole Milanas exactly what he deserves. Date rape drugs, men paying to date rape women, selling young girls and murdering men in the ring, and all for another paycheck. Well, he'll not be getting anymore I'm positive of that.

Walking into the kitchen I don't see Axel anywhere and the place is very quiet. Meat isn't in the kitchen either which is a shock as it's still classed as breakfast.

"Where's Meat and everyone else?" I ask Bitty and Amelia, who are emptying the dishwasher and cleaning the counters.

"Oh, they are all in the shed. Axel, Meat, Wings, Drag and Buzz. Not sure who else, but they've been out there all night apparently," Bitty throws that at me as if it's a normal occurrence.

Stomping out the kitchen I speed walk up the compound to the shed. Standing outside the shed is Knuckles, BS, TwoCents and Beer. "What's going on?" I ask as soon as I reach them.

"Axel, and the others have been in the shed with this fucker since they got him back. I'm not sure there'll be much left of him by the time Axel comes out of here. But, we are standing guard no matter how long it takes, or what he does while in there. Whatever he puts this asshole through he deserves it," BS responds while leaning against the shed with his arms folded over his chest.

"Why are you not inside?" Now, BS is an officer so you'd expect him to be inside as well as TwoCents and Beer.

"Axel said to guard, so we are on guard. Nobody in, and only Axel and our brothers out," TwoCents grins. "It's a good thing we had this place soundproofed or the whole state would hear this fucker singing and screaming. I went in for a few minutes to take bottled water and he has a scream like a teenage girl. Makes me sick, all these assholes make out they are the bee's knees, in fact, they are cowards."

"I think we can all agree on that score, TwoCents," I'm replying while trying to see past to the door. Maybe I can step inside and see what the fuck is going on!

The door however slams open and Axel walks out, he has a crazy look in his eye, and I think whatever happened in there has his PTSD itching somewhat. Goddamn I hope it's not set Meat's PTSD off too, because I don't want Blake to see Meat's cock swinging in the wind on that damn treehouse walkaround. Maybe that won't happen with Star being around, I'm sure she'll not want all the Ol' Ladies seeing it either.

"Clean up by bagging and sending to Nell for the gators to snack on," Axel calmly states and walks down the compound back to the clubhouse as though he's not been torturing someone.

Meat steps out next and that fucker is humming under his breath. Not sure what the heck it is, but it's a jaunty tune. Looking at him he's as bright as a button, and not showing any of the PTSD signs we've seen in the past. Star appears from nowhere and throws herself into Meat's arms, clinging to him like a spider monkey, kissing his face before slamming her lips on his, too much for me and as I'm about to step inside the shed BS says 'wait'.

BS stands in front of me looking into the shed doorway, but we can't see anything from here so I turn my head to look at him, and see why we are waiting around. "Look, this is not going to be pretty.

Why don't I clean up with Buzz, Wings and Drag who are still inside. They may have most of it cleared away now. Take off and we'll deal with this."

Beer, Knuckles and TwoCents all nod in agreement so I sigh and nod too. Whatever happened in the shed will stay in the shed, we all know the score on that. I'm just happy to know the fucker is taken care of, but if it's a bag it up job then it's likely there isn't much of Milanas to be seen anyway.

"Come on, Mav, let's go have a coffee and grab one of the cookies that Bitty and Sybil have been hiding in the pantry," Knuckles slaps my shoulder hard enough that I take two steps forward, but I follow him down the compound to the clubhouse kitchen, with Beer, and TwoCents right behind me.

Before we reach the kitchen door a commotion starts at the front of the clubhouse. Walking around the side of the building we all four come to a stop when we see Vitale and Axel nose-to-nose once more.

Vitale has no idea that Axel is already on a high from his overnight spree in the shed, so we all edge nearer getting ready to grab Axel because if he kills Vitale we'll have a mafia war on our hands, and we can't win that no matter how much fighting experience we have. The Vitale Mafia have us outnumbered by more than ten to one, and Vitale's second in command will want as much retribution as he can get.

"I don't know how you got the fucker, but I want him back, and I want him back now," Vitale shouts at Axel.

Oh, fuck...I can see it, please don't do it Axel I'm thinking. But I close my eyes when he takes out his phone and mumbles something to whoever he's speaking to.

Five minutes later after the tension in the air is so great I feel like putting a bullet in my own head, Buzz, BS, Wings and Drag saunter past carrying black garbage bags and throw them at Vitale's feet.

Motherfucking fuck!! Yeah, he did it, he's given Vitale exactly what he asked for. He's given him Milanas in pieces in garbage bags.

Before Vitale can respond a vehicle drives into the compound, causing dust to fly when he comes to a grinding halt. Nell along with Graham and Tank jump out of the vehicle and Nell storms over to Vitale prodding his chest with her finger. I'm not sure what she's saying to him but she has her teeth clenched together and Vitale leans down closer so he can hear what she's saying.

Graham is standing near, but not too close. He knows the consequences of Nell's temper, the same as Tank who is also staying back, but close enough he can surge forward if needed.

"Deal." Vitale points at two of his men and the garbage bags, which are quickly thrown into the bag of their Escalade. Grinning like a fool Vitale jumps into the vehicle, winks at Nell and leaves the compound.

Nell however whirls around and points at Axel, "I don't give a shit you are President of this place...you owe me big and I will collect. Oh, you can buy me a fucking trike as part payment of the debt you owe."

Now, Axel grins but gives Nell a slight nod before turning and walking inside the clubhouse. I'm standing here looking like a fool, with my mouth probably hanging open. "You lot need to make sure not a single thing is going to come back on you, and you all owe me so don't think just because I called out your President I'm not calling you all out too." Nell grabs Tanks arm and near enough drags him to the vehicle, but Graham stays where he is with a grin on his face like a fool. "Oh, and you think it's so funny Graham? Find your own way home."

We all, including Graham watch Nell drive out of the compound. Graham throws his head back laughing. "Someone needs to give me ride. But boy this is gonna be fun to stand back and watch."

"What is?" TwoCents asks.

"Vitale got himself another date," Graham laughs some more and I have to admit I do chuckle at that comment.

Walking inside the front doors of the clubhouse and through the common room, we all make our way to the kitchen where Axel is sitting calmly eating pancakes with syrup and fresh fruit. Nobody would guess what he had been doing all the hours previously. Buzz, Drag and Wings take a seat with him, and I stay back because honestly, I don't want to get involved in whatever shit may happen.

"What happened with the others?" Axel asks Graham, which surprises me as this is usually a conversation had in church or his office where women can't see or hear any of it.

"The usual, but it was a quick clean. Vitale wanted it all gone, nothing left to chance. He did take some with him as he is going to see if they are worthy of being foot soldiers. But you know most those were dragged into it to save their family members. Innocent of any crime until the fucker entered their lives. It's a good day in hell is all I say. But you have nothing to worry about, Axel." Graham grabs a plate from Meat who is cooking up a storm of pancakes.

Looking around I notice the Three Stooges are not in the kitchen and neither is Mia or Jo, who are the usual ones to be hanging around in here. Beer leans over as he must have realized the same thing. "Bet they were sent to the kids' playroom when Axel came inside."

Before I can respond Mia storms into the kitchen looking around wildly, spotting me she storms over, "Come on, Mav we've got to get to school. The boys have been up to something and I was told they could get expelled."

Axel busts out laughing, which gets him a filthy look from Mia, and she points at him while snapping, "This is all your fault, they take after you and your crazy foolishness. If you gave my boys your PTSD in their genetics there will be hell to pay."

Now, we all struggle to keep a straight face at her comment because we know one slip and we'll be on the receiving end. I'm thinking maybe I'll stop coming to the clubhouse so much, but Blake is at work so I had no reason to hang around the house this morning. I also had to be here in case I was needed. I am part of the security and muscle of the club at the end of the day. No hiding from the shit shows and drama that happens here, no matter I would like to dodge it at times. But, fuck, some of it is hilarious I have to admit.

Axel walks over to Mia, kissing her thoroughly, which takes the wind out of her sails somewhat, before he slaps her ass, chuckles and walks away with Buzz, Drag and Wings right behind him, giving Mia 'sorry' looks.

"Come on, Mav," Mia murmurs, and I follow her out the back door and to the SUV which has the twin's seats in the back. Riding along to see what is going on, I turn to give Mia a smile when she asks, "They can't really expel them can they?"

"I don't know, Mia," I have no good vibes to give her because I've no idea what power some of these people have. But we are talking kindergarten kids, I mean really, come on, expelling them is a bit over the top.

Standing in the Secretary's office at the school I have to put the palm of my hand over my mouth because what I am seeing is the funniest damn thing I've seen in a long time.

The twins are running around the office, stark naked, but with paintings all over them. I would imagine they've done it to each other as they have it all over their backs too. But it's the purple and green dicks that has me wanting to roll over laughing. They are fluorescent colored, and it's obvious they painstakingly covered every inch of them. But the contrasting color on their balls is what has me because they painted them to look like eyes, so they have a pair of eyes for balls and a colored dick sitting on top, it looks like a turkey neck they are sporting.

Mia I see out the corner of my eye is opening and closing her mouth, and it's obvious she has no idea what to say or do. Glancing at the Secretary, who is standing behind her desk and looks like a bygone era's school mistress. She'd only need something for corporal punishment and the boys would probably not be able to sit for a week, or more.

"Boys, get dressed," Mia snaps as she comes out of her daze. "I'm sorry, I'll speak to their father and see what we can do about their behavior. Honestly, I don't know why they are misbehaving so badly, they are angels at home."

I swallow spittle down the wrong way and start to cough, and Mia gives me a *shut-up* look, but slaps me on the back doing her best to look like a caring mother hen.

"Yous okay, Unc Mav?" Carter asks as he starts to pull up his pants. I notice he's no underwear on but keep that comment to myself.

"I'm good, Carter. You be good and get dressed so we can take you home."

"Yous wunts a green cock, Unc Mav?" Hunter asks, and the Secretary along with Mia gasp with shock, I chuckle before responding.

"No, I'm fine with it just as it is thanks for asking, Hunter." Mia gives me a frown, but keeps quiet.

As soon as the boys are dressed we are out the building and have them fastened in the back in their child seats, Mia has an odd look on her face, and I'm not sure if she wants to laugh or take a shit. But half way back to the clubhouse she bursts out a laugh so loud it has me jump in my seat. I grip the steering a little further as I side-eye to see what's going on.

"Do you want a green cock, Uncle Mav?" Mia sing-songs, then busts out laughing some more. But the cherry on the top is the boys who are hilariously laughing along with their mother.

CHAPTER THIRTY-TWO

The week is buzzing past, and it's Wednesday already. Tonight, I'll be with my seniors and I'm becoming more and more protective of them. I'm watching Pru closely as she has had a nasty cough the last two weeks. I may mention it to Alf and see if he can have someone check what's going on with her health.

I'm nearly ready for my second job, and I pack the cupcakes I purchased as treats for my seniors into single cupcake boxes. I know they'll not eat more than the one tonight, but I have one for tonight and one for them tomorrow. I know Ed will watch what I take for him, as he does every Wednesday evening.

Later that evening I arrive at Ed's and still have a feeling that Pru is not as well as she is trying to convince me. I'm lucky that my clients all live close to each other and I'm going to use that to my advantage.

"PawPaw, I need you to do something for me," I quickly ask as I place the cupcake boxes on the kitchen counter.

"What do you need me to do?"

"If you would check on Pru for me sometime tomorrow. I'm worried she has this cough that isn't going away. I'm going to speak to Alf and see if he can get someone to look at her. You know he has everyone's health information, so he'll be able to get the right person to check her."

"You worried about Pru?" Ed opens the small box and takes out the cupcake. I don't miss he has a cheesy smile on his face.

"Yeah, I am. She has allowed no one to check on her, but I'm going to speak to Alf tomorrow. But if you can check in at her place for me, it will ease my mind."

Ed takes a bite of the cupcake, hums with enjoyment and looks up, giving me a nod, before mumbling he will check on Pru. But I smirk at him as he has frosting all over his top lip and looks like a little boy.

Before I know what he is doing, Ed picks up his phone and makes a call. "Alf, you need to check on Pru. She's not well and is ignoring it."

I'm not sure what is being said as all I hear is a mumbling sound, with Ed giving a 'Yeah,' 'Okay,' 'For sure.' But when he turns to look at me and hands me his phone, I take it and give a tentative 'Hello'.

"Hi, Blake, it's Alf. Look I'll have Pru checked and Ed will go around to her home and see if he can get her anything. I know you have seen her tonight, so she'll be fine until the morning. I'll make sure she is okay even if I have to get her to emergency. The other thing is your house is cleared out and clean. They did a fantastic job of it and worked hard to get it done quickly. I gave them a bonus, and the realtor has an offer on the place. They said if you accept, then they will do the yard, it's up to you. I'll get the realtor to contact you, and you can get it completed. It's an excellent offer, and I would accept."

"Oh, thank you Alf. I was worried about Pru because that cough wasn't going away, and she wouldn't hear of me taking her to be checked out. You stepping up is great and makes me feel much better about it. As for the house, well, I want it gone. It was never my home, so I have no emotional attachment to the place. I'll do what's needed to get the place off my hands."

"Okay, you don't be late leaving Ed's place. I know he's one for taking up more of your time," Alf chuckles more to himself than me, but he's right that Ed keeps me here longer than is really necessary but I love the old fool so it's not a bother to me.

Handing the phone back to Ed, he gives me a smile with some frosting on his top lip, which has me rolling my eyes and grinning more to myself than to him. But I quickly get to the reason I'm here and head to the utility room, where I know I'll see a pile of laundry waiting. It is Wednesday after all!

After finishing all my chores upstairs, I head back to the kitchen where I overhear Ed talking with someone called Glo. "Oh, you're all done then. That's good. Hum-hm, okay, yeah, that's great."

I finish wiping the hob and counter tops and rinse out the cloth I was using as I hear Ed say bye. He's not long before he talks to me.

"That was Glo. She's one of the ladies that was working at your other house. She's all done. They got it cleaned out, and she said to thank you for the bonus. Well, Alf gave them a bonus. Anyway, it's done, so you just have to get with the realtor as Alf said and get it off your hands," Ed chats away while I finish up in the kitchen.

"I'll check with the realtor tomorrow. Alf has organized everything so I hope all I have to do is sign something. Any news about my yard yet?"

"Yeah, the contractor my friend is sending will see you on Friday morning if you are about when he comes to look. I'll be there with you, and I suggest you have it paved and have a few plants in pots, so's you don't have extra work," Ed grins when he gives me the so's comment.

"Okay, I'll see what they suggest on Friday, but I don't want a lot of cost because I'll make a small profit on the house sale and I want to keep it as a safety net, as much as I can, anyway."

"Your man will help you out with finances now, I'm sure. He's living with you and he's not the kind to not pay his way, or look after his woman. It's easy to see that, and if I thought he was going to do you wrong, I'd make sure he paid for it." Ed gives me a hug after I put my jacket on, ready to leave for the night.

"Yeah, I think he's a good one too, PawPaw."

Cuddled in bed next to Mav later, I look up from where I'm resting my head on his chest. "Do you think having the front yard done will cost me a lot?"

"I think we should see what the man suggests and then tell Hammer what we want. This way we only have to pay for the materials." Mav chuckles. "Yeah, I know that's sneaky, but hey we all got to do what we got to do."

"Okay, let's see what he suggests. Ed is going to come over and see, too. He's going to make sure you don't do me wrong, too." I giggle when I hear Mav mumble to himself, *'do you wrong, never.'*

"Oh, Mia said I have to have a hog or a trike? Now, I've never driven a motorcycle, Mav, and only been on the back of yours. So, if being in this girl gang means I have to own one, can you teach me so I can get my license?"

"I can do that, but do you have which one you would like in mind?" Mav kisses the top of my head as he responds, and wraps his arms tighter around me, tucking me close to his body.

"I think a trike, because it's got three wheels and will more than likely be easier to learn to drive."

"Okay, we'll ask Mia if you can learn on hers and if you are good with it, I'll buy you one. A damn good one that you can have custom painted."

"Oh, that would be awesome. I'll call her and speak with her about it," I kiss his chest before sighing and closing my eyes.

"No, I'll speak to her. Now go to sleep."

Once Mav has left for the clubhouse in the morning I quickly clean the kitchen after breakfast and make a coffee before sitting at the table and making a call to Bitty. "Morning, mama. I wanted to ask if Raven was alright after she had that bash on the head?"

"Oh, she's fine. She had a headache apparently, but she's okay, she's at work." Bitty talks to someone in the background before continuing our conversation. "I heard you are having someone look at your yard tomorrow."

"Yeah, it's a friend of Ed's who is sending someone. But Mav said we'd listen to ideas, then get Hammer to do the work, so we only have to pay for the materials."

"Good idea, Mav has his head screwed on right. He's here and helping finish the treehouse extension. The tree next to the original one is going to be the children's nursery and playroom. Meat has it set up so they can't escape, or so he thinks, but you never know with the twins," Bitty giggles. I can imagine she is seeing something in her mind's eye that the twins could get up to. Again, someone speaks to Bitty in the background, "I've got to go, Blake, but I'll see you soon."

I look at my phone because she's gone already, not giving me a chance to say goodbye. People, honestly they all are so busy, and here I am wondering what to do until I go to work tonight.

Now, I shouldn't have thought that because my phone rang and I was surprised it was the realtor. After making arrangements, I quickly go into town, using the van as I've now Alf's permission to use it outside of work hours. I get the offer, sign the paperwork and it's done. All I have to do now is wait for all the legalities to be completed.

Late afternoon I finish making the cookies I'm taking for my seniors tonight, and the lasagna dish for Mav and I. Hearing his bike, I quickly place plates and cutlery on the table and take out the lasagna so it's sitting on the table ready to serve. Opening the fridge, I grab the bowl of salad I made earlier and pop that on the table, right on time to turn and give Mav a huge smile as he walks into the kitchen.

Placing a box on the countertop, Mav grabs me into his arms and kisses me thoroughly before pushing his nose into my neck and taking a huge intake of breath. "You smell great, just what is needed after a day with Meat."

"You're just a sweet-talker," I giggle, but I love the way he holds me and makes me feel special.

"Oh, I have something for you." Mav picks up the box he brought inside with him, and opens it, taking out a jacket that I see when he turns it around has what is called a property patch. 'Property of Mav' it states clearly for all the world to see. My eyes tear up because this shows how invested in our relationship Mav is and I know he's given me all the information about being an Ol' Lady, and what it means to a biker.

Placing the jacket on me, Mav again wraps me close against his body and kisses the top of my head. "I'm such a lucky fucker to have found you, and I promise to love you and cherish you the rest of our lives."

A tear trickles down my cheek with the emotion that is bubbling from my soul. For Mav to say that means everything to me, and I look up with a single tear still falling, "I love you too, and I'll cherish you until our time on earth ends."

I can't help but think we sound like a movie or a romance novel, but I don't care and looking at Mav, he doesn't either, and that's all that matters.

CHAPTER THIRTY-THREE

The weekend has come around once more and I'm excited about this evening's theme night. I've got to get to the costume shop and grab our clothes for tonight. I had Lily pick out one of the best ones, and I'm hoping Blake will be thrilled about what I have for us. I didn't tell her what the theme night was as I want to surprise her when she sees her outfit.

Back at the clubhouse, I head to the treehouse and stand underneath as the hatch is closed. Meaning Meat doesn't want visitors, or some shit. Who knows with him?

"MEAT?" I shout loudly, because honestly, if he doesn't want to respond he won't, but there will be no excuse that I didn't try. No reply, and after many shout-outs I'm done. The damn treehouse is completed anyway, but I felt it was polite to check he needs nothing else done.

Walking to where my house is being built, I can't hold back the smile because I'm sure Blake is going to love this place. Large kitchen with a walk-in pantry, utility room, and every other room we'll need. The foundations are in, and the size of it looks damn impressive.

"Hey, Mav, you okay?"

Turning, I give a chin lift to Hammer who is heading back to the clubhouse from my house build. "Yeah, I thought I'd check how things were going, and if you'd spoken to anyone about Blake's places."

"I was given our marching orders on the place she's selling. Alf's dealing with all that with the realtor, as you know. But the new people, if the sale goes through okay, want to do the yard themselves." Hammer rubs the back of his neck before continuing, "Your place, well, Blake's place where you are both living. I've gotten the information about the front yard. It seems she wants it all resin, which is great for us. She wants it in a sandy, goldish color and then she's going to get pots and have plants around. Seems that is Ed's idea, and she likes it. I'll give you the price, but it's not going to be anywhere near as much as she thinks it'll be."

"Oh, that's good. It'll be easy to keep nice and if we lease the place, it'll be parking off the street. My hog will stand nice on resin," I grin at Hammer, and we make our way back to the clubhouse together. I give him the go-ahead and to get TwoCents to take the money out of the bundle I have in the safe.

"I'll get the team on the job that does the resin work and it'll be next week. But you can cross it off your list of things to be done and concentrate on your Ol' Lady," Hammer winks before walking into the kitchen and heading into the common room.

Blake is at work this morning, and I'm sure she'll have a brilliant afternoon as I'm going to get Mia's trike, or someone else's, for her to learn on. That thought reminds me I best get Mia's permission first.

I'm looking forward to the evening and hope we have no issues with any asshole trying to cause trouble, whether it be a male or female asshole.

Walking to the playroom, I find the Three Stooges with Mia, along with the twins and Summer. But what the fuck is Ed doing here? "What are you doing here?" I blurt out in my surprise.

"Well, I do know all these ladies. We've known each other since, well, forever, and I thought I best come and see where my Blake is going to be hanging out. Where she'll be living when this house of yours is built." Ed is giving me a very serious look, and I know he's testing me for a reaction of a negative kind, but fuck him, I can play his game. We've all seen shenanigans with Star's father and Meat, so we know the signs.

"Oh, that's cool. I'll take you and show you where the house is being built. Everyone here will answer any questions you may have, nothing to hide here," I calmly respond, and ignore the smile that Amelia has plastered on her face. "You'll have to excuse me a moment, as I need a private word with Mia."

Mia looks up and seeing my serious look stands from where she'd been sitting on the mat playing with the twins. "Let's pop into the common room, Mav."

"Okay, thanks Mia." I follow her out of the playroom and through to a quiet corner of the common room. I wait for Mia to sit before taking a seat myself.

"Blake told me she is part of the girl gang now, and I wanted to say thanks for doing that, Mia. It shows me you have embraced her as my Ol' Lady, and welcomed her to the MC."

"Mav, I am more than happy to welcome any brother's woman into the club, into the girl gang. But, if we ever have a horrid Ol' Lady, like BS's ex-wife, then I'll do everything I can to make her feel unwelcome." Mia gives the feral smile she has obviously learned from Axel, and she wears it well, I have to admit.

"She was horrid, wasn't she?" I ask, more than comment.

"Yeah, she truly was," Mia giggles at the memory and I wince because his ex-wife was rotten to the core, and we could all see it. "So, is that what you wanted to say?"

"Oh, no, I wanted to ask if I could use your trike to teach Blake how to drive. She's leaning toward a trike instead of a bike, and if I'm honest, I think she'll love a trike. But I don't want to go buy her one until I know she's good with it."

"Of course you can use my trike. But one scratch on her and you'll owe me a visit to Hot Hogs."

"I'll make sure she doesn't scratch her up." If I wasn't feeling so confident I would cross my fingers for good luck.

Mia stands and runs her hands down her thighs, straightening out her jeans. "The key to her I leave behind the kitchen door. Meat put me a hook up and you'll see it, as it has a pretty pink and two blue feathers attached."

"Ah, feathers for the kids?" I ask, giving her a smile.

"Yeah, the boys gave me them and when I had Summer, I picked up a pink one for her." I give Mia a quick hug and walk away because I'm going to get my woman and get her on this trike.

Once Blake had finished her shift and arrived home, I waited patiently for her to shower and change. Reaching the clubhouse, I park my hog and tell her to keep her helmet on. "Wait here. I'll be back in a second." I run to the kitchen, grab the trike key and take it out with me, where I grab Blake's hand and lead her to Mia's trike. Which I'd placed near the front of the clubhouse ready.

"This is Mia's trike, and she's kindly said you can learn to drive on her. Now, I'll go over all the controls before you start her up." That's exactly what I do, I take Blake through everything. I have her sitting on the trike and have her repeat everything enough times to know she has remembered where and what everything is.

The lesson goes far easier than I expected and I have to admit she is a natural and won't have any issues. I'm excited about buying her a trike, and having rides out with her behind and wrapped around me, or on her own trike alongside me.

"You're a natural, and I want you to think about what you'd like your trike to look like. The brothers at Hot Hogs & Cages will do you a respray to make it special and stand out from the crowd."

"Oh, I'll think about it for sure. But I'll not have any money until the house sale is completed, and the profit is deposited into my account." Blake mutters.

"Hey, I'm buying you the trike. You're my Ol' Lady and I will make sure you get a first-class trike and anything else you need. You keep that money safe in your account when it is deposited. It will be a safety net for a rainy day." I kiss Blake softly. It's my way of showing her I'm taking care of her in the best way I can.

The afternoon has flown by and we dash home to eat and get ready for the evening. The outfit is an enormous success and I can't help but swell with pride when I see how beautiful she looks in it. I wear my outfit and strut around, which has Blake giggling loudly.

"Come on, let's get to the bar and have some fun." I announce, taking Blake's hand and tucking it into my arm. Leading her out of the house, locking up and to the SUV I took from the compound. Hm, a random thought pops into my mind, 'I'm gonna have to buy a truck or SUV.'

Walking into TJs, I smile looking at everyone dressed up and dancing already. I'm in a pinstripe waistcoat suit, and as I'm not used to a vest it feels a little restrictive. But the black suit on whole feels comfortable. I've a black button-up shirt and a white tie on, but completed the outfit with a hat that gives the gangster vibe a finishing touch.

Blake is wearing a dress that is also black, but has fringes over it, and as she moves they swing with her. She has a band around her head that has a black feather atop, and to finish it, long white gloves and a set of long pearls. False ones, of course, as they came with the outfit. But she looks stunning, and we have the 1920s theme down, and we match each other perfectly.

Finding one whole side of the room covered in brothers and Ol' Ladies, all dressed similarly has me smirking, because we probably would all be congregated like this if it was at that time in history. I can just imagine Axel and Mia as Bonnie and Clyde, but without the death at the end.

The evening flows extremely well. I dance with Blake and enjoy her laughter as I swirl her around the floor. We do some very odd old-fashioned dances too, but it's all fun and with no trouble rearing its ugly head. I think the night is a tremendous success and then Meat calls his team over to do a dance on stage. That's when I put my foot down and take a seat with Blake, refusing to have anything to do with the stage striptease.

We all bust out laughing when we see Star giving Meat hell, and chasing him out of the bar, through the kitchen and to fuck knows where. But it seems our Star doesn't want her man showing his dick to any other woman, and I can see from the look in all the Ol' Ladies' eyes they agree with her. I blow out a relieved breath that I made the right choice of refusing to dance on stage, because if I had I can just imagine the cluster fuck result it would have gotten me.

Wrapping my arm around Blake's shoulders I pull her to my side, kiss the side of her head, and take a moment to appreciate how lucky I am to have found her.

CHAPTER THIRTY-FOUR

-:- BLΛKE :

Last night was awesome. We had a great time and I love the other women, or Ol' Ladies, as they are called. I didn't get to wear my new jacket that Mav gave me, which claims I am his property. It was a bit of a shock, but he is showing he's a caveman just like the others I've met so far. He is, however, sensitive, loving and mine...and I know that I'm feeling possessive, but if he says I'm his property, then he has to be mine in return.

I was watching Winter at the bar last night and she has a fantastic relationship with her man, Target. Winter, I've noticed, is held in high regard by everyone. I decided I'm going to have lessons with her to learn to use a weapon. I keep thinking that I want to be Winter when I grow up. Hm, saying that Raven, Star, or Eden...Grief, I think I just need to get the confidence all of them have, and I'll be as sassy as they all are!

My phone rings, which pulls me from my thoughts, and seeing it's Alf, I quickly answer, "Hello, Alf."

"Hi, Blake. I wanted to let you know I've had Pru checked, and she has bronchitis. She's now on medication and I've arranged a carer to be with her for the next seven days. She'll live at the house with her, make sure she does as she's been told."

"Oh, I'm pleased I mentioned it to you now. It would have been bad if it had turned to pneumonia. Shall I still go on my shift or wait until the carer has finished living with her?"

"You can take her a cookie now and again, in the day or evening, but it's not working. The carer is doing all the chores, so you just get a smile out of her and leave," Alf chuckles, "She loves you going on your shifts, and taking cookies, cupcakes and other treats."

"I'll do that, and Ed is popping in to see her, too. I'm sure he'll keep her on her toes."

"Oh, my, he will. Anyway, you won't be working for Pru this next week, but I'll not be taking anything out of your week's salary. It's not your doing that she has someone else with her. She'll be delighted to get you back, I'm sure, because she already told me this woman is a battleaxe," Alf is chuckling to himself, and I grin because I can imagine Pru saying just that. Alf excuses himself and cuts the call.

With it being Sunday, Mav is at church, and I would never have thought he was religious, but I'm saying nothing, because they are a cult, after all!

Ed walks into the house, pours himself a cold drink from the fridge and takes a seat at the table across from me. "Morning, Blake. I've come over to update you on what I know."

"Morning, PawPaw." Now, before I can say more, Ed launches into his report, which has me silently wanting to laugh.

"Okay, first off I went to the clubhouse where Mav was living to see what it was like and to see this house he's having built. Because if it was shit, I was going to tell him to take a hike and leave you alone. As your PawPaw, I take your health and safety seriously."

Nodding to show I'm following along, although I'm not sure why he thinks I may have a safety problem. It seems Ed just wants to get everything off his chest he continues.

"The place seems okay. I saw nothing that either you or I needed to worry about. Bitty, and her witches have the place covered, so

I'm not worried at all about you going there. I also saw the plot for the house Mav is building, and the foundations are solid. It looks like it will be a large place, and he told me it will have a front and back porch."

"It sounds lovely, and I've not seen it yet. Mav has shown me the plans and what it will be like finished and I'm excited, but want to wait until I can walk inside."

"I'll keep my eye on it as your PawPaw, just to be sure nothing goes wrong," Ed states proudly, and I give him one of my sweetest smiles, then he continues, "I've visited Pru, and she has this woman looking after her. I had to stop myself from laughing because she was rather harsh in manner and looks. Poor Pru looked like she wanted me to take her home with me when it was time for me to leave."

Giggles pop out before I can stop them, and knowing I'll be visiting next week, so I best be ready and don't upset this woman. But if she's harsh with Pru, I will tell her. Thoughts of Winter cross my mind, and have me steeling my backbone, ready for anything this woman may throw at me if I have to stand up to her.

"Oh, did you hear anything yet from the realtor?"

"Yes, I'm just waiting for the paperwork to be done. The realtor will let me know when that's done, and then I'll get the money from the sale. I'm not worried about the money, PawPaw. I just want it gone and done with."

"Yeah, but it won't take long, I'm sure."

Later that afternoon, I set up the grill and place a table next to it where Mav can stand the tray of meat I have for him to cook. He does not know I'm doing this, but I feel like sitting outside at the patio table and enjoy the fresh air. Of course, Ed decided it was a good day to stay and eat with us, so he is talking to Mav now about anything and everything he can think of. Mav is so good with him, patience flows from him when dealing with Ed's constant stream of chatter.

Turning as though he can hear my thoughts, Mav gives me a huge smile. "I forgot to tell you that Hammer is organizing for resin to be laid in the front yard. I've given him the finances, so you don't have to worry about that either."

"Oh, I can give you it back when the house sale money comes to me."

"No. I've paid for it. If we lease this place it'll pay for itself given time. I think one of the brothers may be interested in leasing it which will be perfect." Mav throws ribs I marinated earlier onto the grill and the sizzle and steam has my mouth watering in anticipation.

The evening is enjoyable, Mav and Ed get on well, and I enjoy listening to them bantering about cars, houses, and even the price of groceries. The loneliness I had been feeling has been washed away and I think I'm so lucky to have these two men in my life. But not only them, Bitty too, who has shown what a mother should be like. Constantly calling, checking I'm alright and including me when she has been going shopping, well if I've been available that is. But it is so nice to have these people in my life that I count my blessings daily.

-:- MAV -:-

What a busy week this has been, what with Ed always being around at our place and Bitty popping in and out too. I've been twice with

Blake to visit one of her clients called Pru, and she's a great senior, one hell of a sense of humor. She needs that humor with the carer she has because that one must have lost her humor when she graduated from diapers. I've yet to see her crack a smile no matter what is said to her.

Saturday afternoon and I'm taking Blake over to Nell's. She is one of the girl gang, and she's just learned how to drive a trike. I thought they would get on well and I want to catch up with Graham to make sure all the trash had been taken out.

Walking into Nell's kitchen, I can't help but take a lung full of the gorgeous smell that is hanging in the air. "What is that smell?" I can't help but ask

"Cake...chocolate, red velvet, carrot. You name it and Nell has been baking it," Tank replies as he hands me a beer and a soda to Blake.

"Why? Is she okay?" Blake asks.

"She's fine. Graham had contact with their father, and they both hate his guts, so it wasn't particularly pleasant. Now Nell wants to get rid of him once and for all. But it's left her with a bit of a temper. She'll be pleased to see you both, and maybe Blake can cheer her up." Tank cuts an enormous chunk of red velvet cake and hands it to me just as Nell walks in through the back door.

"I told you to leave those cakes alone. Now look what you've gone and done, fucking men, I think I'm going to like women... get married to a woman, that'll piss off all you men."

Blake giggles, attracting Nell's attention, but when Blake walks over and gives Nell a hug, links arms with her and leads her outside, I think both myself and Tank are relieved.

"Fucking hell man, she is upset. I've never seen Nell like that."

Tank chuckles, "Oh, she can be fiery like a dragon, but when she's upset, she lets everyone know it, but never, and I mean never, do you want to see her cry. It breaks your heart to see that, and I've only ever seen it once, and I will kill the next fucker that makes her shed a tear."

"What did her father want?" I can't help but ask.

Graham walks into the kitchen just as I asked, so he shakes his head as he grabs a chunk of cake as he replies. "Fucker wants to bury the hatchet. Be family again. He's still with the gold-digging whore, so he has no chance of either of us being family again. I hate her, and I hate him. He can stay away from us. We don't want or need him." After eating a couple of bites of his cake, he continues, "Nell wants to grab him and feed him to Jaws, but I told her to ignore him. He isn't worth it."

Nodding and handing Tank my empty plate, I lean back in my seat. "Family… sometimes you just have to let them go."

"Yeah, I agree. Oh, did I tell you Vitale has had Nell on another date? It's fucking hilarious how he's trying to win her over. You'd never know he could cut someone's throat and never look back, but if Nell scowls, he wants to know why and who did it," Graham chuckles.

"He's not giving up, is he?" I can't help but smirk because we've all seen Vitale trying to get round Nell.

"Not sure he'll win, but it's fun to watch," Tank laughs.

Hearing an engine noise we all run out the back door and look out over the back of the property, and there is Nell driving a trike with Blake in the back seat laughing her ass off. We all three stand with our mouths dropped open to our chests, because these two are going for it. Nell is laughing right along with Blake, and you know I have this awful feeling that my Blake may have found her BFF, as they call them. But fuck, couldn't she have found someone calm and you know, sedate?

Later that evening, we are sitting in the kitchen at the clubhouse eating and enjoying the camaraderie of the brothers and their Ol' Ladies. Mia has taken one of the twins outside, and it looks like she's not amused about something.

Ten minutes later, Axel walks past with Drag and Buzz, and it's the shit-eating grin on his face that catches your attention. But when he loudly states, "The fucker asked me if I wanted a nice purple cock just like his…" that I spit the mouthful of beer I had been about to swallow. The room cracks into laughter as we all know that is the twins talking because they've asked nearly every one of the brothers at this point if they want a green or purple cock, just like theirs.

Blake looks around and smiles, then loud enough for everyone to hear states, "It is a cult, isn't it? But I don't mind, I quite like it here."

Again, the room is in an uproar with laughter, and I wrap my arms around my woman, kissing her silly. I don't give a fuck if she thinks we're a cult or not. Life is good, and that's all that matters.

Books by J.E. Daelman

SATAN'S GUARDIANS MC

Book One — Brand / Book Two - Shades

Book Three — Odds / Book Four - Torch

Book Five - Ace / Book Six - Nash

Book Seven - Ink / Book Eight - Shadow

Book Nine - Christmas at the Clubhouse - Novella

Book Ten - Whisky

Book Eleven — Halloween at the Clubhouse - Novella

RAGING BARONS MC

Prequel - Truth and Lies / President - Axel - Book Two

Silver - Book Three / Fox — Book Four

Grease — Book Five / Hammer — Book Six

BS — Book Seven / Target — Book Eight

Knuckles — Book Nine / Stitch — Book Ten

Forest — Book Eleven / Meat — Book Twelve

TwoCents — Book Thirteen / Rock — Book Fourteen

Jig — Book Fifteen

TRIPLE KINGS MC

PARANORMAL

KINGDOM OF WOLVES

STANDALONE

ACKNOWLEDGEMENTS

Firstly, thanks to Richard, who edits & Alpha reads. You work so hard, and I'm so grateful for all you do. You have so much to put up with, my questions, throwing ideas and having you read chapters back to me so I can hopefully see the story from the readers point of view. Love you sweetie xx

My business manager Vic, thank you for taking a load off my shoulders. It is incredible and gives me more time for my imagination to flourish.

Thanks to my Alpha Readers on this book, Gabi & Marie. You are both amazing and I am truly grateful for all you do.

Proofreader Team: Editing Divas aka Rose, also Linda and Allena.

For my BETA Readers, Jenni and Stacey. Thank you for finding all those errors that could easily slip through the net.

My ARC Team, you all keep me tapping the keyboard, giving me the confidence to carry on and enjoy my imagination. For writing the incredible reviews. Every word means such a lot to me.

Thank you to Elaine for running the street team and ARC team. Plus, the ladies of the street team for jumping in to help and keep me seen on social media.

A huge thank you to Paul Henry Serres who takes the most amazing photographs of the gorgeous models we use on our covers.

Lastly, thank you to my readers, who have reached out and given so many lovely comments about the books. Each of your reviews mean so much and encourages a new reader to give the books a try. Thank you ♥

You can find me here

Facebook Author page:
https://www.facebook.com/Jan.SGMC

Facebook Reader page:
https://www.facebook.com/groups/335434258378835

Twitter:
https://twitter.com/daelman_author

Instagram:
https://www.instagram.com/jandaelman_author/

MeWe:
https://mewe.com/i/jandaelman

Blog:
https://jdaelman-author.blogspot.com/

Goodreads:
https://www.goodreads.com/author/show/21391970.Jan_Daelman

BookBub:
https://www.bookbub.com/authors/j-e-daelman

SIGN UP FOR THE NEWSLETTER
https://www.subscribepage.com/u9r7b4

Made in United States
Cleveland, OH
11 March 2025

15086666R00154